OUT OF TIME

SECRETS OF BROOKHAVEN

BOOK THREE

CHAPTER
ONE

Fallon Ray turned into her driveway, her home a welcome sight after a long day of being on her feet. She pressed the button on the remote, watching as the garage door lifted smoothly, the motor's hum blending with the muted buzz of insects outside.

She pulled into the garage and cut the engine, the gentle purr fading into silence. Wearily, she climbed from the driver seat, then moved to the trunk of the car and gathered a handful of grocery bags. Balancing the bags in one hand, she moved toward the entry door to the house and used her elbow to hit the switch to lower the garage door. The mechanism groaned as the door began its descent, the sound echoing in the confined space.

Fallon headed inside, kicking the door closed behind her before striding into the kitchen. As she began to put the groceries away, she mentally checked her list, ensuring she hadn't forgotten anything essential—milk, bread, a bottle of her favorite red wine. Satisfied she hadn't missed anything, she headed back out to retrieve her purse and cell phone from the car.

As she stepped into the garage a cool draft washed over her, sending goosebumps sprouting over the backs of her arms. She frowned, her attention drawn to the large bay door. It stood wide open, the cool night air drifting through the space.

She swore she'd closed it. Fallon shook her head. She must be more exhausted than she thought.

Shrugging off the unsettling feeling, she tapped the button again and remained frozen in place, watching as the door descended fully this time, sealing her safely inside. A sense of relief rushed through her at the sight, and she let out a soft, self-deprecating laugh as she hopped off the step and crossed the narrow space.

Just as her fingers landed on the door handle, a faint whisper of movement reached her ears. Her heart skipped a beat, her senses suddenly on high alert. Before she could react, a large hand clamped over her mouth and nose, and a damp cloth covered her face.

Instinctively she sucked in a breath, and she drew in a lungful of the noxious fume that emanated from the fabric. The acrid smell was sharp and overpowering, and it caused her eyes to water. Her throat felt as if it were on fire, and she choked reflexively, trying to expel it from her system.

Panic surged through her, and she thrashed wildly, fighting against the attacker. The arm banded around her waist held firm, the hand holding the cloth immovable. Her vision blurred, the edges going dark as the drug sank into her system and took root. She struggled to stay conscious, her thoughts becoming a jumbled mess of fear and confusion, even as her limbs grew heavy and unresponsive.

Her breaths came in ragged, desperate gasps, each one drawing more of the chemical into her system. The world tilted, and her balance slipped away as everything faded to black.

Fallon's eyes fluttered open, slowly adjusting to the dim light that cast eerie shadows across the room. Her head pounded, a dull, relentless ache that matched the cold, damp chill seeping from the concrete walls. Her body felt heavy, sluggish, and she licked her cracked, dry lips.

She blinked hard, taking in the dingy basement, the block walls stained with age and moisture. Confusion settled over her. Where was she?

With startling clarity the events of the evening came back to her, and a wave of panic surged through her.

Oh, God.

Fallon's pulse kicked up, her heart thudding painfully in her chest. Her breaths came in rapid pants, throat aching, mind still reeling from the effects of the drug. Shoving through the foggy delirium that clung to her, she forced her muscles to move. Her hands refused to cooperate, and something cut into the flesh of her wrists.

A sickening sense of dread descended as she realized they were bound with coarse rope and suspended high over her head.

No. No, no, no.

She yanked on them to no avail, her heart slamming against her ribs, lungs hyperventilating with fear. She had to get out of here. But how?

She glanced frantically around the small room once more, and every cell of her body froze.

A man hovered on the periphery of the shadows, only his silhouette visible in the faint glow of the single, naked bulb that hung from the ceiling.

"Please." Her throat, cracked and dry, struggled to form words. "Let... let me go."

The man shifted, moving more fully into the circle of

light, and she studied his features. Something about him was familiar... Did she know him?

He smiled, a gesture that should have been reassuring but only served to amplify her fear. She recoiled as he moved closer.

"Don't worry," he said with a small shake of his head. "Everything is just fine."

Fallon trembled violently as he leaned over her, his hands moving with practiced precision as he checked the restraints. She winced, expecting pain, but his touch was gentle, almost tender. He adjusted the bindings, ensuring they were secure but not tight enough to cut into her skin.

"There now," he murmured. "We don't want you hurting yourself."

Her eyes darted around the room, searching for any avenue of escape. As she turned her head, her chin grazed something on her left bicep, and her attention was drawn downward to a thick, white bandage that stood out in stark relief against her pale skin. Fear mingled with confusion.

"What happened?" She hated that her voice shook.

The man's expression softened as he stroked his hand over her hair. The gesture felt disturbingly intimate, and her stomach revolted.

"You don't need to worry about anything now. We're going to be happy..." His eyes lit up with a strange, fervent excitement as his gaze dropped to her midsection. "The three of us."

Fallon's breath caught in her throat as he placed a hand on her belly. Her stomach swooped violently, and her blood turned to ice as her gaze moved once more to her upper arm. Horror dawned as the cold realization of truth washed over her.

"You... you took out my implant?" she whispered, her

voice barely audible over the rush of her own frenzied heartbeat.

The man nodded, his smile widening. "Yes," he said, his voice filled with twisted pride. "Now we can be a real family."

Tears welled up in Fallon's eyes as she struggled against the restraints, the reality of her situation crashing down on her. She was trapped, helpless, at the mercy of a man who had taken everything from her. Desperation clawed at her throat, but she forced herself to stay calm, to think.

"Please," she said again, her voice breaking. "You don't have to do this. Just let me go."

But the man shook his head, his expression firm. "We're meant to be together. You'll see."

As he turned away, the dim light casting his shadow across the room, Fallon's mind raced. She had to find a way out, a way to survive. She had to fight, not just for herself, but for the life she had never imagined carrying within her. Determination hardened her resolve. She would find a way to escape. She had to.

CHAPTER
TWO

Detective Sawyer Reed's phone rang, jolting him from a deep, dreamless sleep. He groaned, reaching blindly for the phone on his nightstand. The harsh glow of the screen blinded him for a moment, and he blinked rapidly to clear his vision. When he finally opened his eyes again, Sheriff Dare Jensen's name swam into view.

Sawyer tapped the button and held the phone to his ear. "Reed."

"We've got a murder downtown." Dare's voice was tight with anxiety. "Meet me in the alley next to the Italian restaurant. Looks like it might be Lindsey Gill."

Sawyer bolted upright, the last remnants of sleep vanishing. "On my way."

He ended the call and swung his legs over the side of the bed, mind already focusing on the night—or morning, as the case might be—ahead. He dressed in record time, and forgoing coffee for the time being, grabbed his badge, gun, and keys, then dashed out the door.

The cool night air slapped his face as he stepped outside, but he welcomed the jolt to his senses. The streets were empty, a small blessing of small-town life—no traffic to slow him down. He navigated the familiar roads quickly, the only sound the purr of his car's engine and the faint hum of the tires as they spun along beneath him.

As he approached the scene, the red and blue lights of patrol cars bounced off nearby buildings, casting eerie shadows in the dark. He parked behind Dare's familiar SUV and hurried toward the alley, his pulse quickening. The air was thick with the scent of dirt and refuse, mingling with the more tantalizing aromas garlic and basil that floated from the open doorway of the restaurant.

Cam McCoy was on the sidewalk, questioning a visibly shaken restaurant employee. The young man's face was pale, his entire body trembling where he sat on the curb in front of the restaurant.

Cam tossed a quick look at Sawyer before turning his attention back to the man in front of him. "Sam, this is Detective Sawyer Reed. Could you please tell him what you just told me?"

The man—Sam—glanced up at Sawyer. "I—I found her when I took the trash out for the night. I wasn't really paying attention, and I... tripped over her."

His face took on a green tinge as he swallowed hard. "I didn't mean to. I was tired and it'd been a long day, and..."

He trailed off, and Cam offered a kind smile. "I understand. Do you happen to remember what time this was?"

"A little after one. I—I called the cops right away."

Sawyer studied the man. "Is that normally when you take the trash out?"

Sam nodded. "We close around twelve on Fridays, but it takes awhile to get everything cleaned up—especially the kitchen. I usually drop the trash right before I leave."

"Where do you park?"

The man gestured in the direction of the alley. "Behind the building."

At the end of the alley, it opened into a small gravel parking area beyond. "Is that where all the employees park?"

Sam nodded. "Yeah. The side door locks behind you when you leave, so I usually just head out and go straight to my car."

Sawyer glanced around. "Did you hear or see anything unusual tonight? Anyone hanging around the alley?"

The young man shook his head vehemently. "No, nothing. I just came out to take the trash and... she was there."

"Thanks, Sam." Cam dipped his chin. "We'll let you know if we have any more questions. Do you need a ride home?"

Sam stood, looking slightly less shaken than before. "N-no, I think I'll be all right."

He cast a quick look down the alley, then with a small shudder turned away and headed around the back of the building to retrieve his car.

Sawyer turned to Cam. "We're sure it's Lindsey Gill?"

Cam straightened, his expression grim. "Victim is female, early- to mid-twenties. No ID on her, but the description matches."

Fuck. Sawyer felt a cold knot form in his stomach. "Any other witnesses?"

Cam shook his head. "Not so far. We're checking into the other businesses in the plaza, but most close down early. Sam was the last employee to leave."

Sawyer and Cam ducked under the crime scene tape and joined Dare where he stood just a few feet away from the woman sprawled facedown next to the dumpster.

Sawyer's gaze swept over her pale form, completely nude from head to toe, her skin filthy and mottled with grime and blood. "Jesus."

The sheriff glanced over at him and nodded. "Someone did a number on her."

Dark streaks of blood stood out in the harsh light of the fluorescent work lamp that had been set up at the mouth of the alley. Bruises and lacerations covered her body, evidence of a prolonged and vicious assault.

Dare crouched down and, using a gloved hand, gently brushed the woman's hair away from her face. The extent of her injuries became more apparent. Her face was swollen and bruised, almost unrecognizable.

Sawyer's heart sank as he got his first glimpse of the woman. It took a moment for the pieces to click into place— her disheveled hair, so encrusted with blood and dirt that it looked brown, the once delicate features now marred by violence.

Dare lowered the thick curtain of hair back into place. "It's definitely her."

Damn it. Sawyer swallowed hard as a wave of anger and sadness washed over him. Lindsey Gill's recent abduction from her home had captivated the small town of Brookhaven. The beautiful blue-eyed blonde had worked as a nurse at a nearby hospital, her bubbly personality enriching the lives of everyone she met. For weeks the community had held onto the hope that she would be found alive. But now, all those hopes had been dashed in the most horrifying way.

Over the past month, two other women had been found dead. But their deaths were nothing compared to the brutality Lindsey had suffered. Sawyer shoved down the turmoil swirling in his stomach and focused on Lindsey's body.

"She was definitely killed elsewhere," he said unnecessarily.

Dare exhaled a deep breath through his nose. "Let's see what we can collect. I'll hold off on letting anyone else back here until you're done."

Sawyer tipped his head in acknowledgment, then moved back to his car to retrieve his kit. Cam began to set up evidence markers throughout the alley, and Sawyer moved back toward the dumpster.

While the other victims had been painstakingly posed and cared for, Lindsey's murder appeared to lack the same methodical precision. From his place near her feet, he studied her. It was almost as if she'd tripped and landed facedown. One arm seemed to be trapped underneath her torso, the other extended slightly away from her body. Her legs were sprawled slightly apart, and blood marred the inside of her thighs.

A shudder of revulsion started low, and Sawyer clenched his molars, pushing it down.

"We need to notify her family," Cam said quietly, pausing in his task of photographing the scene. "They need to know."

Sawyer agreed, but first they had to ensure every piece of evidence was collected. "I'll take care of it. Make sure we get everything—we can't miss a single detail."

As they continued to work, Sawyer's mind raced. The brutality of the crime, the methodical removal of fingerprints —it all pointed to a killer who was both ruthless and calculated. Someone who had done this before, or at least thought about it long enough to know how to cover their tracks.

Sawyer was momentarily distracted as Medical Examiner Tom Seidel arrived at the scene, his expression grim. He ducked under the crime scene tape, pausing to speak with Dare before moving toward Sawyer. "Detective."

"Morning, Doc." Sawyer and Cam watched as he knelt beside Lindsey's lifeless form, his assessing gaze carefully inspecting her injuries.

"Blunt force trauma," Dr. Seidel murmured, his eyes scanning the extensive bruising and lacerations. "She was beaten severely. But I won't be able to determine the official cause of death until I can conduct a full examination."

Sawyer nodded, stepping back to give Dr. Seidel space to work. "Understood. We'll need every piece of information you can get us."

Dr. Seidel continued his preliminary assessment, his brow furrowed in concentration. After a few minutes, he stood up and signaled to the team to prepare Lindsey's body for transport. As the medical examiner's team took over, Sawyer and Cam moved aside, watching in silence as Lindsey was placed into the van, the door closing with a heavy finality.

"We'll come back in the light of day to reassess," Cam said. "We might find something we missed in the dark."

Sawyer nodded, his gaze still fixed on the departing van. "Let's collect what we can for now. I don't want to lose anything overnight."

The alley was scoured for anything that could provide a clue—a piece of fabric, a stray hair, a discarded weapon. Every detail mattered.

As they worked, the first gray light of dawn began to lighten the sky, casting long shadows over the ground. The weight of the case pressed heavily on Sawyer's shoulders, but he refused to let it slow him down. This was his job, his duty, and he wouldn't rest until the killer was caught.

Around five o'clock Sawyer and Cam finally paused, their initial sweep of the scene complete.

"We'll regroup later," Sawyer said, his voice tinged with exhaustion. "I'm going to visit the Gills."

"Want me to come?"

Cam shot him a sideways glance, but Sawyer shook his head. "I'll handle it. Why don't you get some rest, then get started sorting through his stuff." He gestured toward the collection of evidence. "Maybe we'll find something in there."

Cam clapped a hand on his shoulder. "We'll get this bastard."

He sure as hell hoped so. They both knew the clock was

ticking. The longer the killer remained free, the greater the danger to the community. And for Sawyer, it was personal. He had to find justice for Lindsey Gill. He wouldn't rest until they had answers—and until the monster responsible for this horror was brought to justice.

CHAPTER
THREE

Sawyer sat in his car, the engine idling quietly as he gathered the strength to face the task ahead. The exhaustion from the long night weighed heavily on him, both physically and emotionally. His mind replayed the gruesome scene from the alley, the brutalized body of Lindsey Gill haunting his thoughts. Now, he had to do the hardest part of his job: notify Lindsey's parents of her death.

Sawyer drew in a deep breath before stepping out of the car and making his way up the walkway. The morning sun had just broken over the horizon, casting a warm glow over the neighborhood that felt completely at odds with the grim news he was about to deliver.

He climbed the steps of the small front porch, his heart pounding in his chest. He paused for a moment, steeling himself, then knocked, the sound seeming to echo in the stillness of the morning.

A few moments later, the door opened to reveal Lindsey's mother, Mary Gill, her face etched with worry. "Detective Reed. Have you found Lindsey?"

Sawyer swallowed hard, his throat tight. "Mrs. Gill, may I come in?"

Mary's face paled but she stepped aside, allowing him to enter. The house was filled with pictures of Lindsey—smiling, vibrant, full of life. The sight of them made the task even more heart-wrenching.

Lindsey's father, John, appeared in the doorway of the kitchen, his expression a mixture of hope and fear. "Detective, any news?"

Sawyer took a deep breath, struggling to find the right words. "Mr. and Mrs. Gill, I'm very sorry to have to tell you this, but we found Lindsey last night. She... she didn't make it."

Mary's knees buckled, and she sank into the nearest chair, a strangled sob escaping her lips. John's face crumpled, and he reached out to steady himself against the wall, his eyes filling with tears. "Are—are you sure?"

Sawyer gave a small nod. "I'm sorry."

"No... No, not our Lindsey," Mary cried, her voice breaking. "She can't be gone."

Sawyer felt a lump rise in his throat as he watched their world shatter. He wished he could do more, offer some comfort, but he knew that nothing he said could ease their pain. "I'm so sorry for your loss. We're doing everything we can to find the person responsible."

John clenched his fists, his knuckles white. "She was our baby girl. How could this happen?"

Sawyer shook his head, his heart heavy. "We're going to find out—I promise you that. Lindsey deserves justice, and we're not going to stop until we get it."

Mary sobbed uncontrollably, and John moved to her side, holding her tightly. They clung to each other, their grief palpable. Sawyer stood there, feeling utterly helpless.

"Is there anything we can do?" John asked after a long moment, his voice hoarse with sorrow.

Sawyer glanced at Mary, then tipped his head at Mr. Gill. "Could I speak with you for a moment?"

John patted Mary on the shoulder, and with a few reassuring words, moved toward Sawyer, a question in his eyes.

"Mr. Gill, we'll need someone to identify her. If you're not feeling up to it—"

"No." John's voice was hard when he spoke. "I want to see her."

Sawyer dipped his chin. "Of course. I can take you to the Medical Examiner's office."

John's face fell, but he nodded resolutely. "Let me get my coat."

Sawyer knew that look; there was still a small part of the man that held out hope the police were wrong, that Lindsey was still alive and well. He understood the need to see her with his own two eyes.

The ride to the Medical Examiner's office was quiet, the silence thick and heavy with dread. John stared out the window, his hands clenched in his lap. Sawyer could feel the man's anxiety, and his stomach twisted violently. He hated this part of the job.

When they arrived, Dr. Tom Seidel met them at the entrance. He spoke gently to John, his voice soft and soothing. "Mr. Gill, I'm very sorry for your loss."

John nodded a little distractedly. "Can I see her?"

"Of course." The doctor gave a slow nod. "Before we go back, I should warn you—due to her injuries, Lindsey might look a bit different."

John's brow furrowed in confusion. "What do you mean?"

Sawyer stepped in, his tone respectful but direct. "She was

badly beaten, Mr. Gill. We can do a physical viewing of the body, or if it's too difficult, we can use a recording. It's your choice."

John's eyes filled with tears, but he shook his head. "No, I need to see her. I need to be sure it's her."

Sawyer and Dr. Seidel led John to the back room. The cold, clinical atmosphere seemed to amplify the tension. Dr. Seidel pulled back the sheet, revealing Lindsey's battered body. Sawyer stood close by, ready to support John if he needed it.

John sucked in a sharp breath. "Oh, God... Lindsey..."

Sawyer's heart ached as he watched John break down, his shoulders shaking with sobs. Lindsey's face was almost unrecognizable, her features distorted by the violence she'd endured.

"I'm so sorry, Mr. Gill," Sawyer said softly. "I wish we could have found her sooner."

John nodded, unable to speak. After a moment, he took a deep breath and turned to Sawyer. "Thank you for letting me see her."

Sawyer and Dr. Seidel gently led John out of the room and back to the car. When they reached John's house, the older man looked at Sawyer, his eyes red and filled with pain. "Promise me you'll find the person who did this, Detective. Promise me."

Sawyer met his gaze and held. "I promise, Mr. Gill. I'll do my best to bring them to justice."

John nodded, his expression resolute despite his grief. "Thank you."

"Mr. Gill, if I may..." Sawyer passed him a card. "Dr. Nadine Turow is a grief counselor. You might want to give her a call."

John studied the card as he extracted it from Sawyer's fingers. With a small smile of thanks that didn't reach his eyes, the older man slipped from the car and was gone.

Sawyer watched as John walked back into his house, the weight of the promise he had just made pressing heavily on his shoulders. The faces of Mary and John Gill, broken by grief, lingered in his mind.

He would do everything in his power to catch Lindsey's killer. She deserved that much. And so did her family.

CHAPTER
FOUR

The sound of yelling pierced the early morning stillness, and Brynlee Layne jerked from sleep. Dread curdled in her stomach as she launched from the bed and raced toward the front of the house, her heart pounding.

Throwing open the front door, Brynlee winced at the sight that greeted her. Next door, her neighbor, Sawyer Reed, was waving his arms wildly, shouting at her cat, who had once again made himself at home on the roof of Sawyer's meticulously maintained car.

"Scooter, no!" Brynlee called for the cat as she raced outside barefoot, her feet slipping on the dewy grass. "Get off there!"

The cool morning air sent goosebumps sprouting over her arms and legs. She reached the car and snatched Scooter off the roof, cuddling him close despite his protests, his claws digging into her arm.

Sawyer turned to her, his face a mask of fury. "Goddamn it, Brynlee, this is the third time this week! As if I don't have enough to deal with right now. Keep your cat off my damn car!"

"I'm so sorry, Sawyer." She could see the paw prints on the car's roof, evidence of Scooter's repeated escapades. "I've been trying to keep an eye on him, but he keeps slipping out the animal door."

"Maybe try a little harder," Sawyer snapped, his eyes flashing with irritation.

Dark circles ringed his eyes as he glared at her. His neatly pressed suit and polished shoes contrasted sharply with the oversized tee shirt and shorts Brynlee had slept in, and she shifted slightly, clutching Scooter close to her chest.

Next to him, she felt like a little girl. He was always clean cut and professional, and he stared down his nose at her like she never quite measured up. He knew how he saw her: she was just some airhead hippie who worked in a salon. Not that she cared, but he put her on edge, and she didn't like it.

She gritted her teeth together and forced herself to meet his gaze. "I promise it won't happen again."

His lips pressed into a firm line as he regarded her for a moment. Then, as if deciding she wasn't worth the time or aggravation, he climbed into his car and slammed the door. The engine roared to life, and Brynlee fought the urge to stick her tongue out at him as he pulled away and disappeared down the street.

"Grumpy prick," she murmured as she turned to go back inside.

Every time they took one step forward, they seemed to take two steps back. Sawyer was meticulous—almost obsessively so. He washed his car several times a week, and she truly did feel bad about the cat ruining his hard work.

She had tried everything to keep Scooter inside, even fixing the animal door multiple times, but the clever cat always found a way out. The scratches on the inside of the door and the tiny footprints all over Sawyer's car were a testament to her routine battles with the feline escape artist.

Ironically, Scooter always bolted straight for Sawyer's car, and never her own. She wasn't sure if that was a good thing or not.

"Bad kitty," she murmured, rubbing his head as she carried him back inside. "You better behave from now on."

She set him down gently, giving him a stern look that he completely ignored, his tail flicking dismissively. With a sigh, she headed to the bathroom to get ready for work.

Standing in front of the mirror, she brushed her hair and applied a touch of makeup, frustration from this morning's confrontation lingering in her mind. The man was going to be the death of her.

She could admit that she would be mildly annoyed if he had a cat that continually came over to her place and made a nuisance of himself, too. But Brynlee tried not to get too worked up over little things like that. Sawyer was far too rigid. It seemed like Brynlee could never do anything quite right in his book. No matter what she said or did, his gaze constantly followed her, silent judging her and finding her lacking.

Shaking her head, she dismissed the thought and focused on the day ahead. Saturdays at the salon were always hectic, and she couldn't afford to be distracted. She checked her hair and makeup once more to make sure she looked okay, then dressed and grabbed her purse. She paused next to the door, giving Scooter one last admonishing look. "Stay inside today, okay?"

The cat blinked at her, unimpressed, before turning to groom himself. Brynlee rolled her eyes with a smile despite herself and locked the door behind her.

As she walked to her car, the morning air cool against her skin, she couldn't help but glance over at Sawyer's empty driveway with a sigh. Maybe one day they could find some common ground. This constant friction was terrible for her mood. She would definitely need to meditate and take some time to rebalance herself once she got home.

The drive to the salon was uneventful, the familiar route offering her a chance to clear her mind. She parked in her usual spot at the back of the lot, leaving the best spots for the customers, then headed for the front door. Unlocking the door, she pushed it open, the bell overhead chiming softly as she entered. The familiar, welcoming scent of lavender mixed with hair products greeted her, and she smiled.

Walking in here—into this place she'd created—never failed to lift her spirits. She'd opened Blissful Beauty just over a year ago and so far things were going exceedingly well. For several years Brynlee had worked as a massage therapist for a spa in the next town over. When the spa closed, leaving Brynlee without a job, she'd begun to advertise around town and worked out of her home.

Soon, she seemed to have enough interest to open her own place. It was a stroke of luck that her friend, Melanie, was a certified stylist. Brynlee had run the idea of opening a small salon and spa by her friend, and Melanie had immediately jumped on board. At first it was just the two of them, but business had grown steadily over the past year, and Brynlee had hired an additional four stylists to round out their staff.

Brynlee moved to her office and set her bag down, then checked her schedule, a small smile forming when she saw a few familiar names.

In desperate need of coffee, she made her way to the small employee break room next door and brewed herself a cup of coffee. Just as she lifted the rim of the mug to her lips, the jingle of the front door echoed through the salon.

Suddenly alert, she popped her head out to see who had come in. A smile curled her lips when her gaze landed on her friend and employee, Melanie.

"Hey, Mel!" Brynlee greeted. "How's it going?"

Melanie smothered a yawn as she cut across the salon. "Tired. Didn't get nearly enough sleep last night. How about you?"

"Same old." Brynlee rolled her eyes as she turned back toward the break room. "Had another run in with Sawyer this morning."

Melanie's face clouded over. "Oh, that reminds me—did you hear about the murder?"

Brynlee stopped mid-step, glancing over at Melanie with wide eyes. "No, I didn't. What happened?"

Melanie bit her lip and made a face. "They think it was Lindsey Gill. Poor thing. They found her body this morning—or late last night, technically."

Brynlee's heart sank. She had held out hope that Lindsey would come home safely, that she was just missing and not... gone. "That's awful," she murmured, her voice heavy with sorrow. "I was really hoping she'd be found alive."

Melanie nodded, her eyes glistening. "Me too. It's just so tragic."

Brynlee's thoughts drifted back to Sawyer. He'd looked exhausted this morning, dark circles under his eyes and a severe frown etched on his face. He was extra grumpy—even for him. He must have been up all night working on the case, trying to find answers.

A pang of guilt assailed her, and she made a mental note to make sure Scooter couldn't get out from now on. The last thing Sawyer needed was more stress, especially with a case like this weighing on him.

Steering the conversation to lighter topics, Brynlee and Mel chatted for a bit as they readied the salon for the day. The morning sun streamed through the large windows of Blissful Beauty, casting a warm glow over the gleaming floors as Brynlee flipped the sign to "Open."

The scent of fresh coffee filled the air, mingling with the

subtle fragrance of hair products and essential oils. The stylists were all in place, bustling around their stations and preparing for their first clients—all except for Jessica.

Brynlee frowned as she glanced at the clock. Jessica's first appointment was due any minute, and there was no sign of her. Just then, Jessica's client, a regular named Mrs. Hughes, walked in. She chatted warmly with Brynlee as she checked in, then took a seat in the waiting area. Brynlee's stomach tightened with anxiety as the minutes ticked by, each one making Jessica's absence more conspicuous.

After five minutes, Brynlee made an executive decision. Jane never hesitated to step up when needed, and Brynlee sidled up beside her. "Jane, could you do me a favor? Would you mind taking Mrs. Hughes for Jessica? She's not here yet, and I don't want to keep her waiting."

Jane grinned and nodded without hesitation. "Absolutely. I'll take care of it."

Relief washed over Brynlee as she watched Jane escort Mrs. Hughes to her station. Brynlee was at the reception desk when Jessica sauntered in, twenty minutes late, an iced coffee in one hand and her cell phone glued to her ear. She didn't seem to notice—or care about—the disapproving look Brynlee shot her way.

Brynlee caught up with Jessica halfway across the salon. "Jessica, I need you to end your call and come with me to the office, please."

Jessica rolled her eyes but ended the call and followed Brynlee to the small office at the back of the salon. Brynlee shut the door behind them, drawing in a deep breath before turning to face her wayward employee.

"Jessica, this is unacceptable," Brynlee began, striving to keep her tone calm and professional despite her frustration. "You were twenty minutes late for your appointment, and this isn't the first time. Your attitude and work ethic have been a problem for a while now. I've given you multiple warnings, but nothing has changed."

Jessica had been with her since the beginning, one of the first stylists Brynlee had hired. At first, she was enthusiastic and dedicated. But over the past few months her attitude had changed. She talked back, made snide comments, and acted catty with both Brynlee and the other employees. Brynlee had corrected her behavior numerous times, but it only seemed to get worse.

She knew what she had to do, and the thought made her stomach churn. Firing Jessica was a risk. Several of her friends worked here, and Brynlee worried they might leave in solidarity. But she couldn't let one person's toxicity ruin what she had built.

Jessica crossed her arms, her expression defiant. "You're overreacting. It's just a few minutes. What's the big deal?"

"The big deal is that your clients depend on you, and so do your colleagues," Brynlee said, her frustration bubbling to the surface. "This isn't just about today. It's about the pattern of behavior you've established. I can't keep covering for you. I have to think about what's best for the salon and our clients. I'm sorry, Jessica, but I have to let you go."

Jessica's face flushed with anger. "You can't do this to me! I'm the best stylist you have!"

Brynlee fought to remain calm. "Unfortunately, your lack of dedication outweighs your talent."

Jessica gaped at her for a moment, her eyes darkening with fury. "My lack of dedication? Are you kidding me? My clients love me."

"When you show up on time," Brynlee agreed. "But this isn't the first time I've had to have another stylist cover for you, and if I allow to you stay here, it won't be the last. Your behavior is affecting everyone here, and I won't allow it to continue."

"You'll regret this, you'll see. You think you're so high and mighty, but you're nothing without me." She stormed out of the office, her voice rising several octaves. "I don't need this place anyway!"

Heads turned as Jessica made her way through the salon, her tirade drawing everyone's attention. Brynlee followed, feeling the weight of her decision but knowing it was the right one.

Jessica paused in the middle of the room, her gaze sweeping over the dozen pairs of eyes that watched on. "Guess what, everyone? Brynlee just fired me!" she said loudly, her voice dripping with venom. "If you want a real stylist, I'll be working out of my house for now."

"Jessica—" Brynlee warned.

But that was all she got out before Jessica whirled her way. "Screw you, Brynlee!"

The iced coffee in the woman's hand suddenly launched across the room, soaking Brynlee from head to toe and splattering the wall behind her. For a moment Brynlee was too shocked to move—then anger, hot and fierce, swept through her. She sucked in a breath, ready to unleash several months' worth of fury on the woman. At the last moment, she swallowed down the words, biting back the urge to snap at the woman.

Jessica was only making things worse for herself. Brynlee needed to remain professional; she didn't want to say or do anything she would later regret. It took every ounce of restraint to stall the flow of angry words. "Please leave."

"Whatever." Jessica spun on a heel and flounced out the door, slamming it behind her.

The salon was silent for a moment, the tension palpable. Brynlee could feel the eyes of her other employees on her, the uncertainty swirling in the air. She knew she had taken a gamble, but she also knew it was the right thing to do.

She drew in a deep breath before turning toward her audience and forced a small smile to her face. "I'm sorry you all had to see that. I assure you that everything will be taken care of."

She looked around, meeting the eyes of every staff member and client. "We're here to provide the best service possible, and I promise that's exactly what we'll do."

Jane shifted closer and tipped her head next to Brynlee. "I have a spare shirt in my locker."

Brynlee shot her a grateful smile and nodded, then inched her chin up as she glanced around the salon. As she turned to leave, Mrs. Hughes broke the silence.

"Brynlee dear, would you mind getting me a cup of coffee?"

She smiled at the older woman, grateful for her easy acceptance. "Absolutely."

Just like that, the salon gradually buzzed back to life. As Brynlee headed toward the break room, a mixture of relief and lingering unease roiled in her stomach, but she knew she'd made the right choice.

CHAPTER
FIVE

Sawyer leaned back in his chair and scrubbed a hand over his face. Nothing about Lindsey's death made sense.

Dare leaned against the battered filing cabinet and hooked the heel of his boot on the drawer's handle. "Is there any connection to the other murders?"

Sawyer took a deep breath and shook his head. "There's not—not yet, anyway."

The recent murders had shaken the once-quiet town of Brookhaven to its core. Last month, Jayla Simms had been found dead, her body posed on a park bench in the center of Brookhaven. Official cause of death was asphyxiation.

A few weeks later, Hilary Swanson's remains had been found on a popular hiking trail, her body posed, just like Jayla's. However, instead of asphyxiation, the medical examiner concluded that Hilary had died of severe blood loss as the result of what he suspected was a miscarriage.

Lindsey Gill had been abducted from her home in Brookhaven shortly after Jayla Simms had been found. From the state of her home, it appeared as though she was getting ready to leave for work when she was distracted by arrival of a visitor. Now, she was also dead, apparently due to blunt force trauma.

The pieces of the puzzle didn't fit. Aside from the fact that all of the women had blonde hair and blue eyes, there were no common threads, no overlap in their lives aside from their looks. In the case of both Jayla and Hilary, the killer had scrubbed down every inch of the women's bodies, using bleach to remove any trace of DNA. Lindsey's fingers had been removed, most likely for the same reason.

But Lindsey's manner of death was completely different. While she'd been placed where she would be found quickly, her death lacked the care taken with the other two women. Why?

"Lindsey Gill appears to have been brutally raped and beaten," Sawyer said as he glanced at the crime scene photos. "Jayla and Hilary were both posed, as if the killer had cared for them. But Lindsey..." He shook his head. "He literally threw her away like trash."

McCoy leaned forward, his eyes narrowing. "What are you thinking? A copycat?"

Sawyer ran a hand over his hair. "It's possible. The level of brutality is higher, more chaotic."

Dare rubbed his chin thoughtfully. "So we're looking at a different killer. Someone trying to emulate the original but lacking the same level of control and planning."

"That's my theory," Sawyer said. "Both Simms and Swanson were kept for nearly a year before they were killed. Lindsey Gill was only missing for a couple of weeks. I think we need to treat this as a separate case for now. The killers' methods are different, and the timeline doesn't fit. We could be dealing with someone who's aware of the previous murders and is trying to replicate them, but with their own twisted variations."

Dare sighed and rubbed his temples. "We already have the

public in a panic over the Simms and Swanson cases. If word gets out that there's a second killer on the loose…"

Yeah. It was going to be a clusterfuck. Sawyer glanced at Cam. "Why don't you see what you can find out here? I'm going to head back to the alley, make sure we didn't miss anything, then get the footage from the restaurant."

Cam nodded. "I'll keep you posted if I find anything."

Sawyer's eyes burned with fatigue, and his entire body felt weighed down by the emotional toll of the past twenty-four hours. The gruesome images of Lindsey Gill's brutalized body were seared into his mind, and the memory of her parents' devastated faces when he delivered the news gnawed at his heart.

He had been a detective for years, but it never got easier. Telling a family that their loved one was gone forever was the worst part of the job. It was moments like those that made him question why he chose this line of work. But deep down, he knew the answer. It was the need for justice, the desire to bring closure to families torn apart by violence and loss.

He sighed deeply and ran a hand through his disheveled hair. He had barely slept, managing only a quick nap before heading back to the station. The morning's confrontation with Brynlee was still fresh in his mind, adding another layer of frustration to his already foul mood. They always seemed to get off on the wrong foot.

Sawyer rubbed his temples. Despite his attempts to keep things cordial, their interactions always devolved into bickering. He knew Brynlee wasn't entirely to blame. She was spirited and unpredictable, qualities that infuriated him as much as they intrigued him. But her free-spirited nature clashed with his need for order and control. It was like trying to mix oil and water.

And her damn cat, Scooter, was a constant thorn in his side. He'd returned home long enough this morning to grab a quick nap, shower, then head back outside—only to find the cat once again perched on the roof of his car. What a fucking pain in the ass.

He took a deep breath, trying to shake off the emotional fog. He needed to compartmentalize, to push his personal feelings aside and concentrate on the task at hand. Lindsey deserved justice, and he was determined to see it through. He needed to find answers—needed to bring the killer to justice, and to make sure this never happened again.

Grabbing the handle, he pushed the door open and stepped out onto the sidewalk. The sunlight was harsh now, revealing every detail of the grim scene with stark clarity as he ducked under the threshold of the crime scene tape. He approached the area where Lindsey's body had been discovered, his gaze sweeping over the grim surroundings.

Last night they'd collected what they could, but he wanted to go over it once more, scrutinize every inch of the alley in the daylight. They couldn't afford to miss a single thing. The smallest piece of evidence could lead them to the monster responsible for Lindsey's death.

He knelt down, carefully examining the ground near the dumpster. Pieces of broken glass, crumpled paper, and stained fabric littered the area. Each item was a potential clue. He carefully collected samples, placing them carefully into evidence bags.

His attention shifted to a nearby stack of cardboard boxes. The alley smelled of refuse and decay, the odor a harsh reminder of the brutality that had taken place. He rifled through the boxes, checking for any signs of tampering or discarded items that might have been missed during the initial sweep.

His mind flashed back to the Gills, the anguish etched into their faces when he had delivered the news. The memory of their tears and pleas for answers was a relentless burden, fueling his determination to solve the case. He couldn't bear to see that kind of devastation again. They needed justice, and he was going to give it to them, no matter the cost.

Sawyer moved to the far end of the alley, where the grime and detritus accumulated more densely. He scrutinized every inch of the area, pushing aside trash and debris with methodical precision. Each piece of evidence was cataloged and bagged, each small detail noted in his notebook.

As he worked, the sound of distant voices and the hum of traffic arose as the small town stirred to life around him. Sawyer remained focused, his eyes scanning the ground for anything that might have been overlooked.

He stood up with a sigh, surveying the alley one last time as the weight of the day settled heavily over him. He couldn't afford to let his guard down. The killer was still out there, and Lindsey's case was far from closed. They would need to follow up on every lead, analyze every piece of evidence. Sawyer was determined to find the monster responsible and bring them to justice. For Lindsey, for her family, and for every victim who deserved closure, he wouldn't rest until the case was solved.

Sawyer turned in place, taking in his surroundings. The alley was fairly narrow, maybe only eight feet wide. It was flanked by the restaurant on one side, a small floral shop on the other. There was a single outdoor bulb situated over the door of the restaurant, but nothing on the side where the florist was located.

His gaze swept along the roofline of the restaurant, and he noticed a camera situated high in the corner. Following the trajectory, he imagined it would cover the area near the door to catch people coming and going from the alley. He needed that footage.

CHAPTER
SIX

Sawyer's jaw tightened as he strode out of the alley and approached the restaurant. The sign on the glass door informed patrons that the restaurant didn't open until early afternoon, but he knew from speaking with Sam last night that most workers would be here already, prepping for the day ahead.

He knocked hard on the door, hoping to catch someone's attention. Ten seconds passed, then twenty. Sawyer knocked once more, a little harder this time, then moved toward a side window. Cupping his hands around his face to block out the sunlight, he managed to catch a glimpse of the interior.

A shadowy figure was moving across the dining area, and Sawyer knocked on the window to capture their attention. The figure paused, then turned his way. A moment later, a man appeared in the window, shaking his head, indicating they were closed. Sawyer unclipped his badge and held it up to the window for the person to see.

The man's face registered surprise, and he pointed toward the door. Sawyer met him there a moment later, and the front door swung inward.

"Sorry about that," the man apologized. "I didn't recognize you. I'm Dan Reynolds, the manager here."

"No problem. I'm Detective Reed," he introduced himself, extending his hand for a quick shake. Sawyer tipped his head toward the alley. "I'm following up on the murder from last night."

Dan made a face. "Terrible, what happened to her. And poor Sam. I can't imagine."

Sawyer nodded in commiseration. "How is he holding up?"

"He took the day off—understandably—but he seems to be okay."

"Good." Sawyer gestured toward the restaurant. "I noticed you have a few cameras outside. I need to see your security footage from last night."

The manager's eyes widened slightly, but he nodded. "Of course, Detective. Follow me."

He led Sawyer to a small office at the back of the restaurant, where a monitor displayed several camera feeds. The manager pulled up the footage from the previous evening and handed the controls to Sawyer.

"We have two cameras outside—one positioned at each doorway," Dan added.

"What about out back?"

"You mean where the employees park?" Dan's mouth curved down in a slight grimace. "Sorry. Everyone leaves through either the front door or the alley, so that's where they installed the cameras."

Sawyer nodded slowly. "Who all parks behind the building?"

"Mostly the cooks." Dan lifted a shoulder. "The waitresses generally finish up sooner, so they park out front, across the street. Since the cooks are here longer, the lot out back is reserved for them since it's closer."

"How many people worked last night?"

Dan glanced upward in thought. "About twenty, including all the cooks, waiters, and other staff."

Sawyer stewed over that for a moment. How was it that no one else had seen Lindsey? "How many cooks did you have last night?"

Dan let out a little laugh. "On a Friday? Several. It's one of our busiest nights. We had five people back here."

"Sam was the last person here—What time did the others leave?"

Understanding immediately what Sawyer was asking, Dan's expression turned serious. "I'll check the time cards."

"Thank you." Dan left to retrieve the information and Sawyer focused on the screen, enlarging the feed that spanned the alley. He rewound to the previous evening, beginning the footage at sundown, his eyes scanning every movement in the alley.

Time crawled by as he slowly advanced the video. The alley remained empty as the light faded, the shadows growing longer. The restaurant's side door occasionally opened, revealing employees stepping out for a smoke break or to take out the trash, but nothing out of the ordinary.

The office door opened, and Dan stepped inside. "Here you go." He passed Sawyer a list of employees and the times they'd clocked out.

"Perfect. Thanks for your help."

Sawyer rolled the footage, watching as the employees began to trickle out after their shift. He cross-checked the time on the camera to the time on Dan's list, marking off each employee. Finally, only Sam remained.

Just before one o'clock, a figure appeared at the edge of the screen. Sawyer's heart rate quickened as he watched the man enter the alley from the rear. The man kept his head down, his movements jerky and hurried as he strode toward the dumpster.

From the bulky outline of the shadow, Sawyer could tell that the man carried Lindsey over his shoulder, her arms dangling limply. Sawyer winced and anger burned through him as he watched the man bend, then drop her to the ground. Her body hit the ground hard, limbs tangling as she landed face down.

Sawyer curled one hand into a fist, bile rising in his throat. It was as if he were discarding trash—not a human. Fury raced through his veins as he focused on the man, desperate for a glimpse of him. But the man kept his face tipped downward, hidden within the shadows.

"Goddamn it," Sawyer muttered savagely. The man knew exactly where the camera was; he must have scouted the place before choosing to leave her here.

On screen, the footage continued to roll until, less than ten minutes later, Sam left through the side door and angled toward the dumpster. Everything happened exactly as he'd said —he'd literally tripped over Lindsey's body on his way out.

Sawyer paused the video and scrubbed a hand over his chin. The man had entered through the back parking lot. Had any of the other cooks seen anything suspicious? He glanced at the time log again, noting the last person who'd left before Sam—Jay Cochran.

"Dan?"

Clearly hovering nearby, the manager stuck his head in the open doorway. "Yes?"

"Could you please get me Jay Cochran's information?"

"Of course."

Sawyer turned back to the screen and rewound to when the man entered from the back. He watched once more as he dumped Lindsey's body, then retreated the same way he'd come. A few moments later, Sawyer noticed a slight lightening near the edge of the screen.

Headlights.

Sitting forward in his seat, Sawyer mentally tracked them, trying to figure out which direction he'd gone. Movement from the left side of the screen caught his attention, and Sawyer tapped the button to freeze the screen. He squinted but could make out nothing.

He slowly rewound until a large object moved into view and tires filled the upper portion of the screen near the road. Sawyer tipped his head, staring hard as he watched the vehicle slowly roll across the screen. Too long to be a car, it had to be a van, SUV, or truck. The body was lighter in color, possibly white or silver.

Hope exploded in his chest. They had a lead—*finally*.

"Here's Jay's information."

Sawyer nodded. "Is he working today?"

"Yes, but his shift doesn't start until four."

Good. That gave Sawyer plenty of time to speak with the man. "By the way—can I get a copy of this?"

"Sure thing."

Dan copied the footage, then sent it to Sawyer who stood and shook the man's hand. "Thanks again for your help."

"I hope you can find something," Dan offered.

"Me, too."

Sawyer left the restaurant and paused on the sidewalk. Less than twelve hours ago, a vehicle had passed by this very spot. Was it the man who'd killed Lindsey? His gut told him yes.

Shielding his eyes against the bright morning sun, he lifted his gaze and studied the surrounding buildings. Someone had to have a camera that pointed in this direction—and he was damn well going to find it.

CHAPTER
SEVEN

Sawyer pulled his car to a stop in front of the apartment complex, then glanced at the address once more, confirming he was at the right place. He climbed out and headed up to the second floor, to apartment 2F.

Sawyer gave a quick, hard knock, then waited. A few moments later, the door creaked open, revealing a very exhausted-looking man. His hair was disheveled, a mixture of brown and gray strands sticking out at odd angles, like he'd just rolled out of bed. Clad in a wrinkled t-shirt and plaid pajama pants, he squinted his eyes against the daylight. "Yeah?"

"Jay Cochran?"

"Uh... Am I in trouble?" Jay's voice was thick with sleep, his expression puzzled as he took in the sight of the detective on his doorstep.

"Not at all." Slipping his hands into his pockets to keep his stance non-threatening, Sawyer leaned back against the wall. "Mr. Cochran, sorry to disturb you so early, but I'm investigating a situation that occurred last night. We're trying to get some information, and I'd appreciate it if I could ask you a few questions."

Jay rubbed a hand over his face, clearly trying to shake off the last remnants of sleep. "Yeah, sure. Come in."

Sawyer followed him inside, where they settled in the living room. Jay covered a yawn. "Sorry. What did you say this was about?"

"There was a murder in the alley next to the restaurant where you work," Sawyer said. "A woman was found near the dumpster."

Jay's mouth dropped open in shock, his fatigue gone in the blink of an eye. "Murder? You're serious?"

Sawyer nodded. "Unfortunately."

"Jesus, that's…" He gave a slow shake of his head. "This is the first I'm hearing of it. I… I just woke up."

Sawyer studied him carefully, noting the genuine shock on Jay's face. "You worked last night, right?"

"Yeah, I did. I left after my shift, came straight home, showered, and went to bed." Jay gestured vaguely behind him, his hand trembling slightly. "Didn't hear or see anything after that."

Sawyer nodded, taking in the details. "When you left, did you notice anything out of the ordinary? Any people around, anything unusual near the restaurant?"

Jay frowned, his brow furrowing as he tried to recall the night before. "Not really. I parked out back, like I always do. Didn't see anyone around when I left, though. It was quiet."

"Were there any vehicles parked near the alley when you left?" Sawyer pressed.

Jay thought for a moment, then nodded slowly. "There was a vehicle parked on the side road—you know, over by the church—but I didn't think anything of it at the time."

"Did you happen to notice the make or model?"

"Might've been an SUV or a van, I think. Maybe white?"

Sawyer filed that away, a small piece of the puzzle, perhaps, but a piece nonetheless. "Did you notice if the vehicle was running? Anyone inside?"

Jay shook his head. "No, it was just parked there. No lights on, no one around that I saw."

Sawyer stood, offering a nod of thanks as he walked toward the door. "I appreciate your time, Mr. Cochran. If you remember anything else, don't hesitate to reach out."

Jay looked relieved that the questioning was over, his hand gripping the doorframe as if to steady himself. "Sure thing, Detective. I'll let you know if anything comes to mind."

With that, Sawyer turned and walked back to his car, his mind already working through the new information. A white vehicle, maybe an SUV or a van, parked near the alley on the night of the murder.

He started the car and drove away, the quiet neighborhood fading into the background as he headed back to the station. The pieces were slowly coming together.

Inside the police station, activity buzzed around him as he stepped inside. Phones rang, voices carried on muted conversations, but his focus was singular as he headed straight for the small conference room where Dare Jensen and Cam McCoy were waiting.

The fluorescent lights glowed brightly overhead, illuminating the photos on the wall. Dare was leaning against the table, arms crossed, his expression more stoic than usual.

"Got something for us?" Dare asked.

Cam glanced up from where he was seated, flipping through a notepad, his attention now focused solely on Sawyer.

Sawyer nodded, relaying the events of the morning as he pulled a USB drive from his pocket and plugged it into the computer connected to the monitor. "I stopped by Jay Cochran's apartment after I left the restaurant. He claims he didn't see or hear anything unusual when he left the restaurant last night, but he did mention spotting a light-colored vehicle parked near the church down the street. I've pulled the footage from the restaurant's cameras to see if we can spot anything."

He clicked through a few files, bringing up the video feed from the restaurant's back alley. The footage was grainy, but clear enough to make out shapes and movement. Sawyer fast-forwarded until he found the timestamp that matched Jay's departure.

"There," he said, pointing to the screen. A light-colored vehicle moved slowly through the frame, the headlights flickering as it passed by the alley. "That's the vehicle Jay mentioned."

Dare leaned in, his brow furrowing as his gaze narrowed on the screen. "Looks like a van or an SUV. Hard to tell in this light."

Cam squinted at the image, his pen tapping lightly on his notepad. "You think this is our guy?"

Sawyer shrugged. "It's a lead. Jay said the vehicle was parked near the church when he left. We need to scout the area, see if we can find any cameras that might've captured a clearer image."

Dare pushed off from the table, already heading for the door. "Let's get moving then. I don't want this asshole slipping through our fingers."

They split up, combing through the streets around the restaurant, checking every angle for possible cameras. But the results were far from satisfying. Hours later, the three of them found themselves back in the station, the frustration weighing heavily on their shoulders.

Dare glanced their way. "Either of you come up with anything?"

"Not a damn thing worthwhile," Cam said. "It's like he knows where every camera in town is, and managed to avoid all of them."

"Wouldn't surprise me." Dare let out a little growl. "Reed, you find anything?"

Sawyer slumped into a chair at the table and rubbed his temples. "Only one camera managed to capture anything remotely useful," he said, pulling up the footage they had retrieved.

"Got this from that dance studio across from the church." The video flickered to life on the screen, showing a distant shot of the side road near the church. The camera was located inside the lobby of the studio, and the image was blurry, the distance making it difficult to make out any clear details.

Dare stepped forward, head tipped in contemplation. "What does that look like to you?"

The area was dark, no street lamps or anything to illuminate the vehicle's shape, and Sawyer shook his head. "Van or SUV?"

The vantage point wasn't great, but from here they could see the front right corner of the restaurant, and part of the road. The footage rolled for several minutes, and they watched as several of the restaurant employees pulled out of the back lot, turned on to the road, then headed home.

Sawyer checked the timestamp and pointed to a sedan pulling out of the restaurant's back lot. "This must be Jay Cochran."

The sedan turned left onto the main road, in the direction of Cochran's apartment complex. As soon as the car disappeared, the white vehicle parked along the side road began to move. The headlights remained off as the driver steered the vehicle into the parking lot, then disappeared behind the restaurant.

"Rewind that."

Sawyer did as Dare asked, then tapped play as it pulled away from the curb once more.

"Look at the shape." Dare dipped his chin. "Doesn't that look like a van—the type contractors use?"

"Fucking great." Cam rolled his eyes. "That should be easy to narrow down. Every business only has a dozen of those."

"Something is better than nothing," Dare softly admonished as he watched the vehicle disappear behind the restaurant again. Less than two minutes passed before the screen grew brighter and the vehicle appeared again.

Cam used his finger to trace the headlights on the car. "Older style. Maybe ten, fifteen years old?"

Dare nodded, and they all watched as the van turned left out of the lot, heading away from town.

"Goddamn it. No decals, nothing to identify it," Cam noted, his tone laced with frustration. "And we can't even see the damn plate."

"It's a start," Dare said, though even he didn't sound particularly convinced. "We'll run a check on all registered work vans in the area, see if we can narrow it down. But this... this isn't going to be easy."

Cam sighed, flipping his notepad closed. "When is it ever?"

Sawyer knew Cam was right. Investigations were rarely straightforward, but the nagging sense of urgency clung to him. A woman had been murdered, and somewhere out there was a killer who thought they'd gotten away with it.

Sawyer stared at the screen, the white van taunting him from the fuzzy footage. It was a lead, but one that was frustratingly out of reach. "We'll get him," Sawyer said, more to himself than to anyone else. "We have to."

Dare and Cam nodded. There was still much to do, more leads to chase, and a killer to bring to justice. They were closer than they had been that morning, but still, not close enough. And until they were, he wouldn't rest.

CHAPTER
EIGHT

As the evening settled over the city, Brynlee flipped the sign to "Closed", relieved that the day was almost over. Only one client remained with Jane, but they would hopefully be finished soon.

Brynlee moved on autopilot, gathering towels and loading them into the washer, then checking the bathroom to make sure it was clean and well-stocked. The stylists were responsible for their own stations, but Brynlee did a quick once-over to make certain everything was in its place.

After Jessica had slammed out the door this morning, the remainder of the day had been a blur of appointments and stilted conversation. A few of Jessica's friends had come to her over the course of the day to express their concerns but also to show their support, understanding why she had made the decision she did. It wasn't an easy conversation to have, but it was a necessary one.

She had built this salon from the ground up, and she wasn't about to let anyone tear it down. She had weathered storms before; she would weather this one too.

"Thank you so much, Jane," Elisa gushed as the stylist

guided her toward the reception desk. The woman turned to Brynlee. "She did an amazing job. I'll definitely be coming back."

Brynlee smiled warmly. "We're glad to hear that, Elisa."

She led Elisa to the front desk, giving her the total, and Elisa handed over cash, glancing around the salon appreciatively.

"Is there a restroom I can use before I go?" she asked.

"Of course," Brynlee replied, pointing down the hallway. "It's just past the massage rooms, on the left."

Elisa nodded, following Brynlee's directions. While she was gone, Brynlee continued her end-of-day routine, sanitizing surfaces and organizing supplies. She made sure everything was in its proper place, ready for the next day's appointments.

Elisa headed toward the door with a little wave. "Thanks again. Have a great weekend!"

"You too, Elisa," Brynlee replied, waving as Elisa walked out the door. She then turned to Jane, who was gathering her things. "Enjoy your day off tomorrow, Jane. You've earned it."

Jane grinned. "Thanks, Brynlee. You have a good weekend too. See you Monday!"

With one last smile, Jane headed out, leaving Brynlee alone in the now-quiet salon. She took a moment to breathe in the calm, the peacefulness that came with the end of a busy day. Then, she set about turning off all the lights, each room falling into darkness one by one.

She gathered her belongings, then stepped out into the cool evening air. Pulling her jacket tighter around her shoulders, she locked the front door, then climbed into her car and headed home.

As she pulled into her driveway, the sight of the sight of a small package on the porch caught her eye. She groaned, the sight of it triggering a wave of apprehension.

She sighed deeply as she shifted the transmission into park, finally mustering the energy to step out of the car. Stepping out of the car, she approached the porch with a sense of foreboding. Climbing the steps, each one felt like a small mountain. The knot in her stomach tightened with every step.

It was the third time this week that Zane had left something for her. He had been returning her belongings one by one, an unwelcome reminder of their past and his betrayal. At first, it had been small things—a book, a piece of jewelry, a sweater. But each package felt like a stab, reopening wounds she was desperately trying to heal.

She wished he would just stop and leave her alone. She didn't know what he was trying to accomplish, but each item felt like a small, calculated intrusion into her carefully rebuilt life. He had cheated on her, moved on with someone else, and yet he still found ways to disrupt her life.

Brynlee picked up the package, her fingers trembling slightly. She could see his handwriting on the label, neat and familiar, and it made her heart ache. The sight of it brought back memories of happier times, tainted now by his infidelity.

For a moment, she contemplated throwing it into the trash without opening it, but her curiosity and the need for closure got the better of her. Inside the box was a small stuffed bear, a red rose clutched in one paw, a heart in the other. She remembered it vividly. He'd given it to her for Valentine's Day —just days before she'd found out he'd been unfaithful.

Brynlee felt tears prickling at the corners of her eyes. She would gladly give up everything she left behind if it meant never having to see or hear from him again.

Brynlee unlocked the door and stepped inside, the familiar scent of home doing little to calm her. She tossed the bear into a box in the hall closet and slammed the door shut, the sound echoing through the empty house. She leaned against the door for a moment, closing her eyes and taking a deep breath.

She'd dealt with enough today; she didn't need to add Zane's ridiculous excuse for absolution, too. Pushing off the door, Brynlee headed into the kitchen. She needed something to take her mind off the day—a hot shower, a glass of wine, maybe even both. Anything to drown out the echoes of her confrontation with Jessica and the unwanted reminders from Zane.

Scooter was lying contentedly in a patch of evening sunlight that streamed through the back door, and she paused to pet him. "Were you good today?"

Meow.

Brynlee chuckled. Figured the cat would behave—Sawyer wasn't home yet. It seemed like the cat lived to torment her neat-freak neighbor. "We have to get that door fixed."

Pushing to her feet, she dropped her purse and keys on the counter then made a beeline for the bathroom. Inside, she turned on the water for the shower, letting it run until steam filled the bathroom. As she stepped under the hot spray, she let the water wash away the stress of the day. But no matter how long she stood there, she couldn't shake the feeling that her past was closing in on her, one small, unwelcome reminder at a time.

A moment of clarity hit her all at once. This would be the last time he had the power to disrupt her peace.

She needed to focus on moving forward, on healing. Brynlee knew it wouldn't be easy, but today had shown her that she had the strength to make tough decisions. She had faced one difficult goodbye already; it was time to face another.

Stepping from the shower, she grabbed up her phone and pulled up Zane's information. With a deep breath, she tapped the option to block his number.

No more packages, no more reminders. As she stood there, a sense of calm washed over her. It was time to reclaim her life, one step at a time.

CHAPTER
NINE

The sun was beginning to set as Sawyer dragged himself through the front door, the weight of exhaustion and frustration settling deep into his bones. It had been another long ass day, doing nothing but chasing dead ends.

Feet dragging, he made his way to the kitchen at the back of the house. His body protested every movement as he slipped off his holster and set his pistol, badge, and phone on the counter. He needed a stiff drink and about twelve hours of sleep.

Yanking open the door of the fridge, he drew in a deep breath as a refreshing blast of cool air washed over him. He snagged a bottle of beer, popped the top, then drank deeply. The cold liquid instantly soothed his frazzled nerves, and he leaned against the counter near the sink.

He couldn't help but shake his head at the sight that greeted him. Outside, Brynlee stood in the backyard on her side of the duplex. She was barefoot, her arms stretched heavenward, eyes closed. She didn't move. She just stood there for what felt like forever, frozen like some pagan goddess in the midst of a sacrificial ritual.

Brynlee never ceased to baffle him. Still, he couldn't ignore the odd sense of balance her presence brought to his life—even if it was wrapped in crystals, essential oils, and a bunch of other shit he really didn't understand.

Grabbing his beer, he walked outside, letting the screen door slam behind him. He paused for a moment, just watching her. He knew she had heard him, but she refused to acknowledge his presence, maintaining her serene pose.

"What are you doing?" he finally asked, his voice tinged with both curiosity and exasperation.

Brynlee opened one eye and glanced at him before closing it again. "Grounding myself," she replied, as if it were the most obvious thing in the world.

Sawyer snorted. "Grounding yourself? You do know this is a backyard in a suburban duplex, right? Not some mystical forest."

Brynlee lowered her arms and turned to face him, a sickly sweet smile dancing on her lips. "And you do know that grounding can be done anywhere, right? Even in a suburban backyard."

He took a swig of his beer and shook his head. "You're such a hippie."

"Maybe if you tried it once in a while you wouldn't be so grumpy all the time."

"Is that why I'm grumpy? And here I thought it was because someone is killing women and leaving them out in the public eye."

Brynlee winced slightly. "I'm sorry. I heard about Lindsey as soon as I got to the salon this morning."

Sawyer waved off her apology, knowing he was extra tense because of the recent cases. "It's fine."

"Still..." She made a little face. "You doing okay?"

He lifted a brow her way. "You getting soft on me, Layne?"

She cracked a smile that slipped right through his ribs and pierced his heart. "Never."

Sawyer cleared his throat. "Enjoy your..."—he gestured toward her with the beer bottle—"whatever that is."

He turned to leave Brynlee to her grounding ritual when he spotted Scooter lounging on the patio table, looking smug and content.

"Your cat is a menace," he grumbled, sliding a glare at Brynlee.

She glanced at Scooter and then back at Sawyer, unfazed. "He's not a menace. He just likes his freedom. And he's smart. No matter what I do, he keeps breaking out of the animal door."

Sawyer's irritation flared once more. "Then fix the door so he can't escape."

Brynlee rolled her eyes. "You think I haven't tried?"

"Fine." Sawyer made a split-second decision. If she couldn't—or wouldn't—take care of it, then he would. Abruptly, he turned on his heel and strode back to his side of the duplex. He grabbed what he needed and retraced his steps, determined to put an end to Scooter's escapades.

Returning to the backyard, he bypassed Brynlee and walked right through the back door and into the kitchen that mirrored his—with a few minor exceptions. Her house smelled fantastic.

"What is that?" He almost bumped into Brynlee as he turned around.

"What is what?" Her brows drew together in an aggravated frown. "And what the hell makes you think you can just walk in here—"

"It smells delicious."

"Oh." She blinked up at him, looking taken aback. "I made soup."

"Clearly." He moved toward the slow cooker and peered through the lid, spotted with condensation. "What kind?"

She stared at him for a moment before he raised his brows, prompting her to answer. "Um... ham and potato."

He nodded. "Good, I'm starving. You can pay me in soup."

"Pay you—What?" Brynlee followed him as he turned back toward the door and set the toolbox at his feet. "What are you doing?"

"Fixing the problem," he replied curtly, not bothering to look back.

"Sawyer, I can—"

"No, you can't, or it would already be fixed," he interrupted, kneeling down in front of the small door. "Just let me handle it."

With a beleaguered sigh she dropped into a chair next to the table. He could feel her eyes on him as he worked, but she didn't say a thing. A smile tugged at the corners of his mouth, but he bit it back, focusing on the task at hand. Fixing something, working with his hands, was a welcome distraction from the grim events of the past twenty-four hours.

Sawyer removed the plastic swinging door that hung limply on its hinges. Almost immediately the cat bolted through the open space, startling Sawyer and nearly knocking him on his ass.

He glared as the cat sauntered past him. "You're welcome, you furry little asshole."

Scooter tossed him a look ripe with disdain from where he sat near one of Brynlee's potted plants, his tail flicking lazily. Brynlee sat back and crossed her arms over her chest, still barefoot and slightly bemused by the whole situation.

"You're really something, you know that?" she said with a shake of her head.

"Yeah, well, I can't have your cat causing chaos all over the neighborhood," Sawyer muttered.

He leaned in to examine the frame, noticing the scratches and bite marks Scooter had left in his attempts to break free. "Persistent little guy, isn't he?" Sawyer said, more to himself than to Brynlee.

"He's determined, I'll give him that," Brynlee replied, watching him with interest.

Scooter gave a low meow, as if he knew they were talking about him, and Sawyer rolled his eyes. "You better appreciate this, you little shit."

He reinforced the frame, making sure there were no gaps or weak points, then layered a small square of wood over the space. He tightened the screws with a final twist, then stood to inspect his handiwork.

"That should do it," he said as he gathered his tools and replaced them in his bag. "Scooter won't be breaking out of here anytime soon."

A smile curved Brynlee's mouth, though he wasn't entirely certain if it was born out of amusement or appreciation. "You didn't have to do that, you know."

He lifted a brow her way. "I did if I want to keep my sanity."

The corners of her mouth twitched. She was definitely laughing at him. He rolled his eyes and moved past her, opening cupboards until he found what he was looking for.

"Need something?"

He ignored her as he removed the lid of the slow cooker and ladled a healthy portion of soup into the bowl. His stomach growled as the savory scent wafted up to his nostrils.

He opened a drawer in front of him, looking for a spoon, but found a drawer stuffed with junk.

"To your right," came Brynlee's voice, saturated with mirth.

He moved to the drawer she'd indicated, pulled out a spoon, and scooped up a large serving of the soup. It exploded over his taste buds, and he closed his eyes in appreciation.

He swallowed then turned her way. "This is damn good."

"Glad you like it."

He cleared his throat as he gathered up his tools and headed for the door. Since his hands were full, Brynlee opened the door for him, stepping aside to let him pass.

He tipped his head at the cat. "If you have any more issues with Satan over there, let me know."

Brynlee couldn't hold back her laugh this time. "You'll be the first person I'll call."

Yeah, he knew that was a lie. He stepped outside, but the sound of her voice had him pausing once more.

"Sawyer?"

He glanced over his shoulder. "Yeah?"

"Thanks for your help. Really."

He winked, a small smile tugging at his lips. "Anytime, sun goddess."

As he walked back to his side of the duplex, Sawyer felt a little lighter than he had when he'd gotten home. Maybe Brynlee's grounding ritual had some merit after all. At the very least, it had given him a momentary escape from the darkness that had been clouding his mind.

Fixing an animal door wasn't going to solve his problems or bring justice to Lindsey's killer, but it was something he could control, something he could fix. For now, that was enough.

CHAPTER
TEN

Brynlee Layne wiped her hands on a dishtowel, looking around the bustling kitchen of the family farmhouse. The scents of roast chicken and freshly baked bread filled the air, mingling with the faint smell of gardenias from the porch. It was the perfect setting for a Sunday lunch, and yet, Brynlee couldn't shake the feeling of being a bit out of place today.

Sunlight streamed through the large windows, casting a warm glow over the familiar space. The Layne house, with its wraparound porch and inviting charm, had always been a haven of comfort and love. Today, as every Sunday, it was the center of their close-knit family gathering.

Charlene Layne, Brynlee's mother, was at the stove, finishing up the gravy. "Bryn, can you set the table, sweetheart?"

"Of course," Brynlee replied, grabbing the stack of plates from the counter.

Brynlee moved toward the dining room and set a plate in front of each chair—except one. The seat next to her own remained empty and probably always would. A sigh escaped before she could stop it, and she spun toward the window.

Immediately his gaze landed on the group of people gathered on the back patio.

Next to the grill, her father, Garrett, was expertly flipping steaks on the grill. His laughter mingled with the chatter of the others gathered around him. Her gaze snagged on Ainsley and her fiancé, Sheriff Dare Jensen, and she couldn't help but smile.

Dare had one arm wrapped around Ainsley's waist, and she leaned into him, face tipped up, eyes full of love and devotion. It was obvious they adored one another. Ainsley deserved it after everything she'd been through recently. Her ex had been abusive and possessive, but she'd managed to escape, and now had found someone who truly loved and cared for her.

Brynlee had suspected something was going on for months before Ainsley returned to Brookhaven. She'd been quieter, more reserved, and Ainsley's bright smile had been conspicuously absent for longer than Brynlee could remember. When she'd heard that Dare was looking to rent out the suite attached to his family home, Brynlee had casually mentioned it to her mother in passing, knowing that Charlene would try to convince Ainsley to move home.

Everything had worked out perfectly—almost. Ainsley's ex-boyfriend, Joel Parsons, wasn't at all thrilled that Ainsley had left him, and he'd stalked Ainsley for weeks for attacking both Ainsley and Kinley. Thankfully, the police had shown up in time to stop anything truly horrible from happening. The man was now dead and Ainsley was getting married to the man of her dreams soon.

Brynlee's gaze slid to her middle sister, Kinley, and her boyfriend, Cam McCoy, who were absorbed in their own conversation. The love between the two was palpable. They'd been best friends for years and had finally decided to take the next step.

Of course, almost losing the love of your life tended to put things into perspective. Kinley had nearly drowned just a couple of weeks ago after a threat from the past resurfaced. Cam had been more protective of Kinley than ever, barely letting her out of his sight for a second. Brynlee had a feeling they'd be announcing their own engagement soon enough, but they were giving Ainsley and Dare their time to shine.

Brynlee's chest swelled with happiness for her sisters, even as a pang of loneliness moved through her heart. She loved her job as a massage therapist and took immense pride in her salon, but her personal life felt... incomplete.

The back door opened and laughter poured in through the open space, shattering Brynlee's reverie. She quickly gathered the flatware and finished setting the table as everyone filed into the room and took their seats.

As everyone gathered around the large wooden table, Charlene brought in the final dish. "All right, everyone, dig in," she said, taking her seat next to Garrett.

Kinley dropped into a chair next to Cam and glanced across the table at Ainsley. "Everyone in town is talking about the wedding. Have you narrowed down your guest list yet?"

Ainsley shook her head and slid a quick look at Dare. "We were kind of thinking of keeping it small. Just family and friends."

That didn't surprise Brynlee at all. Her sister hated being the center of attention. "I think that's smart, actually," she put in. She smiled at Ainsley. "Have a small ceremony, then go enjoy your honeymoon."

Ainsley bit her lip. "Won't people be disappointed?" She threw a look at Kinley. "Are people really talking about it?"

Guilt flooded Kinley's face. "Oh, I just meant... A couple people mentioned how happy they are for you."

Ainsley didn't look convinced. "But—"

"It's your wedding," Brynlee interjected. "You could elope if you wanted."

Charlene looked horrified. "Or... Like Brynlee said, you could just keep it small."

Brynlee rolled her eyes with a smile, then turned her gaze to Ainsley. "Who cares what everyone else thinks? All that matters is what you want."

"I keep trying to tell her the same thing," Dare said. His arm was draped over the back of her chair, and he gave Ainsley's shoulder a little squeeze. "We don't have to do anything you don't want to do."

Brynlee loved that he understood her sister so well and always seemed to have exactly the right answer. Ainsley had been pressured enough over the years; she didn't need anyone dictating this for her, too.

"I guess we'll have to think about it," Ainsley said slowly as she glanced at Dare. "But for now... I think we're planning a ceremony by the lake."

Charlene perked up at that. "Have you set a date?"

Talk turned to potential dates, and Brynlee smiled, happy for her sister but feeling a little left out. Both Ainsley and Kinley had found love, the kind of deep, unwavering love that their parents had. Brynlee longed for that connection, for someone to share her life with.

The conversation flowed easily, filled with laughter and shared memories. They talked about the quirks of small-town life, the upcoming wedding, and the latest happenings in Brookhaven.

"Dare, how's the sheriff's office these days?" Garrett asked, his tone light but curious.

"Busy as always," Dare replied.

Brynlee listened, contributing here and there, but her mind often wandered. She loved her family dearly and cherished these moments, yet she couldn't help but feel a sense of longing. Her professional life was thriving, and she found great fulfillment in helping others through her work. But in the quiet moments, she wished for someone to share it all with.

"Bryn, could you pass the rolls, please?" Charlene's voice pulled Brynlee from her thoughts.

"Sure, Mom," Brynlee replied, her voice bright despite the tug of discontent she felt. She picked up the basket of rolls and walked over to the table, placing it in the center where everyone could reach.

"Thanks, Brynlee," Dare said with a smile as he reached for a roll. "Everything looks amazing."

"I'm glad you think so," Brynlee said, forcing a smile. She took her seat next to Kinley, trying to immerse herself in the cheerful chatter about Ainsley's upcoming wedding.

The conversation continued, filled with enthusiasm for the wedding plans and light-hearted jokes. Brynlee tried to join in, but her responses felt hollow compared to the genuine excitement around her. It wasn't that she didn't care about her sister's happiness—she did, deeply. It was just that seeing everyone so wrapped up in their own bliss made the stab of loneliness feel that much sharper.

"So, Bryn," Charlene began, her eyes twinkling with curiosity, "how's the salon going? I've heard you've been quite busy lately."

"It's going really well," Brynlee said, straightening a bit in her chair. This was something she could get excited about. "We've got a steady flow of clients, and everything's been going great so far."

"That's wonderful," Charlene said, beaming with pride. "I always knew you'd make a great massage therapist."

"I love what I do," Brynlee agreed, her smile more genuine now. "The salon is my happy place."

"I can't imagine running a business like that," Kinley said. "It's exciting but I don't know how you juggle everything."

Brynlee smiles. "I really do enjoy it, so it makes it that much easier."

"I've heard a lot of great things," Cam said. "You've had a few of the guys in, haven't you?"

Brynlee nodded. Several of the deputies had scheduled appointments with her, and she was glad she could help relieve them of their stress.

Despite the warmth of the compliments, Brynlee couldn't shake the feeling of being on the outside looking in. She was content with her professional life—she took pride in her work and felt fulfilled by it. But in the personal realm, it was a different story. Watching her sisters bask in the glow of their relationships, and hearing their plans for the future, made her own sense of longing even more pronounced.

As the conversation turned back to wedding plans, Brynlee's thoughts drifted. She imagined what it might be like to have someone by her side who looked at her the way Dare looked at Ainsley, or the way Cam looked at Kinley. She craved that deep, unwavering connection, that kind of love that seemed to come so effortlessly to her sisters.

Charlene's voice brought her back to the present. "So, Brynlee, have you met anyone interesting lately?"

Brynlee hesitated, her fork pausing mid-air. "Not really. I've been so focused on work that I haven't had much time to think about dating."

"That's understandable," Kinley said sympathetically. "But you never know when you might meet someone special."

"Yeah, you're right," Brynlee said, forcing another smile. "I guess I just haven't found the right person yet."

The conversation continued around her, and Brynlee tried to stay engaged. Despite the warm embrace of her family's love and support, she couldn't shake the lingering feeling of being on the periphery of the happiness that surrounded her. She longed for the kind of love her parents and sisters had, a love that seemed so elusive in her own life.

As dessert was served and the laughter grew louder, Brynlee took a deep breath, reminding herself that even though her journey was different, it didn't mean it was any less meaningful. She would find her path, her love, in her own time. For now, she took solace in the warmth of her family and the hope that someday, her own story would be just as joyful and fulfilling as the ones unfolding around her.

As the meal wound down, Charlene raised her glass. "To Ainsley and Dare," she said, her eyes misty with emotion. "May your wedding day be as beautiful as your love for each other."

"To Ainsley and Dare," everyone echoed, raising their glasses.

Brynlee clinked her glass with the others, smiling brightly. "Here's to a lifetime of happiness," she added, her voice steady despite the flutter in her heart.

The afternoon sun dipped lower in the sky, casting a golden glow over the room. Brynlee watched her family, their faces filled with joy and love. She knew she was incredibly blessed, and she held onto the hope that one day, she would find the kind of love her parents and sisters had.

For now, she would cherish these moments, finding solace in the warmth of her family's embrace and the love that surrounded her. And maybe, just maybe, the future held the promise of her own happily ever after.

CHAPTER
ELEVEN

"Sir?"

The men glanced toward the doorway where Webb stood, a sheaf of papers in his hand. "I have the information you asked for."

"Thanks, Tony."

Dare grabbed the papers, then dropped them to the desk. "Every white van registered in the state."

Cam let out a low whistle as he flipped idly through the pages. "This is going to be like finding a needle in a haystack."

"Over five hundred vans," Sawyer muttered, rubbing the back of his neck. He felt the familiar ache of exhaustion settling in, but pushed it aside. There was too much at stake. "It's not impossible, but it's damn close."

Dare was already pulling out a map of the surrounding counties. "We need to narrow this down. Let's focus on the counties near Brookhaven first. The van was seen at the restaurant on the night of the murder; it's likely local or at least nearby."

The three men began to work, marking off counties one by one. After an hour of meticulous cross-referencing and eliminating vehicles registered in distant counties, they managed to reduce the list. When they finished, Sawyer leaned back, his fingers tapping against the edge of the table.

"We're down to 72," Sawyer said, though the relief in his voice was minimal. "Still a lot, but better than 500."

"Most of these vans belong to businesses," Dare pointed out, scrutinizing the list. "We need to rule out the ones with decals or any kind of signage. The one Cochran saw was plain white, no markings."

Cam was already pulling up his laptop, the screen reflecting the intense focus in his eyes. "I'll start with the small businesses, see if we can find any information on their vehicles. A lot of these companies have websites or at least social media. If they've got pictures of their fleet, we can cut down the list even more."

They fell into a rhythm, each man tasked with scouring the web for details. Websites, social media pages, even local news reports—anything that might show whether a business had marked vehicles. It was tedious work, but slowly, the number of potential vans began to shrink. One by one, they crossed names off the list, marking the businesses that had identifiable vans.

"Down to 34," Cam said after a couple of hours. "This is getting better, but still too many to just go knocking on doors."

Dare nodded, his expression grim. "We'll need to dig deeper into these last few. It's a start, but we're going to need more information before we can pinpoint the right one."

Sawyer tapped his pen against the table, thinking. "We should hand off the list to a couple of deputies, have them run background checks on the drivers. Maybe one of them has a record that stands out."

"Good idea," Dare agreed. "We can't afford to miss anything. Every detail counts."

With that, Sawyer grabbed the list and headed out to the main office. Two deputies, Webb and Landry, were at their desks, filling out reports. Sawyer handed them the list, explaining the task at hand.

"I want you both to run background checks on every name here," he instructed. "Look for anything that might connect these drivers to the case—criminal records, outstanding warrants, anything that raises a red flag."

Landry nodded, already reaching for his computer. "We're on it."

As Sawyer returned to the office, Cam looked up, his expression fierce. "At least we're moving in the right direction. If there's a link to be found, we'll find it."

Sawyer stared at the whiteboard, tension rippling through him. "We have to. Whoever's behind this has been careful, but they've slipped up somewhere. It's just a matter of time before we catch them."

There were still too many unknowns, too many questions left unanswered. But with every name they crossed off, they were one step closer to finding the truth.

And once they did, there would be nowhere left for the killer to hide.

Sawyer and Cam were seated at their desks, reviewing case files when Yvonne knocked on the doorjamb. "Maureen Ray would like to speak with you—both of you."

Sawyer lifted a brow at Cam, who shrugged. Though Sawyer had moved to Brookhaven nearly a year ago, he still didn't know a majority of the residents. Apparently, Cam wasn't familiar with Mrs. Ray, either.

"Show her to the conference room."

Yvonne nodded and disappeared, and the men headed

toward the conference room down the hall. A minute later, an older woman joined them, her expression strained.

"Mrs. Ray?" Sawyer asked, moving forward to greet her. "I'm Detective Sawyer Reed, and this is Lieutenant Cam McCoy. How can we help you today?"

Maureen's voice was choked with emotion as she began to speak. "I'm here to report my daughter, Fallon Ray, missing. She didn't show up to work for the past two days, which is completely unlike her. Her employer called me, as I'm listed as her emergency contact. I tried calling and texting her, but there's been no response."

Sawyer and Cam exchanged a quick, concerned glance. They gestured for Maureen to sit down at the empty table beside them.

"Go on," Cam encouraged gently.

"I went to her house this morning," Maureen continued, her hands trembling slightly. "The door was locked, and I had to use the spare key to get in. Everything seemed... normal. There's nothing out of place, nothing missing. Her car is still in the garage, which means she should be here. It's like she just... vanished."

Sawyer took notes as Maureen spoke, trying to piece together the timeline. "Did Fallon mention anything recently that seemed out of the ordinary? Any arguments, changes in her routine, or personal issues?"

Maureen shook her head. "Not really. She'd picked up some extra hours at work and seemed a bit stressed, but she didn't say anything about problems. She was just her usual self, really."

"Where does she work?"

"Boho Boutique." At Sawyer's blank look, she elaborated. "It's a small shop in the same plaza as the hardware store."

Cam nodded. "We'll need to start by checking her recent activities and any potential contacts who might have seen her or had interactions with her recently. We'll also need to look into her workplace and see if anyone there noticed anything unusual."

Maureen's eyes filled with tears, her voice breaking. "Please, you have to find her. Fallon is everything to me. I can't imagine what could have happened. I've already checked with her friends and colleagues, and no one knows anything."

Sawyer placed a reassuring hand on Maureen's shoulder. "We understand how distressing this must be for you, Mrs. Ray. We'll get started on this immediately. We'll check with her workplace, her friends, and anyone who might have seen her recently. We'll do everything we can to find your daughter."

Maureen nodded, her eyes filled with a mix of hope and desperation. "Thank you. I just want her back safe. Please, don't stop until you find her."

Sawyer and Cam assured her they would do everything possible, and Maureen left the office, her shoulders slumped with misery. As the door closed behind her, Sawyer turned a concerned look Cam's way. "Another missing girl?"

Cam grimaced. "And she's apparently been missing for at least two days already."

It didn't bode well—not at all. "We need to get on this yesterday," Sawyer said, standing up. "Let's start with her house."

An hour later Cam and Sawyer, accompanied by deputies Evan Landry and Tony Webb, arrived at Fallon Ray's home. Maureen Ray's distress was still fresh in Sawyer's mind as they prepared to delve deeper into the scene.

As Maureen had reported, nothing seemed out of place. Personal items were in their usual spots, and there were no signs of a struggle inside. Sawyer scanned the rooms, noting the calm, almost too calm, state of the house.

Sawyer glanced at the deputies. "Check all points of entry.

We'll need to print the windows and doors. Look for anything out of place."

With a nod to the deputies, Sawyer pulled on a pair of gloves and made his way to the garage. He was determined to find something—anything—that could provide a clue to Fallon's disappearance.

He paused at the bottom of the steps that led into the kitchen, his gaze sweeping over the small space. As Mrs. Ray stated, Fallon's car was parked in its rightful spot inside the single car garage. A solid steel door situated in the wall across from him drew his attention, and he crossed over to it. The door was locked from the inside, and he tested it to be sure. Opening the door, he inspected the outside. There was no sign of forced entry.

Locking up once more, Sawyer turned his focus back to the car. Peering in through the window, he studied the inside. The car's interior was clean, organized, and seemingly untouched. Sawyer popped open the driver's side door and started his examination. The first thing he noticed was Fallon's purse still sitting on the floorboard in front of the passenger seat.

The sight of it gave him pause. If she'd been planning to leave, she would likely have taken her purse with her. Of course, people occasionally left everything behind in an attempt to disappear. Without a lot of cash, though, it was significantly more difficult.

Sawyer pulled the purse out and opened it briefly. It was filled with the usual items—wallet, phone, keys. He set it aside, his mind racing with questions. Assuming she had, in fact, been kidnapped, why was her purse still in the car? Had she intended to leave or was she simply arriving home?

His gaze flicked upward, and he noticed a depression on the driver's side visor. He reached up and checked it carefully.

It was a slim line, the kind a clip left—like from a garage door opener.

Sawyer continued his inspection of the car. Without a garage door opener, Fallon's car had no way of getting into or out of the garage unless the door was manually operated or left open. Moving swiftly, Sawyer checked under the seats and in the trunk, looking for any overlooked evidence. Everything appeared to be in order except for the missing garage door opener.

Sawyer moved on, checking the back seat, the trunk, inside the console and glove box, but there was no garage door opener in sight.

Sawyer moved back into the house where the others were still taking photos and collecting evidence.

"Hey," Sawyer called out, his voice carrying through the small home. "I need you guys to check the house again, especially around the entry points. See if you can find a garage door opener."

Evan and Tony exchanged puzzled glances but nodded and went inside the house. Cam strode across the living room toward him. "Find something?"

"Maybe. Fallon's purse is still in the car, along with her wallet and phone."

"Interesting." Cam's brows dipped together. "Her keys are on the kitchen counter."

The deputies returned from their search, shaking their heads. "Nothing in the house," Tony reported. "But the garage door opener isn't anywhere to be found."

Sawyer nodded slowly and glanced at Cam. "If it's the same guy, we know he's meticulous. He obviously studies these women—knows their habits, their schedules..."

Cam nodded, following his train of thought. "We still don't know if this was the same guy who killed Lindsey, but this reminds me of Lindsey's house. No forced entry, nothing missing..." He propped his hands on his hips and glanced around. "Maybe that's how he got in and out."

"Could be," Sawyer agreed.

He glanced over the exterior of Fallon's small condo. She lived in the end unit of a triplex, with two neighbors to her left, as well as an identical condo unit across the street. "We need to find out if anyone saw her that night."

The deputies joined them, and Sawyer turned their way. "We'll need to check with Fallon's neighbors, see if they noticed anything or anyone out of the ordinary over the past couple of weeks. We need to find out who might have had the opportunity to access her home or observe her routine. Cam and I are going to head over to the shop where she worked, see what they can tell us. Keep us posted if you find anything."

The deputies nodded their assent, prepared to canvass the neighborhood, and Sawyer and Cam climbed into the car. Finding Fallon was the top priority, and every minute spent on this case could mean the difference between finding her alive or too late.

CHAPTER
TWELVE

Brynlee arrived at her salon, a bounce in her step. But a prickling unease swept over her as she unlocked the door and stepped inside. Instead of the familiar scent of hair products and calming lavender fragrance, the unmistakable smell of damp and mildew tickled her nose.

Her heart dropped to her toes as she took in the glossy sheen of water that had pooled on the floor near the reception desk. Panic rose within her as she ventured deeper into the salon to assess the extent of the damage.

"Oh no, no, no." Her stomach twisted into a tight knot as she reached the massage room and found the carpet soaked. Damn.

The water damage seemed to be the worst at the back of the salon, and she moved from room to room, carefully inspecting the pipes and water valves. She finally found the culprit in a leaky valve under the bathroom sink.

The small vanity was saturated with water, and everything inside was ruined. Tears sprang to her eyes, and she blinked them away as she pulled her phone from her purse, hands shaking. Clearing her throat, she fired off a quick text to all of her stylists, explaining the situation and asking them to cancel all appointments for the day. Next, Brynlee contacted her own clients, apologizing profusely and explaining the unexpected closure.

With the immediate concerns addressed, she knew she needed to act quickly to mitigate the damage. She called her landlord, Mr. Pollard. However, instead of sympathy, she was met with hostility.

"This is your responsibility," the landlord snapped over the phone. "You should have been more careful. It's not my problem."

Frustration and anger welled up in Brynlee as she tried to reason with the unyielding landlord. "I have renter's insurance. I'll contact a plumber, but I need your permission to bring him in."

After what seemed like an eternity of arguing, the landlord reluctantly agreed, leaving Brynlee seething with a mix of emotions. She wasted no time in contacting her insurance company and scheduling a plumber to assess the damage.

Brynlee returned to the bathroom and began to pull saturated rolls of toilet paper and paper towels from underneath the sink, then tossed them in the trash. The vanity would need to be replaced, and she did a quick check online to see if the local hardware store had anything in stock.

She'd just finished arranging a pick up for later this afternoon when the plumber arrived—a middle-aged man named Mr. Henderson, recommended by a friend of Brynlee's father. He greeted her with a reassuring smile as he entered the salon, toolbox in hand. "Let's take a look at this leak," Mr. Henderson said.

His calm tone and professional demeanor put her slightly at ease. There was a lot to fix, but he seemed confident that he could take care of it. Brynlee directed him to the bathroom, where he immediately began inspecting the area around the sink and toilet.

"Here we go," he murmured, pointing to a valve under the sink. "I can fix this right away," Mr. Henderson assured her, kneeling down to work on tightening the valve.

Brynlee nodded, her mind already racing with plans to call a restoration company. "Thank you, Mr. Henderson. Please let me know if you need anything else."

As Mr. Henderson worked, Brynlee stepped outside to make arrangements with a local restoration company recommended by her insurance provider. They promised to dispatch a team as soon as possible to begin drying out the salon and assessing the extent of the damage.

Returning to the salon, Brynlee couldn't help but feel a wave of exhaustion wash over her. The initial shock and adrenaline were wearing off, replaced by a sense of resignation tempered with determination. She knew this setback would be challenging, but she was determined to overcome it and reopen her beloved salon as soon as possible.

As Mr. Henderson finished tightening the valve and assured her it was secure, Brynlee thanked him profusely. "I really appreciate you getting here so soon."

He nodded with a reassuring smile. "My pleasure, Ms. Layne. Looks like everything is good to go, but don't hesitate to call me if you notice anything else."

"I will, thank you."

She closed up after Mr. Henderson, then slumped against the door. As she turned back to the salon, the reality of the damage hit her like a sucker punch. The carpet in the massage studio was soaked through, the fibers bloated and discolored where water had pooled. Cabinets in the adjacent laundry room showed signs of swelling and water stains were slowly crawling up the walls in several places.

Brynlee's frustration and helplessness welled up again as she surveyed the scene. She knew that fixing the leak was just the first step—the real challenge lay in dealing with the aftermath. Taking a deep breath to steady herself, she reached for her phone and dialed the number of a local restoration company she had researched earlier.

"Hello, this is Brynlee from Blissful Beauty," she began, her voice trembling slightly with fatigue and emotion. "I had a water leak and need immediate assistance with cleanup and restoration."

The voice on the other end of the line was professional and reassuring. "Of course, Brynlee. We understand how stressful this can be. We'll send a team over right away to assess the damage and start the cleanup process."

Relief washed over Brynlee as she thanked the representative and hung up. She moved quickly to gather all the linens and towels that were now damp from the water, loading them into her car to take home and wash. Tears stung her eyes as she handled each item, the weight of the situation pressing heavily on her shoulders.

Within the hour, the restoration company arrived with a team of technicians equipped with industrial-grade wet vacuums, fans, and dehumidifiers. Their efficiency and expertise were a stark contrast to Brynlee's feelings of despair. They immediately set to work, assessing the extent of the water damage and formulating a plan to mitigate further harm.

"Brynlee, we're going to start by extracting as much water as possible," one of the technicians explained kindly, noticing her distress. "Then we'll set up drying equipment to prevent mold and further damage to your salon."

Brynlee nodded gratefully, feeling a small glimmer of hope as she watched the team get to work. They moved swiftly and methodically, focusing on salvaging what they could and minimizing the impact of the water damage.

As they worked, Brynlee stepped back, feeling a mixture of gratitude and exhaustion. She couldn't have managed this crisis alone, and seeing professionals take charge gave her a sense of reassurance. The hum of the drying equipment and the rhythmic sound of water being extracted became a background symphony to her thoughts.

Throughout the cleanup process, Brynlee assisted where she could, handing over damaged items and answering questions about the salon's layout and any potential hazards. Each moment brought a renewed sense of determination—to rebuild, to overcome, and to reopen her cherished salon.

By the time the sun began to set, the restoration team had made significant progress. The worst of the water had been removed, and the drying equipment hummed diligently to finish the job overnight. Brynlee stood in the doorway, watching the technicians pack up their equipment and offering heartfelt thanks for their hard work.

"Thank you all so much," she said sincerely, her voice wavering with emotion. "I don't know what I would have done without your help today."

The team leader smiled warmly. "It's our pleasure, Brynlee. We're here to make sure your salon gets back to normal as quickly as possible."

After the restoration team had finished for the day, Brynlee sat in her office amidst the drying machines, feeling drained and overwhelmed. The immediate cleanup was underway, but the reality of the damage was sinking in. The cabinets in the laundry room were irreparably swollen and discolored from the water, and the carpet in her beloved massage studio was beyond salvage.

With a heavy sigh, Brynlee pulled out her phone and began researching replacement options. She found a local supplier who could deliver new cabinets by the end of the week, but installation wouldn't be possible until the following Monday. It was a delay she couldn't afford, but the earliest available date left her no choice.

Next on her list was replacing the water-damaged computer in the reception area. She needed it to manage appointments, process payments, and communicate with clients. The thought of another expense added to her mounting worries about finances.

Feeling the weight of the day pressing down on her, Brynlee decided to take action where she could. She locked up the salon and drove to a nearby store to purchase a few storage shelves. It wasn't an ideal solution, but it would serve as a temporary measure to store towels and supplies until the new cabinets arrived.

Upon returning to the salon, Brynlee made arrangements for the carpet replacement. She found a reputable flooring company willing to install new carpet the following day. It was a relief to know that at least one major aspect of the restoration process would be resolved quickly.

As the day stretched into evening, Brynlee worked tirelessly to address the immediate needs of her salon. She fielded calls from concerned clients, reassured her stylists that they would be back in business soon, and tried to maintain a semblance of normalcy amidst the chaos.

By the time she locked up the salon for the night, exhaustion had settled deep into her bones. She sat alone in the quiet salon, surrounded by the faint hum of drying equipment and the scent of disinfectant, reflecting on the unexpected turn of events.

With a heavy heart, she packed up her belongings and headed home, thoughts swirling with plans for the days ahead.

Tomorrow would bring more challenges—dealing with

insurance claims, coordinating repairs, and reassuring clients. As she closed the door behind her, she hoped that tomorrow would bring a fresh start.

They headed straight to Fallon Ray's workplace, a small boutique downtown. Inside Boho Boutique, they headed straight for the counter and flashed their badges.

"I'm Detective Sawyer Reed," he introduced himself. "This is Lt. Cam McCoy. We're investigating a missing person."

The woman's eyes widened. "Fallon?"

"That's right." Sawyer dipped his chin. "Can you tell me what happened?"

The store manager, Alexis, was visibly shaken as she relayed the events of the past several days. "She'd asked for more hours, but it wasn't originally her day to work, so I figured she just forgot about it." The woman dragged in a shaky breath. "But she didn't show up the next day, either. And with everything going on..."

She trailed off and bit her lip. "I started to get really worried, you know?"

"I understand," Cam said. "You reached out to Fallon's mother first, is that right?"

Alexis nodded. "I thought about calling the police, but I

didn't want to waste your time if it turned out to be nothing. Mrs. Ray was listed as Fallon's emergency contact, so I checked with her first."

"I'm glad you reached out as soon as you did." Sawyer nodded, pulling out his notebook. "When was the last time you saw Fallon?"

"Three nights ago," Alexis replied, wringing her hands.

"Did you notice anything strange, anyone out of the ordinary?"

She shook her head. "Everything seemed normal. She finished her shift and left at her usual time. One of her coworkers, Jenna, walked with her to her car."

"What time was that?"

"Let me check." Alexis turned to the computer and searched for a few minutes until she found what she was looking for, then swiveled the screen his way. "Looks like she clocked out at 7:42 that night."

"Can we speak with Jenna?" Cam asked.

Alexis nodded and stepped away, returning a moment later with Jenna, a young woman in her early twenties, her eyes wide with worry.

"Jenna, tell us what you remember about the night Fallon disappeared," Sawyer said gently.

Jenna took a deep breath. "We finished our shifts and walked out to the parking lot together. We talked for a few minutes by her car, just the usual stuff. I watched her get in, start the engine, and drive away. Everything seemed normal. That was the last time I saw her."

"Did she mention anything unusual? Anyone she was worried about?" Cam asked.

Jenna shook her head. "No, nothing like that. She seemed fine, just tired from work."

"Thank you, Jenna," Sawyer said. "If you remember anything else, please call us immediately."

He handed her a card, then they headed back out to the car. "Let's touch base with Mrs. Ray again, see if she remembered anything, or can give us any more leads."

Fifteen minutes later, Sawyer and Cam stepped out of their car and made their way up to the front door. Maureen Ray, Fallon's mother, greeted them with a tired but hopeful expression. She had been waiting anxiously for any updates.

"Good morning, Mrs. Ray," Sawyer said, offering a sympathetic nod. "We're here to ask a few questions about Fallon. Anything you can tell us might help."

Maureen led them into the living room, her movements heavy with concern. "Of course. I'm just hoping you can find her soon. Fallon's always been so responsible—this is so out of character for her."

Sawyer and Cam took a seat on the couch, their notebooks ready. "We need to piece together her last few days to see if there's anything that might indicate what happened," Cam said. "We'll start with you and then move on to her friends, family, and anyone who might have seen her recently."

Maureen nodded and provided a detailed account of Fallon's recent activities. She mentioned that Fallon had been busy with work and seemed stressed but had not mentioned any specific problems.

"Do you know if Fallon had any enemies? Anyone who might want to harm her?" Cam asked gently.

Maureen shook her head. "No, Fallon is a good girl. She doesn't have any enemies. She's been focused on work and spending time with family. She doesn't even have a boyfriend right now."

Sawyer took notes, his mind racing. "We'll do everything we can to find her. Did she have any plans that night? Anything out of the ordinary?"

Maureen wiped her tears. "No, she was just supposed to come home after work."

"Mrs. Ray, I need to ask you about something we found," Sawyer began, keeping his voice gentle. "Fallon's garage door opener is missing from her vehicle. It appears to be the only thing out of place. Did you take it?"

Mrs. Ray shook her head, her brow furrowing in confusion. "No, I didn't. When I couldn't reach Fallon, I went to her house to check on her, but when I didn't find her there, I left and went straight to the sheriff's department."

Sawyer nodded, jotting down notes in his pad. "Did anyone else have access to Fallon's house?"

Mrs. Ray took a deep breath, trying to recall any details that might help. "I have a key, but I keep it on my keychain. Fallon and her boyfriend broke up a few months ago; he might still have a key, but I'm not sure. I'm not aware of her sharing keys with neighbors or anyone else."

"Do you know if anything strange has happened recently? Anything out of the ordinary?" Sawyer asked, hoping for a lead.

Mrs. Ray's face fell as she shook her head. "No, nothing that I know of. Fallon didn't mention anything unusual to me. She was just focused on work and getting over the breakup."

Sawyer sighed inwardly, feeling the frustration mounting. Every question seemed to lead to a dead end. He looked at Mrs. Ray, her worry etched deeply on her face, and knew he had to keep pressing forward.

"Do you have any idea if Fallon might have given her garage door opener to someone else? Maybe for safekeeping or any other reason?" Sawyer asked, clutching at straws.

Mrs. Ray frowned, thinking hard. "No, she was very particular about her things. I can't imagine her doing that. But... I don't know, Detective. I'm so scared for her."

Sawyer reached out, placing a reassuring hand on her arm.

"We're doing everything we can to find her, Mrs. Ray. If you think of anything, no matter how small, please let me know."

She nodded, tears welling up in her eyes. "Thank you, Detective. I just want my daughter back."

Sawyer stood up, giving her a small, encouraging smile. "We'll find her, Mrs. Ray. I promise."

As he walked out of the house, he felt the weight of his promise pressing down on him. He knew they were running out of time. He needed to find a lead, something that could crack this case open.

Back in his car, Sawyer turned toward Cam. "No one else is supposed to have a key to her house, except maybe her ex-boyfriend."

"You think the ex might be involved?"

"Maybe," Sawyer said, rubbing his temple. "But we need to confirm if he still has a key. And we need to find out why the garage door opener is missing. It's the only thing out of place."

"I'll start digging into the ex-boyfriend's background," Cam replied. "Let's see if we can get anything from him."

He stared out the windshield, the image of Mrs. Ray's tearful face lingering in his mind. He was more determined than ever to find Fallon and bring her home safely. As he started the car and drove away, he knew they were getting closer. Every small detail mattered, and he was ready to follow every lead, no matter where it took him.

CHAPTER
FOURTEEN

Next on their list was Fallon's ex-boyfriend, Mark Sullivan. At a small apartment on the outskirts of town, Sawyer rang the doorbell, and after a brief pause, the door opened to reveal the man in question.

His eyes widened when he saw Sawyer and Cam on his doorstep. "Can I help you?"

"Mark Sullivan?" Sawyer asked, even though he already knew the answer.

"That's me." The man stared at them warily. "What's going on?"

"We'd like to ask you about Fallon Ray."

"Fallon?" His brows drew together first in confusion, then worry. "What happened? Is she okay?"

Cam tipped his head. "Do you mind if we come inside for a minute?"

Mark nodded, stepping aside to let them in. The space was the controlled chaos of a bachelor: minimal decoration, empty food cartons and beer bottles on the coffee table. "We're investigating her disappearance, and we wanted to ask you a few questions."

Mark's expression shifted from curiosity to shock. "Disappearance? What do you mean? Is she missing?"

Sawyer nodded, watching Mark closely for his reaction. "She hasn't been seen for a couple of days, and we're trying to piece together what might have happened. When was the last time you spoke to her?"

Mark ran a hand through his hair, clearly unsettled. "It's been over two months. We broke up after... well, I'm sure you heard about that if you're here. I hadn't heard from her for a couple months now. God, I had no idea she was missing."

Sawyer exchanged a glance with Cam before continuing. "We need to confirm your whereabouts two nights ago. Can you tell us where you were?"

Mark hesitated for a moment, then nodded. "I was out with my girlfriend, Julie. We went to a restaurant—La Trattoria, downtown. I think I still have the receipt."

Without waiting for them to ask, Mark hurried into another room. Sawyer and Cam exchanged a look, both thinking the same thing—if Mark was telling the truth, he'd be ruled out quickly. But they couldn't afford to leave any stone unturned.

Mark returned a minute later, holding a small slip of paper. "Here it is," he said, handing it over. "The receipt from La Trattoria. It should have the date and time on it."

Sawyer took the receipt and examined it. The timestamp showed Mark and Julie had been at the restaurant during the time in question. It was a solid alibi.

"Thanks," Sawyer said, skimming the receipt before passing it to Cam, who also gave it a quick once-over.

Mark let out a breath, relief washing over his face. "I hope this helps. I really hope you find her. Fallon... She's a good person. We didn't end on the best terms, but I never wanted anything bad to happen to her."

"Do you mind me asking why you broke up?"

Mark sucked in a sharp breath, then ran a hand over his short-cropped hair. He was quiet for a long moment before speaking. "I was an idiot. I... cheated on her, and she found out."

Sawyer nodded. "One more thing—do you happen to still have a key to Fallon's place?"

He shook his head. "I never did. There's a small stepping stone in the landscaping by the steps—she used to leave a key under there. If I ever needed to get it, I would just use that."

"We appreciate your cooperation, Mark. Is there anything else you can tell us? Anyone she might have been in contact with, any changes in her behavior before you broke up?"

Mark shook his head, his brow furrowed in thought. "No, not really. She was more withdrawn, but I think that was more because of our relationship problems than anything else. I really don't know who she's been spending time with since we broke up."

Cam stood, signaling that the interview was coming to an end. "Thanks for your time, Mark. If you think of anything else, no matter how small, please don't hesitate to reach out."

Mark nodded, still looking troubled. "I will. I just hope she's okay."

As they left Mark's house, Sawyer couldn't shake the feeling that they were still missing something crucial.

"We've ruled out Mark, but that doesn't mean we're any closer to finding Fallon," Cam said as they walked back to the car.

"No, it doesn't," Sawyer agreed, his mind already turning over the next steps.

Back at the station, Sawyer and Cam reviewed the information they had gathered. The timeline was beginning to come together, but there were still too many gaps. They needed to explore further into her personal life, any recent conflicts or threats, and see if there was anyone who might have had a motive to harm her.

"Everything seemed normal," Sawyer said, frustration creeping into his voice. "She left work, drove home, and vanished. No signs of a struggle, no known threats. It's like she just disappeared into thin air."

Cam rubbed his temples in frustration. "We've got a lot of pieces, but no clear picture yet. We need to dig deeper into her personal life and find out if there were any other issues we haven't uncovered."

They were running in circles, and every new lead seemed to take them back to where they started. Mark Sullivan's alibi was ironclad, as was his girlfriend, Julie's. They were seen together at a restaurant across town, time-stamped receipts and all. Everything checked out, at least on the surface.

A knock at the door drew their attention, and Deputies Evan Landry and Tony Webb stepped inside.

Evan spoke first, his voice steady but tired. "We've wrapped up with the neighbors, but no one heard anything unusual the night Fallon disappeared."

"One neighbor across the street said she saw Fallon's car parked in the driveway that night," Tony added.

Cam made a face. "Well, I guess someone at least placed her at home. Too bad we don't have a lead on whoever abducted her."

"If she was abducted." Sawyer shrugged. "She's an adult; there's nothing to say she didn't leave on her own."

Cam nodded. "True. She could have taken the garage door opener on her way out and used it to close up."

Sawyer scrubbed a hand over his face. It was a possibility, but he didn't like the odds. The resemblance between Lindsey and Fallon's kidnappings were a little too similar for his liking. He wanted to exhaust every resource before throwing in the towel. "Let's hit her friends' houses and see if we can dig anything up that way."

CHAPTER
FIFTEEN

Cam and Sawyer split up to cover more ground and question as many people as they could. Cam was headed to Fallon's house to see if the key Mark had mentioned was still there, then he would question a few of Fallon's friends.

Sawyer now sat in a small coffee shop downtown across from three of Fallon's friends, hoping to piece together her final movements. The group of young women sat huddled on the couch near the fireplace, their expressions a mixture of worry and confusion.

"Thank you all for coming," Sawyer began, glancing around at the young women before him. "We're trying to narrow down the timeline of Fallon's disappearance. We know she left the boutique where she works around 7:45 PM, and she responded to a text message at 8:52 PM. We need to know where she was during that hour."

The friends exchanged glances, trying to recall any details. Finally, one of them, a petite brunette named Lila, spoke up. "I think Fallon was at the grocery store that evening. I called her around 8:30 PM, but she told me while she was checking out, and that she'd call me back."

"Did she call you back?" Sawyer leaned forward, his interest piqued.

She nodded. "Just a few minutes later."

"What time was that call?"

Lila bit her lip, thinking hard. "It must have been just before 8:45 PM. We didn't talk long, maybe a couple of minutes. She kind of laughed about it being a long week, so she'd picked up a bottle of wine and was heading home."

Sawyer jotted down the information. "And that was the last you heard from her?"

Lila nodded, her eyes welling up with tears. "Yes. I texted her a couple of times over the weekend, but she didn't answer."

Cam, sitting beside Sawyer, spoke up. "Did she mention seeing anyone she knew at the grocery store? Or anything unusual happening?"

Lila shook her head. "No, nothing like that. She seemed normal, just like any other evening."

They were getting closer, but there were still gaps to fill. Sawyer turned to the rest of the group. "Did either of you hear from Fallon or see her that evening?"

The friends shook their heads, offering no new information. Sawyer sighed inwardly but kept his frustration in check. Every detail counted, no matter how small.

"Thank you, Lila," Sawyer said, offering her a reassuring smile. "You've been very helpful."

They stood up to leave, and Lila caught Sawyer's arm. "Please, find her. She's a good person. She doesn't deserve this."

"We're doing everything we can," Sawyer promised. "We'll find her."

As he left the coffee shop, Sawyer dug his phone from his pocket and called Cam. "One of her friends says Fallon stopped at the grocery store on her way home. I'm going to head over there, see if I can review the footage."

"I'm just leaving now. I'll meet you there."

Sawyer rested a hip on the front fender and scanned the parking lot while he waited for Cam to arrive, a dozen scenarios flitting through his mind.

Shielding his eyes against the sun, his attention was drawn to Cam's car as he pulled into the lot and parked next to him, then climbed out. "Anything on your end?"

"Nope." Cam grimaced. "Hopefully this pans out, because none of the ladies I spoke with talked to her at all that night."

"Supposedly Fallon was here sometime between 7:45 and 8:45 three nights ago," Sawyer said as they walked toward the entrance of the store. "That should help us narrow it down."

"Let's talk to the manager, see if we can access the security footage."

They entered the store and approached the customer service desk, where the manager, a middle-aged man named Mr. Peterson, greeted them with a cautious expression. "Officers. How can I help you?"

"Mr. Peterson, I'm Lieutenant McCoy, and this is Detective Reed," Cam introduced, flashing his badge. "We're investigating a missing persons report. We need to review your security footage from three nights ago."

Mr. Peterson hesitated briefly before nodding. "Of course. Follow me."

He led them to the small security office tucked away behind the checkout counters. The room was cramped, dominated by a wall of monitors displaying different camera feeds from around the store. Mr. Peterson pulled up the footage from the relevant time frame.

"We'll start with the exterior cameras," Cam instructed, leaning closer to the screen.

The footage began to roll, and they watched intently for Fallon to appear. A few minutes before 8:00, a woman approached the front doors.

Cam pointed at the screen. "Is that her?"

"I think so." Sawyer glanced at the manager. "Do you have a better angle?"

"Sure thing."

He glanced at the timestamp, then switched views so they could better see the woman's face as she approached. Sawyer nodded. "Definitely her. Let's rewind a bit, see where she parked."

Mr. Peterson did as requested, following Fallon's movements as he rewound a couple of minutes.

"There's her car," Sawyer murmured.

They watched as Fallon approached the store, and they switched cameras once more as she entered, then selected a cart and pushed it down the aisle. She took her time selecting her items, but no one approached her; no one appeared to be following her.

"Looks like a routine shopping trip," Sawyer murmured, watching intently.

Cam grunted his agreement, and they watched for several more minutes as she wound her way through the aisles, picking up items, setting them down, and moving on. Finally, she checked out and Sawyer watched as she dug her phone from her bag. She lifted it to her ear for a moment, then dropped it back in her purse.

Sawyer glanced at the timestamp. "That must be the call Lila mentioned."

The footage continued to roll as Fallon paid for her items,

then pushed the cart out of the store and through the parking lot. Sawyer studied the few people milling around, but none stood out. None pair her any undue attention as she reached the car and popped the trunk. Her movements were calm and unhurried as she loaded the bags into the trunk, the roof of the black car reflecting the light overhead.

She returned the cart to a corral in the parking lot, then climbed into the front seat. A moment later, the headlamps flared to life, and the car slowly pulled out of the space.

Cam scowled. "Damn it."

Sawyer's lips pressed into a firm line. "Let's check it one more time. Maybe—"

He abruptly cut off as a second pair of headlights suddenly flashed on and a dark-colored sedan pulled out behind her.

"Freeze that," Cam ordered, pointing at the screen.

The image was grainy, the quality hampered by darkness, and the car was too far away to see the license plate. They could make out the silhouette of a sedan but not the specific make and model.

Fallon stopped at the intersection, blinker indicating that she was turning toward her condo, and waited for a car to pass. Once it was clear, she pulled into traffic and disappeared down the street. The dark sedan behind her paused for a moment, putting a bit of distance between them before following suit.

"Damn," Sawyer muttered, frustration evident in his voice. "Can't make out the plate. But that sedan definitely followed her out of here."

Cam nodded grimly. "We need to find out who was driving that car. Mr. Peterson, do you have any other cameras covering the exits or parking lot?"

Mr. Peterson nodded, adjusting the camera feed to show different angles. They scrutinized the footage, but the dark sedan was only visible for a few seconds before disappearing out of view.

"Anything else?"

Mr. Peterson shook his head with a small grimace. "I'm sorry, officers. That's all I've got."

Sawyer sighed and ran a hand through his hair. "That's all right. This has been a huge help. Thanks for your cooperation, Mr. Peterson. We'll need copies of this footage for our investigation."

As they left the security office, Cam glanced at Sawyer. "We're getting closer."

Sawyer nodded, the weight of the investigation pressing down on him. Halfway across the parking lot, a memory tickled the back of his mind, and he paused midstep. "Remember what Fallon's neighbor said—about seeing her car outside?"

"Yeah." The confusion marring Cam's brow turned to understanding. "Fallon was parked inside the garage. Maybe she actually saw the sedan that followed her out of here."

Sawyer slid a knowing look his way. "And if she saw the car... Maybe she noticed something else."

CHAPTER
SIXTEEN

Sawyer and Cam stopped by the station to check a few notes and print off a handful of photos, then headed back to Fallon Ray's neighborhood. The neighbor's house was identical to Fallon's—another triplex unit with a well-manicured yard, flowers blooming brightly on the small front porch.

Sawyer hopped up the steps and rang the bell, foot tapping anxiously as he waited for someone to answer. Several moments passed before the door swung open and an older woman appeared in the space.

Her brows drew together when she saw them. "Can I help you?"

"Good afternoon, ma'am. We're with the Brookhaven Sheriff's Department. We're following up on some questions about your neighbor, Fallon. Do you mind if we ask you a few questions?"

The woman's brow furrowed with concern, but she nodded. "Of course. I've already spoken with the other officers, but I'll tell you whatever I can."

Sawyer offered a polite smile. "Ma'am, we wanted to follow up on something you mentioned to the deputies earlier. You said you saw Fallon's car parked in her driveway the night she disappeared?"

She nodded slowly. "Yes, that's right. I saw it there when I was closing my curtains for the night."

"Did you see or hear anything unusual the night she disappeared?" Cam asked gently.

She shook her head. "No, it was very quiet. I remember seeing her car in the driveway when I went to bed, but that's all."

"Are you sure it was her car?" Sawyer pressed. "Could it have been another vehicle, similar in color and make?"

The woman hesitated, then sighed. "I suppose it could've been, but it was dark. I didn't think much of it at the time. It looked like her car, so I just assumed."

"Do you remember if the garage door was open or closed?" Cam asked.

The woman's brow furrowed as she thought back. "Let me think... It was closed. Yes, I'm sure of it."

Sawyer's gaze sharpened. "Thank you, ma'am. That's helpful."

Before they turned to leave, Sawyer pulled out a picture of the car from the grocery store parking lot. "One last thing—could you take a look at this for me?"

He handed her the photo, and she stared at the image for a moment. The car was partially obscured, the taillights the most visible feature.

The woman's eyes narrowed as she focused. After a few seconds, she nodded slowly. "That's the car. I remember those taillights. They were on when I saw it parked in the driveway."

"Thank you for your time," Sawyer said, his voice laced with genuine gratitude. "You've been very helpful."

As they walked back to their car, Cam spoke first, his voice low. "That's our confirmation. The car in the driveway was the same one from the grocery store."

"This wasn't just a random disappearance," Sawyer added, his mind racing. "Someone planned this."

They drove back to the station in silence, the weight of the revelation settling over them. They had a lead—a crucial one—but they still needed to connect all the dots. As the station came into view, Sawyer knew they were closer than ever to finding Fallon. But the clock was ticking, and they couldn't afford to lose a single moment.

Sawyer sat at his desk, poring over the latest reports and evidence in Lindsey Gill's disappearance case. Cam was on the phone, coordinating with the tech team to analyze the image of the dark sedan captured on the grocery store's surveillance footage.

"All right, thanks," Cam said, hanging up and joining Sawyer at the desk. "The tech team analyzed the picture of the sedan—it's a 2012 Honda Civic."

Sawyer nodded thoughtfully, his mind racing with possibilities. "That matches the description of the vehicle Lindsey's neighbor mentioned seeing parked near her house before she disappeared."

"We need to talk to her again," Cam said decisively. "Get more details about when and where she saw it."

They printed out enlarged images of the sedan from different angles, highlighting key features like the distinctive taillights and any identifying marks. Armed with these visuals, they headed to Lindsey's neighborhood, hoping for a breakthrough in the case.

Lindsey's neighbor, Mrs. Patterson, greeted them at the door with a mix of apprehension and curiosity. She recognized Sawyer and Cam from their previous visits.

"Mrs. Patterson, thank you for seeing us again," Sawyer

said politely, showing her the printed pictures of the sedan. "We need to ask you about this vehicle. You mentioned seeing a similar car parked across from Lindsey's house a few days before she went missing."

Mrs. Patterson peered at the images, her brow furrowing in concentration. "Yes, that looks like the one I saw. I thought it was strange because I hadn't seen it in the neighborhood before."

"And did you see anyone around the car?" Sawyer asked, jotting down notes in his pad.

"No, I didn't," Mrs. Patterson replied, shaking her head. "I thought about mentioning it to Lindsey, but I didn't want to bother her. She seemed busy that day."

"Did you notice anything else unusual?" Cam inquired, trying to glean any additional information.

Mrs. Patterson paused, deep in thought. "Actually, now that I think about it, I did notice a man sitting in the driver's seat. He was just sitting there, staring straight ahead. I thought he might have been waiting for someone."

Sawyer exchanged a glance with Cam. "Can you describe the man? Did you recognize him?"

Mrs. Patterson shook her head. "No, I'm sorry. I didn't get a good look at his face. He had on sunglasses and a baseball cap pulled low."

"Thank you, Mrs. Patterson," Cam said, handing her a card. "If you remember anything else or if you see that vehicle again, please call us immediately."

Sawyer's heart raced as he climbed back into the cruiser. The same sedan at two different crime scenes... It couldn't be a coincidence. Despite the different manners of death, the cases were linked—he just needed to figure out how.

CHAPTER
SEVENTEEN

Brynlee's hands tightened on the steering wheel as she pulled into her driveway, her mind still swirling with the chaos of the day. The salon, usually her sanctuary, had become a battleground of destruction and frustration.

But as she glanced toward her front porch, her heart sank. There, placed carefully on the welcome mat, was a small box.

"Damn it, Zane," she muttered under her breath. She didn't want reminders of their past, not now, not when she was already struggling to keep herself together.

Her muscles felt like lead as she forced herself out of the car. Each step toward the porch felt heavier than the last, exhaustion threatening to overwhelm her. With a deep breath, she finally reached the front door and picked up the box.

Carefully peeling back the tape, she lifted the flaps and peered inside. Nestled in the bottom, wrapped in tissue paper, was a photo frame, the picture of them smiling on a sunny day, blissfully unaware of what was to come.

The image was a stark contrast to the present reality. They had been so in love, so full of dreams for the future. But that was before Zane's infidelity shattered everything Brynlee held dear. She remembered the pain, the betrayal that cut deep into her soul, leaving scars that still hadn't fully healed.

Seeing it again was bittersweet. She'd given him the photo on their first anniversary and Zane had kept it after they split. Now it was back, along with a flood of unwanted memories.

As she held the photograph in her hands, Brynlee felt a surge of anger. She didn't want Zane's tokens of remorse. She wanted him to leave her alone, to let her move on with her life without dredging up the past.

As Brynlee stood on her porch, contemplating the framed photo in her hands, she heard the familiar rumble of a car pulling into the neighboring driveway. She glanced up and saw Sawyer stepping out of his car. Internally, she groaned. Their interactions often felt like a verbal sparring match, and he was the last person she wanted to see after the tumultuous day she'd had.

As he walked toward her, a smirk twisted his lips. "Look at you, standing out here to greet me after a long day. Lucky me."

Brynlee rolled her eyes, forcing herself to muster a snappy comeback despite her exhaustion. "Piss off, Sawyer. I'm not in the mood for your shit today."

"Does that mean you're usually in the mood for my shit?" He shot her a cocky smile. "I knew you liked me."

"Go away."

"It's okay if you do." He leaned against the post and nodded toward the box in her hands. "Oh, look. You got me a present? You shouldn't have."

She was sorely tempted to throw the thing at his head. "The only present on your doorstep would be a flaming pile of dog shit."

Sawyer laughed. "There she is. I was worried for a minute."

"That would require you to think about someone other than yourself."

"Touchy today, are we?" He peered in the box, brows furrowing when he saw the picture frame. "Who's that?"

Brynlee sighed. "My ex."

"What's it doing out here?"

"I left it behind when we split. He's been returning my things."

"Can't let you go, huh? Can't see why not, considering you're so sweet."

"More like he feels bad for cheating," she shot back, her tone sharper than she intended.

Sawyer's smirk faded instantly, his expression growing serious. He went rigid, a muscle in his jaw twitching. "He cheated on you? Asshole."

The usual sarcasm was absent from his voice this time, and she was momentarily taken aback by his reaction. He didn't make a snide comment or poke fun at her. Instead, he looked genuinely affronted on her behalf.

"Yeah, well, it is what it is," she said, trying to sound nonchalant. "I just wish he'd stop sending me reminders of our past. I'd gladly give up everything I left behind if it meant never having to hear from him again."

Sawyer's eyes softened as he looked at her, and for a moment, she saw a flicker of something she couldn't quite place. "Listen, Bryn," he said quietly. "If you want, I can make it stop. Just say the word."

Brynlee blinked in surprise. She was so used to his sarcastic comments and teasing that she wasn't quite sure how to take this side of him. "Really? You'd do that?" she asked, a small smile tugging at the corners of her mouth.

"Only for you," he replied with a wink. "Because I like you so much."

She couldn't help but laugh. "I'll think about it."

He smiled. "You know where to find me if you need me. Oh, by the way..."

He cleared his throat. "I heard about what happened at the salon. I just wanted to say I was sorry."

"Thanks." Brynlee paused for a moment, caught off guard by his show of sympathy. "It's been kind of a rough day."

"If there's anything I can do to help," he offered, "just let me know. Seriously."

She nodded, touched by his sincerity. "I appreciate that. More than you know."

As they stood there in silence for a moment, Brynlee felt a weight lift off her shoulders. It had been emotionally draining to deal with the fallout from the salon incident, but knowing she had support made it a little easier to bear.

"Anyway," she finally said, forcing a small smile, "I should probably head inside."

"Sure," Sawyer replied, heading for his own front door. "My offer stands. Call me if you need anything."

"I will," Brynlee offered a small smile. "Thanks again, Sawyer. I "really appreciate it."

As he walked away, Brynlee felt a sense of relief wash over her. He had his moments.

CHAPTER
EIGHTEEN

Sawyer stood in his kitchen, nursing a glass of bourbon, when he heard a soft knock at the back door. His brow furrowed, and he set the glass on the counter, the amber liquid sloshing slightly.

He walked over to the door and peered through the small window, his gaze immediately landing Brynlee who stood on the patio outside. He pulled the door open and leaned one shoulder against the doorjamb, his eyes raking over her from head to toe as he studied her.

She looked up at him, one hand on her hip, her expression a mixture of impatience and frustration. "Well?"

Sawyer cocked an eyebrow, not saying a word. Brynlee huffed, her eyes flicking heavenward for a moment. With a little toss of her head, she turned to leave. In one swift motion, he snaked an arm around her waist and yanked her back inside. The door slammed shut behind her as he pulled her against him, their bodies colliding with a familiar heat.

Without a moment's hesitation, Sawyer's lips crashed onto hers in a hard, demanding kiss. It was a familiar dance, one he'd become used to over the past four months since she'd first come to him. Their relationship was a volatile storm of emotions, marked by fiery arguments and even fiercer reconciliations.

Every kiss was a battle, each of them fighting for supremacy and dominance. Their kiss deepened as they stumbled down the hallway, their movements a chaotic blend of urgency and desire. Brynlee's fingers tangled in his hair, tugging him closer, while his hands roamed over her body, reacquainting themselves with every curve and contour. They broke apart only to catch their breath, the space between them charged with an electric tension.

Sawyer's mind raced as they neared the bedroom, the memories of their past encounters flooding back. The arguments, the passion, the nights spent in each other's arms —it all felt like a heady, intoxicating whirl. As they reached the doorway, he lifted Brynlee off her feet, carrying her the rest of the way to the bed.

He lay her down gently in the middle of the mattress, and their eyes locked for a brief moment. In that silence, an understanding passed between them. They both knew this was more than just a physical connection; it was a tempest of emotions neither could easily escape.

And as Sawyer leaned down to kiss her again, he knew that, for tonight at least, they would lose themselves in the storm once more.

Brynlee lay in Sawyer's bed, staring at the ceiling, her mind a whirlwind of conflicting emotions. She hated herself for being so weak, for coming to him again. Every time she swore it would be the last, and each time, she found herself back in his arms. The way he made her feel was the only thing that took the edge off, but deep down, she knew it could never happen again.

Sawyer lay next to her, one arm under her head. With his free hand he lightly coasted his fingers up and down her arm before dropping a kiss on her shoulder.

Her throat grew tight and she pushed to a sitting position, pulling the sheet with her. Sawyer's hand trailed along her spine, tracing each vertebrae and turning her skin to fire.

"You can stay," he murmured.

Brynlee shook her head, sliding off the bed and reaching for her clothes. "I have an early morning," she lied.

She felt his eyes on her as she quickly dressed, then headed for the door. Pausing in the doorway, she turned to face him, her heart aching with a combination of guilt and regret. "Sawyer... This can't happen again."

He didn't respond, just watched her with those intense, piercing eyes that always seemed to see right through her. She turned away, leaving his house and locking the door behind her.

Outside, the cool night air hit her like a slap. She paused by the flowerbed in the backyard, the vibrant blooms swaying gently in the breeze. Unraveling the hose from the reel, she watered them, imagining she could feel Sawyer's eyes on her from just a few feet away, watching every move she made.

Part of her wanted to go back to him, wanted him to ask her to stay again. She swallowed down the emotion in her throat. No matter how good they were in bed, they were all wrong for each other. She couldn't keep doing this to herself.

Returning the hose to its rightful place, she rubbed at the space over her heart before crossing the patio and entering the kitchen of her own duplex.

Scooter greeted her, rubbing against her feet, purring loudly. This was one man she could count on. She scooped him up and cuddled him close, burying her face in his fur.

Inside the house, silence pressed in on her as she made her way toward her own bed and climbed inside. Scooter pranced and turned until he was comfortable, then curled up on the pillow next to her. But his presence was a small comfort. The bed felt even colder, the sheets a stark contrast to the warmth of Sawyer's embrace.

She lay there, staring at the ceiling once more, willing herself to stay strong, to resist the pull that always drew her back to him. Tonight had to be the last time. For her own sake, she had to let go. But as she closed her eyes, the memory of his touch lingered, a bittersweet reminder of the storm she was trying so hard to escape.

CHAPTER
NINETEEN

Sawyer pushed open the heavy door to the Medical Examiner's office, the sterile, antiseptic smell immediately hitting his senses. The familiar hum of fluorescent lights buzzed overhead as he made his way down the corridor, his steps echoing off the tile floor. His mind raced with the grisly details of Lindsey Gill's murder, each piece of evidence forming a grim mosaic in his thoughts.

Dr. Tom Seidel, the city's chief medical examiner, was waiting for him in the autopsy suite. He looked up as Sawyer entered, offering a curt nod of acknowledgment.

"Detective Reed," Dr. Seidel greeted, his voice measured and calm. "I've just finished the autopsy on Lindsey Gill. There's a lot to go over."

Sawyer nodded, bracing himself for the details he was about to hear. He'd seen his fair share of brutality in his years on the force, but something about this case felt different. More sinister.

"Thanks, Doc. What do you have for me?" Sawyer asked.

Dr. Seidel gestured for Sawyer to join him at the exam table, where Lindsey's body lay, covered respectfully with a white sheet. He pulled back the sheet just enough to reveal her face and upper torso.

"Cause of death was blunt force trauma," Dr. Seidel began, "most likely with a heavy object."

Sawyer frowned, leaning in close to examine the damage. The marks were brutal, a clear indication of the killer's rage. "No idea of the weapon?"

"Unfortunately not," the medical examiner replied. "She was also beaten severely," he continued, indicating the extensive bruising on her face and torso. "The facial injuries suggest repeated blows. And there's evidence of sexual assault."

Sawyer's jaw tightened. He had anticipated the brutality, but hearing it confirmed was always a punch to the gut.

"The most peculiar detail, though," Dr. Seidel said, moving to Lindsey's hands, "is that her fingers were removed postmortem."

Sawyer's eyes widened as he saw the crude stumps where Lindsey's fingers should have been. "I'm guessing the killer didn't want any DNA transfer," Sawyer muttered. "No skin cells or blood under her nails to trace back to him."

"Exactly," Dr. Seidel agreed. "But that's not all. We found white fibers in her nose and mouth, likely used to gag her during the attack. We'll need to analyze those further."

Sawyer nodded, making a mental note to follow up on that later. Jayla Simms's cause of death was asphyxiation, and she'd had similar fibers in her airway. If the cases were connected, he needed every piece of evidence he could get to track down the son of a bitch who'd done this.

"There's one more thing," Dr. Seidel said, pulling the sheet back a bit further to reveal Lindsey's upper left arm. "There's a small incision here. It could be a defensive wound, but its placement and precision suggest it might have been deliberate."

Sawyer examined the incision, a neat, almost surgical cut. It didn't fit with the chaotic violence of the rest of the attack.

"It was made by some type of blade," Seidel continued. "See the edges of the wound, how they're straight? Not torn or ragged, like she was pulling away."

"What do you think it means?" Sawyer asked, his mind racing with possibilities.

Dr. Seidel shook his head. "I'm not sure yet. But it's definitely something to consider. I would venture to guess she was unconscious when the incision was made. The killer took great care to eliminate any potential DNA evidence, but this wound... It feels intentional. I'll cross-check her history and see if I can find any correlation."

Sawyer stepped back, the weight of the case settling heavily on his shoulders. Lindsey Gill's murder was more than just a brutal crime; it was a calculated, meticulously planned act. And the killer was still out there.

"Thanks, Doc," Sawyer said, his tone grim. "Keep me updated on those fibers. We need to find this guy before he strikes again."

Dr. Seidel nodded, covering Lindsey's body once more. "I will, Detective. Be careful out there."

As Sawyer left the autopsy suite, his mind churned with the details he had learned. Each piece of evidence brought him closer to understanding the killer's twisted mind. But it also raised more questions, and he knew the answers wouldn't come easily.

The hunt for Lindsey Gill's murderer was just beginning.

* * *

Sawyer pushed open the glass door of the sheriff's department, the weight of the information he had just received from Dr. Seidel bearing down on him. He made his way through the bustling precinct, nodding absently at colleagues as he headed toward the office he shared with Cam McCoy.

The small room was already crowded, with Sheriff Dare Jensen leaning against a desk, his arms crossed over his chest, concern pulling at the corners of his eyes and mouth.

"Sawyer," Cam called, motioning for him to join them.

Sheriff Jensen turned his attention to Sawyer. "What'd you find out?"

"Got some new details from the ME," Sawyer began, dropping into his chair and tossing the file folder on the desk. "Cause of death was blunt force trauma—no surprise there. She was beaten severely and sexually assaulted. Her fingers were removed postmortem, probably to prevent any DNA transfer."

McCoy let out a low whistle, shaking his head. "Jesus, that's brutal."

"There's more," Sawyer continued, glancing at his notes. "White fibers were found in her nose and mouth, likely from whatever he used to gag her. Also, there's a small incision on her upper left arm. Although it could just be a defensive wound, Seidel thinks it might be deliberate."

Jensen frowned, considering the details. "How does this fit with Simms and Swanson?"

"We've placed the same sedan at two scenes: Lindsey's neighbor saw it parked along the street a few days before she disappeared, and Fallon's neighbor across the street saw it the night she was abducted. She thought it was Fallon at first, but I'm guessing her car was already in the garage."

Cam nodded. "This is our guy—we just need to figure out who the hell he is."

"Maybe we can check the businesses next to the grocery store," Dare put in. "See if we get a better look at the plate that way."

"Can't hurt." Cam tipped his head. "But this guy is good. He's managed to avoid every other camera in the area—I would guess he'd be smart enough to stay away from those, too."

Sawyer ran a hand through his hair, frustration evident in his voice. "This is unreal. How does the killer know so much about everyone's routines? It's like he's one step ahead of us every time."

Jayla's body had been very publicly staged in the center of town, where she was certain to be found quickly. Same with Hilary—the killer had chosen a hiking trail used every single morning by the same man. It was almost as if the killer were taunting them with his ability to slip through town, completely unnoticed.

Cam nodded grimly, flipping through his own set of notes. "Jayla was found by Sean, the jogger who runs through town every morning like clockwork. Hilary was discovered by Marty, who hikes that trail religiously. Both of them stumbled upon the bodies shortly after they were left. It's not random—it's calculated."

Dare leaned forward, his brow furrowed in deep thought. "The pattern suggests the killer has intimate knowledge of Brookhaven—knows the residents, their schedules, and habits. He knows exactly when and where to leave the bodies to ensure they're found quickly. And always by an adult—never a child."

Sawyer tapped his pen against the desk, his mind racing. "The killer must have studied this area for a long time, observing, planning. He knows how to avoid detection, how to manipulate circumstances to their advantage."

Cam sighed heavily as he rubbed his temples. "The question is, who among us could have this level of knowledge? It must be someone from Brookhaven, someone who blends in seamlessly."

Sawyer glanced up sharply. "Could it be someone in law

enforcement? A former detective or someone with access to police records?"

Dare shook his head. "Possibly, but not necessarily. It could be anyone—someone with a deep connection to the town, maybe even someone we know."

They fell into a troubled silence, each lost in their own thoughts. The realization was sinking in: the killer wasn't just targeting victims at random. They were executing a meticulously planned series of murders, exploiting their knowledge of the town and its people.

"We need to dig deeper," Dare finally said, breaking the silence. "We need to look at everyone—neighbors, friends, colleagues. Someone here knows more than they're letting on."

Cam nodded, determination hardening his features. "Agreed. We can't afford to overlook anyone."

"We're getting closer," Sawyer said. "Let's find this guy before he strikes again."

As they continued to pore over the evidence, a chilling certainty settled among them. The killer was among them, hiding in plain sight, their identity a mystery waiting to be unraveled. The stakes had never been higher, and the clock was ticking.

CHAPTER
TWENTY

The morning sun filtered through the blinds of the salon, casting a soft glow over the waterlogged carpet and the cabinets that had begun to warp from moisture. Brynlee anxiously awaited the arrival of Mr. Johnson, the insurance adjuster, hoping he would bring some clarity to the chaos that had unfolded.

At precisely 10:00 AM, there was a knock at the door. Brynlee hurried to open it, greeted by a middle-aged man in a suit, briefcase in hand.

"You must be Mr. Johnson," she said as she held the door open. "Please, come in."

"And you must be Ms. Layne." The man offered a warm smile and extended his hand for a quick shake. "Sorry to meet under these circumstances."

"I don't know what happened," Brynlee fretted. "I checked everything Saturday night before we left and it looked fine."

"Let's take a look at the damage and get everything sorted out." Mr. Johnson stepped inside, his gaze sweeping over the salon's interior.

Brynlee led him through the salon, pointing out the areas affected by the water leak. They stopped first at the reception desk where the computer, now a casualty of the incident, sat unplugged, the damaged cords wrapped up to be thrown away.

Mr. Johnson carefully inspected the computer and the desk, jotting down notes on his tablet. "It looks like the computer will definitely need to be replaced," he noted, his voice sympathetic.

"I actually replaced it last night," Brynlee said. "I wanted to make sure we could get up and running as soon as possible."

"Good idea," he said as his gaze slid over the tiled floor. "Doesn't appear to be too much damage to the flooring here since it's tiled."

He squared down to inspect the trim near the floor and around the doors, then made a few more notes on the tablet. Brynlee quietly watched as he made a slow circuit around the room, inspecting all the contents.

He used his pen to point to one of the dryers. "Has anyone tested this yet?"

Brynlee nodded. "Seems to be okay, at least for the moment. Fingers crossed it stays that way."

He turned a concerned look her way. "Make sure to have someone take a look at it. The last thing you want is an electrical fire."

"Of course." She nodded emphatically. "I'll call someone this afternoon."

"Can you show me where the leak started?"

Brynlee led the way to the bathroom, explaining how she'd walked in yesterday morning to find an inch of standing water flooding the entire salon. She pointed toward the toilet. "I called a plumber first thing, who said the valve was leaking."

Mr. Johnson knelt down and ran his fingers over the wall,

the paint slightly discolored where the drywall had absorbed the water. "It's clear the water damage is extensive here," he observed. "Have you had any work done recently?"

"Aside from yesterday?" She shook her head. "No. I had someone check everything over last year before I signed the lease, but everything was okay."

He nodded slowly, then stood. "Based on what I'm seeing, it looks like the damage was caused by human error, which unfortunately falls under your responsibility as the property owner."

Brynlee's heart sank. "What does that mean?"

"The report from the plumber stated that the valve had been loosened slightly." He slid a look her way. "Those typically don't come loose on their own, so it does look a bit suspicious. In my line of work, I've found that it's not unusual for owners to experience... accidents... like these."

She reeled back at his words. "You think I did this?"

She wasn't making a huge profit off the salon, but she had no reason to sabotage it for money. Tears pricked her eyes, and she fought to blink them away. "Mr. Johnson, I swear. I don't know what happened, but I had nothing to do with this."

He closed the lid of the tablet and regarded her for a long moment before speaking. "I would check with your employees, make sure none of them noticed anything. Sometimes people see a problem and try to fix it themselves."

Brynlee nodded, unable to form words over the lump that had formed in her throat. She'd already ordered the cabinets and carpet. If she couldn't get the insurance company to reimburse her, it was going to set her back months, financially speaking.

"I understand this is disappointing," Mr. Johnson said gently, obviously sensing her frustration and disappointment. "Situations like this are never easy to deal with."

Brynlee nodded, trying to maintain her composure.

"Thank you for your understanding. It's just been overwhelming. I had to fire an employee last week, and..." She trailed off, her mind suddenly whirling. The timing did seem suspicious. But Jessica wouldn't have anything to do with this... Right?

Mr. Johnson eyed her critically. "Is something wrong?"

"I'm not sure," she responded honestly, still feeling more than a little off-kilter. "I don't want to assume the worst, but... I know everything was fine Saturday night when I closed up."

Was it possible someone—namely Jessica—had entered after they'd closed up and deliberately sabotaged the valve? The salon was located in a plaza, and though they had security cameras on the exterior, Brynlee seriously doubted they worked properly—or at all. She'd put in a request to install a security system several months ago, but Mr. Pollard had continually put her off. Now she regretted not pushing harder. Thank God the damage wasn't worse.

The insurance adjuster tipped his head her way. "If you suspect it was tampered with, my suggestion would be to file a police report. That could potentially lead to a different assessment of the claim."

Brynlee nodded slowly, considering his advice. "I'll definitely do that."

"In the meantime," Mr. Johnson continued, "let's get started on processing your claim. I'll do everything I can to assist you through this process and ensure you receive the support you need."

CHAPTER
TWENTY-ONE

Sawyer's gaze was fixed on the large map pinned to the whiteboard on the wall, red dots marking the homes of the victims and yellow dots indicating where their bodies had been found. His jaw tightened as he traced the lines connecting each point.

Cam entered the room, a steaming cup of coffee in his hand. He glanced at the map, then at Sawyer, and arched a brow. "Long night?"

Sawyer nodded and let out a ragged sigh. "Couldn't sleep. This case is eating at me, Cam. These women... It's like the killer is taunting us."

Cam dropped into his chair and set his coffee on his desk and turned his attention to the photos on the white board. "Let's go over what we know again. Maybe we missed something."

Sawyer stood and walked over to the map, pointing to the red pins. "Jayla, Lindsey, Hilary, and now Fallon. All blonde and blue-eyed. No common threads, no overlap in their lives except for their looks. There's no pattern in where they were abducted, or where their bodies were found."

Cam joined him at the map, studying the pins. "It's almost like the killer is choosing locations at random, but the victim type is specific. There has to be something we're missing."

Sawyer shook his head, frustration eating at his gut. "I've been going over their backgrounds again and again. Jayla worked at a bank, Lindsey was a nurse, Hilary was studying to be a teacher, and Fallon worked at a boutique. They didn't know each other, didn't frequent the same places. There's no overlap in professions, where they shopped, where they went to school... Not a goddamn thing."

Cam tapped his fingers on the desk, deep in thought. "What about the cars? Anything there?"

"Nothing." Sawyer barely repressed a growl. "I checked everyone close to all of the victims—none of them drive a white van or a dark Honda like the one in the photo. Fallon's ex, Mark, drives a bright blue Ford Escape, and his girlfriend, Julie, drives a small, white Hyundai. We've got shit."

Cam sipped at his coffee for a moment. "What about the DMV records? Maybe—"

Sawyer was already shaking his head. "As soon as we got the footage from the store, I had Webb and Landry check the list to see if any of the van drivers also has a black or navy Honda Civic. We didn't get a single hit."

He propped his hands on his hips and stared at the board. "They checked all the drivers with criminal records first, but they all have alibis. Every. Single. One."

He whirled toward Cam. "What the fuck are we missing?"

Cam made a face. "I wish I knew. We've tracked every lead and come up empty-handed. Whoever this guy is, he's damn good."

"I'm fucking tired of being one step behind," Sawyer snapped. "We need something, goddamn it!"

His phone rang, and he angrily swiped at the screen before lifting it to his ear. "Reed."

"Detective, this is Tom Seidel. I have something I think you need to see..."

Dr. Tom Seidel greeted them at the ME's office, a folder in hand. "Please, have a seat."

Sawyer and Cam did as requested, and Sawyer watched the doctor with a sense of foreboding, his stomach twisting into a tight knot.

Dr. Seidel opened the folder, exposing several photographs, and turned it toward them. "As I mentioned in my original report, while performing the autopsy we found a drop of blood behind Ms. Gill's left ear."

He glanced at the men. "Lindsey sustained severe wounds, predominantly on her face and torso. The blood droplet we found wasn't consistent with her injuries, so I took a scraping and sent it to the lab."

Sawyer arched a brow. "Does it belong to the killer?"

"Not the killer, no." Dr. Seidel adjusted his glasses before folding his hands on the desk in front of him. "But we did get an immediate hit on the DNA."

Cam sat forward in his seat. "Who?"

Dr. Seidel paused for effect, his gaze moving between Sawyer and Cam. "It's a match to Hilary Swanson."

Sawyer blinked at the doctor. "Hilary Swanson? You're sure?"

"Positive." The doctor nodded grimly.

Sawyer's mind spun as Cam turned his way. "Hilary wasn't found until after Lindsey went missing—that places them together. The cases are connected."

"All three women had similar physical features—blonde hair, blue eyes. But their deaths were carried out differently.

Hilary and Jayla were kept alive for months, but Lindsey was killed only a few weeks after her abduction."

Sawyer rubbed his temples, trying to piece together the new information. "Why the change in MO? If it's the same killer, why the sudden shift in behavior?"

"It's possible the killer's motives evolved," Dr. Seidel interjected. "Hilary and Jayla were kept alive, possibly for companionship or some twisted fantasy. Lindsey, on the other hand…"

"Wasn't treated the same way," Cam finished his thought. "It's almost like the killer lost interest or had a different agenda."

Sawyer leaned back in his chair, staring at the ceiling as he processed the new revelation. "Or maybe there's another layer we're missing. Something that connects these women beyond their physical appearance."

Dr. Seidel cleared his throat. "I'd like to discuss something that bothered me during Lindsey Gill's autopsy."

Sawyer leaned forward, his brow furrowing. "What's that?"

Dr. Seidel adjusted his glasses and continued, "As you know, Lindsey had a small incision on her upper arm. Initially, I assumed it was a superficial wound, but upon closer examination, I couldn't find any evidence of a birth control implant, which she was supposed to have according to her medical records."

Cam's eyes narrowed as he processed the information. "Are you saying the implant was removed?"

Dr. Seidel nodded gravely. "That's what it appears. And it's not just Lindsey. I went back and reviewed the medical records for Hilary Swanson and Jayla Simms. Both women were also reported to have had IUDs or implants in their upper arms, but I didn't find any during their autopsies either."

Sawyer scrubbed a hand over his face. "Why wouldn't we have noticed this before?"

Dr. Seidel let out a beleaguered sigh. "Because the killer kept the women for nearly a year. The wounds from the removal of those implants would have healed long ago, leaving no visible traces by the time we examined their bodies."

Cam frowned, trying to connect the dots. "So, the killer removed these implants. But why? What's the significance?"

Dr. Seidel hesitated for a moment before answering. "It's possible the implants were removed as a symbolic act. The killer may have wanted to sever any ties these women had to their reproductive choices, their autonomy. Could be a form of control, a way to assert dominance over them."

Sawyer's jaw tightened. "It fits the pattern of domination and manipulation we've seen in other aspects of the crimes."

Cam nodded in agreement. "And it explains why Lindsey's murder, while connected to Hilary and Jayla's in some way, was executed differently. The killer's motives evolved, but the underlying need for control remained consistent."

Dr. Seidel looked between the detectives, his expression troubled. "I'm sorry to bring such grim news, but I felt it was crucial for your investigation."

Sawyer straightened from his chair. "Thanks, Doc. I appreciate you checking into this."

Cam nodded to the doctor, then fell into step next to Sawyer as he strode from the room. The bright sunlight outside assaulted him, and he slid his sunglasses into place as he cut across the parking lot toward the cruiser.

Cam caught up to him just as he slid into the driver seat. "This could be what we needed."

Sawyer turned to face him. "Something about that whole thing has been bothering me since the beginning. Because Hilary supposedly miscarried, we don't know how far along she was. I kind of assumed that she was pregnant before she was kidnapped, but now..."

He trailed off, and Cam grimaced as he picked up the train of thought. "Maybe that's what they all have in common—maybe he's removing the implants to try to get them pregnant."

Sawyer's stomach flipped over. The thought was revolting. "That's a whole new level of fucked up. And that raises another question—if that's his fantasy, then why get rid of them?"

"Hell, I don't know." Cam shrugged, then started the car and steered out of the parking lot. "Maybe the fantasy outweighs reality. Or maybe that's part of the fascination, too —he holds their lives in his hands and kills them when he's tired of them."

"But Hilary wasn't murdered," Sawyer argued. "She bled to death."

Cam propped his elbow on the door and rubbed his temples. "So he wants them pregnant. Why?"

That was the million dollar question. "You know what I don't understand? Lindsey's death doesn't fit. Not at all. He didn't even keep her long enough to impregnate her."

Cam suddenly straightened. "Maybe that's the point. Maybe she wouldn't let him."

Sawyer's brows pulled together as he turned toward Cam. "What do you mean?"

"That level of brutality is born of passion. He had to be furious to do that kind of damage. And then he cut off her fingers."

"To eliminate DNA," Sawyer added.

"Yes, but he didn't do that with the others," Cam said. "He used bleach to clean them. He cared for them. Because they played into his fantasy."

"And Lindsey didn't." Sawyer dropped his head back. "Fuck."

Cam nodded grimly, and Sawyer drew in a deep breath. "I don't know if that bodes well for Fallon or not."

"It means we need to go back through every single thing. The answer's there—we just have to find it."

CHAPTER
TWENTY-TWO

Sawyer sat at his cluttered desk, his eyes scanning the worn pages of the file in front of him. This case had been haunting him for days, the pieces of the puzzle refusing to fit together. The fluorescent light above flickered slightly, making the words dance on the page as he sipped his lukewarm coffee.

The soft lilt of a feminine voice drifted toward him from the recesses of the outer office, and his ears perked up. He recognized Yvonne's voice, but also... Brynlee?

Sawyer pushed his chair back and strode toward the doorway, his gaze unerringly finding his neighbor standing next to Yvonne's desk, her fingers running through Sarge's thick coat as he stared adoringly up at her.

"Bryn?" Her head jerked up at the sound of his voice, and he studied her intently. "What brings you here?"

Her teeth cut into her bottom lip and she gave Sarge one last pat on the head before drifting toward Sawyer's office.

"I came to speak with Cam or Dare," she said, stepping inside. "But it looks like they're both tied up."

"Anything I can help with?"

"I think I need to file a police report."

His brows jumped toward his hairline. "Did something happen?"

She sighed. "It's kind of a long story. If you don't want to deal with it—"

"It's fine." Sawyer motioned for her to take a seat, pushing the files to the side. "What's going on?"

Brynlee took a deep breath, settling into the chair opposite him. "I had to fire one of my stylists, Jessica, last Saturday. She wasn't performing well, and it was affecting the business. Then, just a few days later, we had a major flooding incident at the salon."

Sawyer leaned forward, his interest piqued. "I remember hearing about that. What happened?"

"According to the plumber, it was a leaky valve," Brynlee explained. "It wasn't even old—just loose. It caused a lot of damage—ruined carpets, cabinets, even our computer. The insurance adjuster came by and said it looked like it was my fault, but I have a feeling it was tampered with."

Sawyer's brow furrowed. "Tampered with? Do you have any evidence?"

"Nothing for sure," Brynlee admitted. "But it just seems too coincidental. I think Jessica might have done it out of spite. I want to file a police report, just in case."

Sawyer nodded slowly and reached for a notepad. "Can you tell me exactly what happened leading up to the discovery of the leak?"

Brynlee recounted the events of the past few days in detail, from the uncomfortable confrontation with Jessica to the moment she walked into the salon and found it in disarray.

While he took notes, he couldn't shake the feeling that this was more of a distraction than a genuine case of sabotage.

"Bryn, I understand your concern," he began carefully, setting his pen down. "But... it sounds like this might just be an unfortunate oversight. Valves can wear out, and leaks happen. Filing a report might not be the best use of our resources."

Brynlee's face fell, her shoulders slumping. "So you think it was just an accident, too?"

He hated the way she said that—like he was giving up on her, too. Unfortunately, the plumber and the insurance agent were most likely correct. Things like this happened. Without solid evidence, there wasn't much they could do.

"I'm sorry," Sawyer said gently. "From what you've described, it doesn't seem like there's any evidence of deliberate tampering. But, to put your mind at ease, I can come take a look myself."

A flicker of hope crossed Brynlee's face. "Would you? I just need to be sure."

"Of course," Sawyer replied, grabbing his coat. "Let's head over to the salon."

The two made their way to the salon in silence, the tension palpable. Once there, Brynlee unlocked the door and led Sawyer inside. The faint smell of damp carpet lingered in the air, and the damage was evident as they walked through the space.

"I've already had a team come through and clean, but..." She shrugged as she trailed off.

"I get it." He tipped his head. "Why don't you show me where the leak started?"

Brynlee showed him to the bathroom, where he inspected the valve first, crouching down to examine it closely. It looked worn, but there were no signs of tampering or recent interference. Next, he checked the doors and windows for any signs of forced entry but found none. Finally, he looked around for any security cameras, noticing the absence of a security system.

"You don't have a security system?" he asked, straightening up.

"No," Brynlee admitted, her voice small. "I'm renting this place, and I assumed it was safe. There wasn't anything mentioned in the lease about needing one."

Sawyer sighed. "Brynlee, from what I can see, there's no evidence of tampering or forced entry. It looks like an unfortunate mistake—maybe the valve was already on its last legs, and it just gave out."

Brynlee's mouth turned down in disappointment. "So you really think it was just an accident?"

"I do," Sawyer said gently. "I know it's not the answer you were hoping for, but sometimes these things happen. It's always a good idea to invest in a security system, though. It might give you some peace of mind."

Brynlee nodded, her expression dejected. "Thanks anyway."

"I'm sorry I couldn't give you better news," he said. "If anything else comes up, you know where to find me."

She managed a small smile, but it didn't reach her eyes. "I will. Thanks again."

A pang of guilt sliced through him as he climbed into his car and pulled away from the salon. He hated seeing her so upset, but he couldn't manufacture evidence where there was none.

Much later that evening, as the sun began to set, Sawyer made his way into the house. Pausing next to the back door, he spotted Brynlee in her backyard, watering her flowers. The colorful blooms waved in the gentle breeze, and she carefully pruned the dead blossoms while Scooter watched from his perch on the table.

He rolled his eyes. Damn cat. At least the animal door seemed to be fixed, because he hadn't noticed any paw prints on his car for the past few days.

For a moment he considered going out to talk to her, but she seemed withdrawn, her body tense. He knew he should leave well enough alone, especially when he had nothing new to offer. Without evidence pointing to foul play, he couldn't justify questioning Jessica further or delving deeper into what might be a simple accident.

Her head lifted for a second and she surreptitiously glanced toward his side of the duplex before turning back to the task at hand. It was clear she was aware of his presence but chose to ignore him, focused entirely on her flowers.

Sawyer sighed and reached into the fridge for a beer. He would never understand her. Brynlee was such a damn enigma. The only place they were compatible was in bed. He could use the release, but he doubted she would be amenable. She barely acknowledged his existence until she needed him, and even then it was only on her terms.

He had a feeling if he walked outside right now and offered to take her to bed, she'd turn him down flat on principle. Hell, last night she'd told him it would never happen again. She probably meant it, too. Which was too bad, because they were fire together. He'd never felt anything like that with another woman. She drove him crazy in all the best and worst ways. It was a dangerous game they were playing, but it didn't seem to affect her at all.

Sawyer popped the top on his beer and took a long pull before sinking into a chair at the table and flipping open the file he'd brought home for work. This, he understood. Dead bodies were a hell of a lot easier to figure out than the infuriating woman next door.

CHAPTER
TWENTY-THREE

Sawyer groaned as he peeled himself off the couch, his body stiff from another night of restless sleep. The clock on the wall read 7:42 AM, and he groaned. Goddamn it. He was late.

He rubbed his eyes and stumbled to the kitchen, the tile cool against his bare feet. He fumbled with the coffee pot, his fingers working on autopilot scooping coffee grounds and pouring water into the machine. As it hummed to life, filling the room with the rich aroma of brewing coffee, Sawyer leaned heavily on the counter.

Sunlight streamed in through the window over the sink and he closed his eyes against the glare, inhaling deeply as he scrubbed a hand over his face.

His mind raced, circling around the same frustrating thoughts that had kept him up all night. The murder investigation was going nowhere. Weeks of tireless work had yielded no substantial leads, and his lack of sleep only fueled his mounting frustration.

The coffee pot sputtered as it finished its cycle, and he grabbed a mug from the cabinet, then poured himself a generous portion of the life-saving brew. He took a sip as he moved across the room, the bitter warmth providing a momentary comfort. But his solace was short-lived.

As he gazed out the back door, a glimmer on the ground caught his eye. The patio was soaked, water pooling around the edges. He frowned. It hadn't rained last night.

"What the hell?"

Setting his mug down on the counter with a soft clink, Sawyer pushed open the back door and stepped out onto the wet patio. His gaze followed the trail of water to Brynlee's side of the yard, which was equally saturated. The sight of the hose still trickling water made his blood boil.

Brynlee.

She must have forgotten to turn it off after watering her flowers last night.

He marched over to the hose, his feet squelching in the wet grass. Water and mud splashed up, splattering his sweats as he reached down and twisted the nozzle shut. With the hose no longer dribbling, he turned his attention to Brynlee's side of the duplex. Her back door was only a few steps away, and he covered the distance quickly, each step fueled by his aggravation.

Sawyer pounded on the door with the side of his fist. "Brynlee! Open up!"

From inside, he could hear the muffled sounds of her footsteps as she entered the kitchen and strode toward the back door. After a moment, Brynlee's face appeared in the window, her hair pulled back in a large clip, her makeup half-done.

She yanked open the door, her face pulled into an expression of annoyance. "Sawyer, what the hell?"

"Did you forget to turn off the hose last night?" He glared at her. "The backyard looks like a fucking lake!"

She looked past him, her expression shifting from annoyance to confusion. "I don't know what you're talking about."

"Bullshit," he retorted. "I saw you out here last night watering the flowers."

She rolled her eyes. "If you were watching me, then you saw me put the hose away."

"I shouldn't have to babysit you and make sure you're doing what you're supposed to," he snapped.

Her eyes narrowed. "I said it wasn't me. Maybe you should check your own side before blaming me."

Their argument escalated, voices rising with every pointed barb they exchanged. Sawyer's frustration from the case and lack of sleep spilled over, mixing with his irritation at the morning's discovery. "Goddamn it! Could you just take responsibility for once?"

"I don't know what happened, but I didn't do this," she said stiffly. "I watered my plants last night, then hung it up like I always do."

"Sure." He rolled his eyes. "How the hell you run a business is beyond me. Oh, wait."

He gave an abbreviated laugh. "Look how that turned out. No wonder you're dealing with flooding at the salon—you just did the same thing here!"

She jerked back at his words, the blood draining from her face. Shit. He probably shouldn't have said that. "Bryn—"

"Fuck you, Sawyer." She turned on a heel, ignoring him completely. He lunged forward, grabbing for the door handle.

"Wait, I—" He yanked his hand back just before the door slammed shut in the space where his fingers had been just seconds before. He growled. Damn pain in the ass woman.

Sawyer's fists clenched as he watched Brynlee retreat into her duplex, her parting words echoing in his mind. The argument had left him seething, yet guilt gnawed at him too. He knew he'd been too harsh, his exhaustion and frustration from the case spilling over into their spat. The sun cast a pale glow over the damp yard, and he could see Brynlee through the window, frantically getting ready for work.

He slogged through the muddy yard and reached the front of the house just as she was locking the front door. She glanced his way for a fraction of a second before hopping off the stoop and striding toward her car.

"Bryn, wait!" he called out, his voice carrying in the quiet of early morning.

She didn't stop, her movements stiff and resolute. She pulled open the car door and climbed inside, not once glancing in his direction.

"Brynlee, just hold on a second!"

She ignored him, fumbling with her keys, and a moment later the engine roared to life. He lunged forward, knocking insistently on the driver's side window. "Brynlee, please, I'm sorry. I didn't mean what I said."

She finally turned to look at him, her blue eyes frigid. She cracked the window just enough to be heard. "You've made your point. Whatever it was, I'm sure it was my fault. But don't worry. I'll make sure I don't make a mess anymore."

"Bryn—"

"I don't like being your neighbor any more than you like living next to me. Just go away, Sawyer, and leave me the hell alone. "

Her words stung, but before he could respond, she put the car in gear. "Brynlee. Goddamn it, wait!"

He called out for her one last time but the car began to move, the tires splashing through the lingering puddles.

Sawyer stood there, a mix of regret and irritation churning inside him as he watched her go. The car approached the intersection at the end of the road, and he waited for the glow of red tail lights to appear. They never did.

His heart lurched as he watched the car glided straight through the intersection, and the sound that followed was a horrendous symphony of screeching metal and breaking glass.

CHAPTER
TWENTY-FOUR

Brynlee pressed down on the brake, but her foot went straight to the floor, and her heart leaped into her throat as she pumped the brake several more times.

Cars became a colorful blur in her peripheral vision as she clenched her fingers around the wheel and sailed past the stop sign and right into traffic. Something large and white appeared in her window, and she didn't even have time to scream before it slammed into the driver's side with a force that sent Brynlee's car spinning.

The impact was deafening. Metal crunched and glass shattered, filling the air with a cacophony of destruction. The force of the airbag deploying hit her like a sledgehammer, and the air rushed from her lungs as her head snapped back against the headrest.

Particles from the airbag filled the cabin, choking the air with a fine, acrid dust. Every breath burned. Every cell screamed in pain. Each tiny movement sent waves of agony through her body as her vision blurred, and she fought to remain conscious.

Somewhere in the chaos, she heard her name being called.

It was faint at first, almost drowned out by the ringing in her ears. But it grew louder, more insistent.

"Brynlee!"

Pushing through the fog of pain, she recognized Sawyer's voice. She turned her head, struggling to focus. Through the haze, she saw him. His face was a mask of concern as he reached for her, his hands strong and sure.

"I'm here, Bryn, I've got you," he said, his steady voice a lifeline in the maelstrom.

He wrenched the door open, the metal groaning in protest. With a gentleness that contrasted sharply with the violence of the crash, he pulled her from the wreckage. Every movement sent fresh jolts of pain through her body, but she clung to him, grateful for his strength, his presence.

"Stay with me, Brynlee," Sawyer urged, guiding her to the ground a safe distance from the car. "Help is on the way. Just hang in there."

He knelt beside her, his hands moving gently over her face and limbs as he checked her vitals. The world around her spun, and she closed her eyes, leaning heavily on him. "I need an ambulance. There's been a car accident..."

Sawyer's words were directed into his phone, his tone remarkably calm as he explained the situation. Once he hung up, he turned to her. "I need to check on the other driver. I'll be right back."

He left and Brynlee closed her eyes again as she reclined against the small tree behind her. The acrid smell of burnt rubber filled the air, mingling with the distant wail of sirens. Her body throbbed with pain, each breath a struggle against the tightness in her chest.

The soft scuffle of footsteps reached her eyes then stopped next to her, and Sawyer gripped her chin, forcing her to look at him. It took a moment for his face to come into focus, and he met her gaze. "You okay?"

She nodded weakly, wincing as a sharp pain shot through her side. The airbag had done its job, but it felt like it had bruised every rib in her body.

Sawyer glared at her, his expression a mix of relief and frustration. "Jesus Christ, Bryn. You could have been killed! Why the hell did you take off like that?" he demanded, his voice harsher now.

Brynlee flinched at his words, the sting of his rebuke cutting deeper than any physical pain. She turned her head away, her eyes filling with tears. "I don't know what happened. I—I couldn't stop it, and I didn't know what to do."

Sawyer shook his head, the corners of his mouth tipped down in a severe frown. "That's exactly the problem, Brynlee. You never think. You just act, and this is what happens."

His words hit her like a physical blow. She pulled away from him, struggling to sit up despite the pain. "You never believe me," she shot back.

"Because it's true!"

The sirens grew louder, and Brynlee's attention was drawn to the arrival of the police and medics as they pulled up to the scene.

"Why the hell are you even here?" She pulled away from him and pressed one hand to the solid ground, then levered to her feet. Sawyer reached for her, but she swatted his hands away. "Leave me the hell alone. You've made it perfectly clear that you don't like me."

Sawyer's face softened, a look of regret replacing the anger. "Brynlee, that's not true. I just—"

"I meant what I said earlier," she interrupted, her tone cold and distant. "I don't want your help, and I don't need it. Just go away."

He stood there stiffly and she stared over his shoulder, refusing to look at him. She sensed he wanted to say something, but he managed to hold his tongue, and for that she was grateful. Moments later the paramedics were by her side, and one went to speak with the other driver while Antonio moved to her side and shot her a gentle smile.

"Hey, Bryn. You holding up okay?"

"Hey." She smiled wearily. "I'm good, just a little banged up."

He nodded, then wrapped a hand around her elbow. "We need to get you checked out, okay?" She nodded, and he gave her a little squeeze. "We'll get the stretcher over here and get you loaded in just a second."

"Oh, I can—"

He shook his head, cutting her off. "You just sit right here and relax. I'll be right back."

She forced another smile. "Thanks."

Sawyer nodded to Antonio, then crouched next to her. "They'll get you fixed up."

She kept her eyes averted, refusing to look at Sawyer. The pain in her body was nothing compared to the ache in her heart.

As the paramedics loaded her into the ambulance, she caught a glimpse of Sawyer standing there, hands on his hips, his face etched with a mix of anger and regret as he stared after her. She turned away, blinking back tears.

Why was she such an idiot? She knew better than to let his words affect her. His moments of concern were few and far between, and more often than not, he was hypercritical of every single thing she did.

They'd bickered relentlessly since the day he moved in next door, and she hated herself a little more for ever going to him. The first time had been a moment of weakness. The other few times over the past couple of months... Well, that was sheer lunacy on her part, apparently.

He was nothing but a temporary distraction, and the past half hour only solidified her decision to stay the hell away from him. He was the last person she needed—or wanted—in her life.

Brynlee's vision swam as she tried to sit up on the gurney, the bright red and white lights of the ambulance flickering around her. She winced, feeling the sharp stab of pain radiating from her side. The paramedics moved swiftly, assessing her injuries and securing her for transport to the hospital.

Amid the chaos, one thought cut through the haze of confusion and fear: she needed to call her family.

Antonio stood next to Sawyer, and she waved one hand to catch his attention. Unfortunately, Sawyer dogged Antonio's footsteps as he approached the ambulance.

"What's wrong?"

Ignoring Sawyer, she focused on Antonio. "Can you please get my purse? I need to call my sister."

Antonio nodded. "Of course. Where is it?"

Brynlee pointed toward the wreckage of her car, the front passenger seat barely visible amidst the crumpled metal and shattered glass. "On the passenger seat." She bit her lip. "At least... it was. I'm not sure where it is now."

Antonio shot her a reassuring smile. "No problem. I'll be right back."

She could feel Sawyer's gaze on her as she watched Antonio move toward the car, then reach inside to search for her purse.

"Do you want me to give Dare a call and let him know what's going on?"

She shook her head and swallowed hard but didn't say a word. After a long moment, a heavy sigh filtered through Sawyer's nose and he cleared his throat. "If you need anything—"

"I won't."

She could practically hear his molars grind together as he

stared at her, but she kept her eyes turned forward, locked on Antonio as he passed her the purse. "Here ya go."

"Thank you." She fumbled with the zipper, her hands shaking, until she finally retrieved her cell phone. She swiped through her contacts and tapped Ainsley's name, holding her breath as the phone rang and rang.

In her peripheral vision she watched as Sawyer finally drifted away to work the scene. After what felt like an eternity, the call connected. "Hey, Bryn, what's up?"

Brynlee drew in a shaky breath, trying to keep her voice steady. "Ains, I... I've been in an accident. I'm okay, but they're taking me to the hospital."

There was a moment of stunned silence on the other end of the line before Ainsley's voice returned, this time filled with concern. "Which hospital are they taking you to? I'm on my way."

Brynlee felt a wave of relief wash over her at her sister's words. "I think they're taking me to Danbury Memorial," she said, glancing at Antonio for confirmation. He nodded as he slid in next to her, giving her a thumbs-up.

"Danbury Memorial," she repeated to Ainsley.

"Just hang in there. I'll let mom and dad know, and we'll be there as soon as we can," Ainsley said, her words slightly muffled as she shifted the phone. "Don't worry, everything's going to be okay."

Brynlee nodded, even though Ainsley couldn't see her. "Take your time. I'll see you soon."

"I'll be there before you know it. Love you, Bryn," Ainsley replied softly.

"Love you too," Brynlee ended the call just as the ambulance doors shut, and she allowed her eyes to drift closed as the vehicle lurched into gear, then sped toward the hospital.

CHAPTER
TWENTY-FIVE

The wail of sirens had faded into the distance, leaving behind the unnerving calm that often followed chaos. Sawyer stood at the edge of the road, assessing the scene. Brynlee's car sat near the median, its front end a twisted mass of metal. Nearby, a tow truck operator finished hooking up the other vehicle involved, its driver already en route to the hospital, much like Brynlee.

Digging out his phone, he called the local garage to have Brynlee's car removed. "Geiser's Garage," came a voice from the other end. "Mike here."

"Hey, Mike. This is Detective Sawyer Reed with Brookhaven Sheriff's Department."

"What can I do for you, detective?" Mike asked.

"I need a favor. Brynlee Layne was in an accident just a little while ago. Her car's in pretty bad shape, and I need you to retrieve it."

"Man, I'm sorry to hear that. Is she okay?" Mike asked, concern evident in his voice.

"Yeah, she's on her way to the hospital now. Can you get someone over here to take care of the vehicle?"

"Sure thing. Just tell me where it is, and I'll head over right away."

Sawyer quickly relayed the location of the accident, his mind flashing back to the scene—the twisted metal, the shattered glass. He shook his head, trying to push the images away.

"Thanks, Mike. I really appreciate it," Sawyer said. "I'll wait here for you."

"Sounds good. I'll be there soon," Mike replied.

True to his word, a large red rollback pulled up less than twenty minutes later, and Sawyer lifted a hand in greeting.

Mike let out a low whistle when he saw the car. "Damn. How's she doing?"

"Some scrapes and scratches, but she wasn't going too fast, thank God."

Mike nodded. "She's lucky she wasn't hurt worse."

Sawyer's lips pressed together in a tight line, guilt and worry clawing at his chest. "No kidding. Thanks for coming out."

"No problem." Mike dipped his chin in acknowledgment. "I'll have this out of here in just a few."

Sawyer watched as he slid under the car to attach the cable. It fell silent for several moments as he worked, then suddenly Mike shimmied out from under the vehicle, his face twisted into a mask of concern. "Reed, come take a look at this."

Brows furrowed, Sawyer moved closer and crouched next to the car. "What is it?"

Mike leveled a look his way. "Someone cut the lines under Brynlee's car."

The car had been tampered with? Fury bubbled in his veins. "Which line?"

"All of them."

The information sent him reeling. "What the hell do you mean 'all of them'?"

"Take a look at this." Mike pointed to a cluster of cut lines hanging loosely beneath the car. "Brake lines, power steering, and a couple of other vital systems. They've been deliberately cut."

Sawyer felt a cold wave of shock wash over him. "Are you saying someone did this on purpose?"

"No doubt about it." Mike shook his head and pointed to one of the severed lines. "Look here. These cuts are clean, made with a sharp tool—could be a knife or heavy duty scissors, but more likely a pair of snips. This wasn't a mechanical failure, and it sure as hell wasn't an accident."

Sawyer's stomach dropped as he stared at the severed lines, reality crashing over him. "You're sure?" He asked the question even though he already knew the answer.

"Positive," Mike confirmed. "Clean cut, too. This was deliberate."

"Thanks, Mike. I owe you one."

Goddamn it. His stomach twisted with dread even as he shook his head, his mind racing. Who would want to harm Brynlee? He pointed at the car. "I'll need to have this taken in for evidence. Can you bring it over ASAP?"

"No problem."

Sawyer pulled out his phone and dialed Cam's number as he watched as Mike began to load Brynlee's car onto the rollback.

"Cam, it's Sawyer. We have a problem," he said as soon as the line connected. He quickly relayed the information about the brake lines.

"Jesus," Cam muttered on the other end. "Is she okay?"

"She's a little banged up." And still pissed as hell at him, but he didn't say that.

Cam made a low sound in the back of his throat. "Any leads?"

"Not yet. I just found out as Mike was getting ready to

load the car. Brynlee thinks it was an accident. We'll need to check with her, see if anything happened recently. Someone wanted to hurt her, Cam."

"I'll let Dare know," Cam replied. "Meet you at the station?"

"Yeah. I'll be there soon." Sawyer ended the call, his resolve hardening.

As he made his way to his cruiser, he couldn't shake the image of Brynlee's eyes, full of terror and pain. Whoever had done this had made a grave mistake. They had targeted someone close to him, and Sawyer would stop at nothing to bring them to justice.

With one last glance at the accident scene, Sawyer climbed into his car, the engine roaring to life. Brynlee needed him, and he wouldn't let her down. Not now, not ever.

CHAPTER
TWENTY-SIX

Guilt gnawed at him as Sawyer navigated the sterile, fluorescent-lit halls of Danbury Memorial, his footsteps echoing softly on the tile floor. He wished he could take back the harsh words he'd said to Brynlee in the heat of the moment. She didn't deserve that, especially not after what she'd been through.

His heart pounded as he approached the waiting area, the smell of antiseptic and the distant hum of hospital equipment serving only to heighten his anxiety.

He spotted Ainsley pacing near the chairs, her arms folded tightly across her chest. Her eyes widened in surprise when she saw him.

"Sawyer?" she asked, clearly taken aback. "What are you doing here?"

There were a million reasons why he wanted to see her, not the least of which was because someone had tried to sabotage her car. Sawyer cleared his throat. "I just wanted to make sure she's okay."

"I haven't heard anything." She gestured toward the large metal doors. "They just got here not too long ago."

Sawyer nodded, his foot tapping nervously on the floor.

She flicked a wry look his way. "You must have been in a hurry. You beat our family here."

"Well, I..." He rubbed one hand over the back of his head. "I feel kind of responsible. We had another fight this morning before she left, and..."

Ainsley's expression softened, a mix of confusion and understanding in her eyes. "You saw it happen?"

The image of the crash played before his eyes again and he blinked it away. "Yeah. I just... If I hadn't snapped at her, maybe she wouldn't have driven off like that."

"Brynlee's tough—she'll be okay." Ainsley gave him a small, reassuring smile. "Let's wait together. I'm sure she'll be glad to know you're here."

Her expression was dubious, and he had to agree with her; he was probably the last person Brynlee wanted to see at the moment. It seemed like all they did was fight and even though part of it was her fault, he couldn't stem the guilt that rose up inside him.

They sat down in the waiting area, the tension between them easing slightly as they shared their concern for Brynlee. Minutes felt like hours as they waited, the hospital's sounds a constant reminder of the seriousness of the situation.

Finally, a doctor approached them, his expression calm but serious. "Family of Brynlee Layne?"

Both Ainsley and Sawyer stood up, and Ainsley moved toward the doctor. "Yes, we're her family. How is she?"

"She's stable," the doctor began. "She has a few bruised ribs and a mild concussion, but she'll make a full recovery. We're going to keep her overnight for observation."

Ainsley let out a relieved breath. "Can we see her?"

The doctor nodded. "Yes, but just for a few minutes. She's resting now."

Sawyer hung back and when Ainsley tossed a look his way, he shook his head. "Just tell her I stopped by, okay?"

Her brows pulled together but she nodded regardless before falling into step behind the doctor as he led the way to Brynlee's room. She was okay; that was enough for now.

Sawyer walked into the office he shared with Cam, and the lieutenant glanced up at him expectantly. "How's Bryn?"

Sawyer lifted one shoulder as he dropped into his chair and rubbed a hand over his face. "I don't know. I didn't stay long enough to find out."

Cam stared at him for a second before nodding slowly. "I'm sure she'll be okay."

Sawyer was certain he would hear the shattering of glass, the screech of twisted metal every time he closed his eyes. He abruptly sat forward in his seat. "What do we know?"

"Mike just towed Brynlee's car over," Cam began without preamble. "The deputies are working on printing and inspecting every inch of it."

Sawyer nodded, taking a seat across from Cam. "Find anything yet?"

Cam sighed, rubbing his temples. "Not much. They compared a set of prints, but nothing's coming up in the system yet. It's like whoever did this doesn't exist."

Sawyer frowned. "What about the brake lines?"

"Cuts are clean, made with a sharp tool—probably snips," Cam replied. "But there's no lead there. No fingerprints, no fibers, nothing."

Sawyer leaned back in his chair, frustration evident on his face. "So we're back to square one."

"Not entirely," Cam said, a glimmer of hope in his eyes.

"The deputies did find something. A single, long black hair under the vehicle."

Sawyer's interest piqued. "A hair? That's something. Have we sent it out for testing?"

"Not yet," Cam admitted. "But it's the best lead we've got so far. We need to find out who that hair belongs to. It could be our perp."

Sawyer nodded, a surge of adrenaline rushing through his veins. "I'll get on that. We need to expedite the testing. This could be the break we need."

Cam leaned forward, his eyes locking onto Sawyer's. "And we need to keep this under wraps. If whoever did this finds out we're onto them, they might disappear. Or worse, come after Brynlee again."

Sawyer's jaw tightened. "Agreed. We'll handle this discreetly. But we need to move fast. If there's a chance to catch this person, we can't waste any time."

Sawyer walked back to his desk, his mind racing with possibilities. They had a lead, however tenuous, and they couldn't afford to let it slip through their fingers. They would find out who was behind the accident and bring them to justice, no matter what it took.

CHAPTER
TWENTY-SEVEN

Sawyer pushed open the door to his house, the weight of the day pressing heavily on his shoulders. The lack of concrete evidence was gnawing at him. He needed a break, even if only for a few minutes.

He dropped his keys on the kitchen counter, grabbed a cold beer from the fridge, and sank into the worn leather couch. Taking a deep swig, he closed his eyes and tried to clear his mind. But the respite was short-lived.

A noise from outside caught his attention, and he tensed, setting his beer down before moving quietly to the window. He peered out, and his heart skipped a beat when he saw a figure skulking around Brynlee's side of the duplex.

The man was dressed in dark clothes, moving cautiously as he peered in through the windows. Sawyer didn't hesitate. He grabbed his gun, slipping quietly out the front door and moving toward Brynlee's side of the duplex.

As he approached, he could see the man better—medium build, young and handsome. Exactly the type of guy he could envision next to Brynlee. He hated the man on sight.

"Stop right there!" Sawyer called out, leveling the gun in his direction.

The man froze, then turned slowly, hands raised defensively. His eyes went wide when he saw the pistol pointed his way. "Whoa, whoa! Wait!"

Sawyer advanced, pistol trained at the man's torso. "Who the hell are you?"

The man's eyes flickered with fear, still locked on the barrel of the gun. "Can you just—could you put the gun down?"

"Depends on your answer." The man had been sneaking around Brynlee's house, peering through the windows like he was checking for an easy entry point. He lowered the pistol a fraction and tipped his chin at the man. "I asked you a question."

"I'm not doing anything wrong."

"And just what the hell were you doing?" Sawyer asked.

"I'm a friend of Brynlee's. I was just leaving something for her."

Suddenly it clicked. This was her ex. "Zane?"

His brows shot up, a mixture of relief and pleasure flooding his features. "She told you about me?"

"Nothing good." The man's face fell, sending a tendril of vindication through Sawyer's chest. He tipped his chin toward the porch. "She said you've been stalking her—"

"That's not true!" The man interjected, his eyes wide. "I—"

"Showing up randomly. Leaving strange gifts," Sawyer continued as if the man had never spoken. "That's trespassing.

"But I'm not doing anything wrong," he insisted. "I just wanted to talk to her."

Sawyer glared at the man. "Talk to her about what?

Because, from what she's told me, the two of you have nothing to talk about."

Zane's face twisted in anger. "Who the hell do you think you are?"

"Detective Sawyer Reed, Brookhaven Sheriff's Department," he introduced himself.

The blood drained from the man's face, and his mouth dropped open a fraction before snapping shut again. "Oh."

Yeah. *Oh.* Sawyer bit back a snort at the look of incredulity carved into the man's face. "Where were you the past twenty-four hours?"

Zane's brows pulled together. "What?"

"Between 8:00 last night and 10:00 this morning," Sawyer clarified. "Where were you?"

Zane gave a slight shake of his head. "I... I was at work."

It was Sawyer's turn to look dubious. "All night?"

"Not at night... no." He gave himself a little shake. "I was home last night, but I had to be at work by eight this morning."

"And last night before bed?"

"I..." His eyes flitted upward, like he was thinking back to the previous evening. "I went to Joe's for a drink."

"I'll verify that," Sawyer said. "Now, since you seem so concerned about Brynlee, I'm sure you won't mind answering a few questions."

"Uh..." Zane eyed Sawyer. "Sure?"

"What do you know about the car accident Brynlee was involved in this morning?"

Zane's eyes widened, a look of genuine shock crossing his features. "What car accident? I hadn't heard about anything."

Sawyer watched him carefully, looking for any signs of deceit. "And the flood damage at her salon? You didn't have anything to do with that either?"

Zane's shock turned to confusion and anger. "No, I

didn't. Why would I? I care about Brynlee. Yeah, we've had our issues, but I would never hurt her."

Sawyer wasn't convinced. He leaned closer, his voice low and dangerous. "Here's the thing, Zane. Someone's been trying to hurt Brynlee. They cut the lines on her car, they trashed her salon. Now, you're telling me you had nothing to do with any of that?"

Zane's expression turned from anger to fear. "I swear, Detective. I had no idea. I've been trying to get her back, not push her further away."

Sawyer crossed his arms over his chest. "Whether you're involved or not, here's what's going to happen. You're going to stay away from Brynlee. No more creeping around her house, no more gifts. If I catch you near her again, I won't be as lenient. Do you understand?"

Zane swallowed hard, nodding quickly. "Yeah, I understand. I won't bother her anymore."

Sawyer's eyes narrowed. "Good. Now, take whatever you brought and go."

Zane's expression shifted, a mix of frustration and desperation. "Can you just tell her—"

"No," Sawyer cut him off. "Get out."

"Where the hell did you come from anyway? You got here awfully fast." Zane stared at him suspiciously.

Sawyer lifted a shoulder. "I was already here."

Zane cocked a brow. "Here? You live around here?"

"Right here." Sawyer paused for effect. "With Brynlee."

The man looked like he'd been punched in the chest, but Sawyer didn't feel an ounce of remorse. The idiot had been trespassing, borderline stalking her. Let him believe Sawyer and Brynlee were together; maybe then he'd leave her the hell alone.

Zane dropped back a step, looking pale. "I didn't realize…"

"Now you know." Sawyer offered a cold smile. "I'll be checking into your alibi—unless there's anything else you want to tell me."

The man shook his head and took another step toward the street. "N-no. I..." He faltered for a moment, then straightened. "I hope everything is okay with Brynlee. I just want the best for her."

Sawyer gave a tight nod and watched him go, still unsure whether the man was telling the truth. Zane's reaction seemed genuine, but in Sawyer's line of work, he had learned that appearances could be deceiving.

He needed to cover all angles, and Zane was just one piece of the puzzle. The nagging feeling that he was missing something important persisted.

CHAPTER
TWENTY-EIGHT

Sawyer pushed open the heavy door to Joe's bar, and the low hum of conversation enveloped him as he stepped inside, the scent of beer and fried food hanging in the air.

Though it was only early afternoon, a decent crowd had already begun to accumulate. He scanned the room, and his gaze landed on the bartender, her dark curls pulled into a messy bun. She was cleaning a glass and chatting with an older man seated at the bar.

Sawyer walked up to the bar, nodding at a couple of regulars who were deep in conversation. He leaned slightly against the counter as the bartender set the glass aside and sent a flirtatious smile his way.

"What can I get you?" she asked.

"Just some information, if you've got a minute," Sawyer replied, pulling out his badge and flashing it briefly before tucking it away. "I'm Detective Reed."

Her eyes narrowed slightly, a hint of caution creeping into her expression. "What do you need?"

Sawyer pulled out his phone and brought up a photo of

Zane. He held it out for her to see. "Do you recognize this guy? His name's Zane. He says he was here last night."

She leaned closer, squinting at the photo for a moment before nodding. "Yeah, I remember him. He was here. Had a couple of drinks, kept to himself mostly."

"What time did he leave?"

The bartender paused, her brow furrowing as she thought back. "Must've been close to ten. He wasn't in any hurry, but I remember it was just before the late crowd started trickling in."

Sawyer nodded, mentally noting the timeline. Zane would have had plenty of time to leave the bar and head over to Brynlee's house. "Did you notice anything unusual about him? Anything out of the ordinary?"

She shook her head. "Not really. He watched the game for a bit, then headed out."

"Thanks for your help." Sawyer offered her a brief smile before turning to leave, his mind already racing two steps ahead.

Zane had been at Joe's, just like he'd said. But there was still the matter of the long hair that had been found near Brynlee's car, something that didn't match up with Zane's short cut.

Could he have worn a wig? Sawyer considered the idea, but it seemed out of character. Zane had been to Brynlee's house multiple times; he wasn't trying to hide his presence before. Why would he start now?

The thought nagged at him as he walked toward his car. If Zane had really cared about Brynlee, and Sawyer was inclined to believe he did, why would he do something so drastic, so dangerous? The brake lines hadn't been just tampered with—they'd been cut with precision, almost ensuring a catastrophic accident. That wasn't something you did on a whim or out of anger. It was premeditated.

Sawyer sighed as he slid into the driver's seat, his hands gripping the steering wheel. The case was getting more tangled by the minute. On the surface, Zane didn't have a clear motive to hurt Brynlee. And yet, the pieces didn't quite fit together.

As he pulled out of the gravel lot, his thoughts kept circling back to the same question: If not Zane, then who? And why would they go to such lengths to disguise themselves?

For now, Sawyer would have to rule Zane out. But the flicker of doubt in his mind refused to go away. Something still wasn't adding up. And until he had more answers, everyone remained a suspect.

According to the lab reports, the hair belonged to a woman—quite possibly the same woman Brynlee had fired just a few days ago. He needed to follow up on Jessica, see if her anger had turned into something more sinister.

Sawyer pushed open the glass door of Blissful Beauty, and the soft chime above the entrance rang out, announcing his arrival. The place looked pristine, the polished floors gleaming under the soft lighting, and the faint scent of lavender lingered in the air. Soft chatter filled the air, and Sawyer noted three women seated in the chairs along the wall, their hair in various states of disarray.

A woman emerged from the short hallway near the bathroom, and she turned a polite smile his way. "Welcome to Blissful Beauty. How can I help you?"

"I'm Detective Reed with the sheriff's department," Sawyer introduced himself as he stepped closer to the counter. "I'm looking to speak with whoever's in charge while Brynlee Layne is recuperating."

The woman's expression shifted from polite curiosity to

understanding. "That would be me," she replied. "I'm Melanie. How can I help you, Detective?"

Sawyer nodded, appreciating her directness. "I'd like to ask you a few questions about a former employee, Jessica. Could we talk somewhere private?"

Melanie hesitated, then gestured toward a hallway leading to the back of the salon. "We can use the break room. Follow me."

Sawyer trailed behind her, nodding to the ladies in the salon area as he passed. The salon was spotless, each station meticulously organized. He could still hear the low hum of the dehumidifier in the massage room, but it already looked far better than it had the other day when he'd been here.

They reached the break room, and Melanie sat down, motioning for Sawyer to take a seat across from her.

"So," Melanie began, folding her hands on the table, "what do you need to know about Jessica?"

Sawyer leaned forward slightly, keeping his tone neutral. "I understand she was fired recently. Were you here when it happened?"

Melanie's brows furrowed as she nodded. "Yes, I was. Jessica came in late that day and Brynlee wasn't having it. She pulled her aside, and the next thing I knew, Jessica was shouting. She was furious, made a huge scene, and then stormed out. It was pretty intense."

"Have you seen her since then?" Sawyer asked.

Melanie shook her head. "No, I haven't. She just disappeared after that. We haven't heard a peep from her."

"Why did Brynlee fire her?"

Melanie drew in a deep breath. "Jessica is a great stylist, but..." She gave a tiny shake of her head. "She's just not a great worker. She was late more often than not, and her attitude over the past couple of months wasn't great. It was starting to affect everyone here, and Brynlee..."

Melanie grimaced. "Well, you know how it is. She had to do what was best for the business."

Sawyer paused, considering his next question. "Do you think she could have been responsible for the flood damage? Could she have accessed the valve in the bathroom?"

She frowned, thinking it over. "I don't think so. Everything happened so fast that day. She showed up late, Brynlee fired her, and she was out the door in no time. I didn't see her go near the bathroom, and honestly, I don't think she had the chance."

Sawyer studied her for a moment, then nodded. "What does Jessica look like?"

"The last time I saw her, she had shoulder-length brown hair with purple tips," Melanie replied. "She changes it up pretty often, though, so I can't know that for sure."

Sawyer noted the description. It wasn't much to go on, but every detail helped. "Thanks, Melanie. I really appreciate your time."

Melanie gave him a small smile, though it didn't reach her eyes. "No problem. I hope you find what you're looking for."

Sawyer stood and made his way out of the salon, the door chiming softly behind him. Another dead end. He couldn't shake the feeling that he was missing something, a crucial piece of the puzzle that kept slipping through his fingers.

Sawyer racked his brain, trying to think if he knew any women with long, nearly-black hair. He didn't think so. He'd have to ask Brynlee later if she was close to anyone who watched the description. They'd yet to question her, but Sawyer wanted to do that himself.

She still had no idea she was in danger, but she was safe enough in the hospital, surrounded by family. Until she was released, though, he had a million other leads to chase down.

CHAPTER
TWENTY-NINE

Sawyer was halfway through the files on his coffee table when he heard the sound of a car pulling up outside. His heart jumped, his thoughts immediately going to Brynlee. Dropping everything, he rushed to the window. Keeping to the side, out of sight, he peered around the edge of the curtain.

A blue SUV sat in Brynlee's driveway, and he watched as she slowly emerged from Mr. Layne's car, pain hindering her movements. Mrs. Layne hovered beside her, trying to help, but Brynlee waved her off, stubborn as always. Sawyer's lips pressed into a firm line. She shouldn't be home so soon. She needed rest, care—things Brynlee was too proud to ask for. Damn woman was far too independent for her own good.

Even from this distance, Sawyer could see the strain on her face, the exhaustion in her posture. After what felt like several minutes, she finally made it to her front door. She paused on the front porch, fumbling with her keys. She dropped them and Mrs. Layne stooped to grab them, then passed them back to Brynlee, who opened the door and stepped inside, disappearing from view.

Sawyer watched surreptitiously as Mrs. Layne spoke with

Brynlee, her face twisted into a mask of concern. Finally, resignation settled over her features and she turned away, heading back toward the vehicle. The Laynes sat in the SUV for a long moment, presumably to make sure Brynlee was okay, before driving away.

The moment their car disappeared down the street, Sawyer let the curtain drop back into place and took off toward the back door. She wouldn't be happy to see him, especially after the things they'd said to each other. But he had some questions to ask her—and, slightly more pressing, he needed to make sure she was okay.

Before he could talk himself out of it, he was out the door, crossing the small patio that separated their duplexes. He reached her back door, hesitating for just a second before knocking. The sound echoed in the quiet evening air, and he held his breath while he waited.

Inside the soft pad of footsteps approached. They paused a few feet away, then, after what felt like forever, the door swung open. Brynlee stood in the open space, her expression a mixture of pain and annoyance. She was still as stunning as ever, even in her disheveled state, but it was the look in her eyes that made his chest tighten. She wasn't just sore and tired—she was pissed. And every ounce of that anger was directed squarely at him.

"What do you want, Sawyer?" she asked, her voice sharp.

He took a breath, trying to ignore the way his heart squeezed at her tone. "I needed to make sure you were okay."

She rolled her eyes, leaning heavily against the doorframe as if she didn't trust her legs to hold her up. "I'm fine. Congratulations, you've done your job, so now you can go."

Sawyer clenched his jaw, refusing to be dismissed so easily. "I have a few questions first."

She glared at him, but there was something else in her eyes —something that told him she wasn't as okay as she wanted him to believe. After a long, tense moment, she sighed and stepped aside. "Fine. Come in."

He followed her inside, keeping a sharp eye on her as she moved deeper into the room. His senses were immediately flooded with the familiar scent of her home: lavender and vanilla, warm and inviting, yet so starkly at odds with the tension that hung between them.

Brynlee crossed her arms, wincing as the movement pulled at her sore muscles. She leaned against the counter, her posture defensive. "Make it quick, Sawyer. I'm not in the mood for this."

Sawyer propped a hip on the small table and regarded her. "Can you tell me what happened yesterday morning?"

Brynlee glared at him. "Well, let's see. You came over and blamed me for leaving the hose running all night—which I didn't—we got into a fight, and then I left. So, pretty much a typical day for us."

Tension gathered between his shoulder blades and Sawyer swallowed hard, stalling the retort that jumped to his tongue. Drawing in a deep breath, he willed himself to stay calm. "I'm sorry for that. I am," he said at her dubious look. "I shouldn't have blamed you—not for flooding the yard, and not for the accident. I shouldn't have let you leave when you were angry. If you hadn't been distracted—"

"So it's my fault?" Her voice rose several octaves in indignation. "Fuck you, Sawyer. Get out."

She started to storm toward the door, but he caught her around the waist, stopping her progress. She sucked in a breath, and he immediately released her. "Shit, I'm sorry. Did I hurt you?"

"No more than usual." Her lethal blue glare landed on him once more. "Now leave."

He held up his hands. "I didn't mean that the way it sounded. I—"

"Really?" She let out a mirthless laugh. "You said I was distracted. Because, you know. It was all my fault my brakes weren't working."

"Listen, I don't want to fight with you—"

"Then don't."

Sawyer ground his molars together and drew in a deep breath before speaking as calmly as he could manage. "Tell me what happened. Everything you remember from the time you got into the car."

She glared at him for several seconds as if weighing his words. Finally, she relayed her side of the story. "We were fighting—again." She shot him a dirty look. "So, yes, I was a little distracted when I backed out of the driveway. Had I been thinking clearly, I would have noticed sooner."

"Noticed what?" he asked softly.

"My brakes. They felt soft, like I had to push down harder to stop. But it didn't really sink in until I got to the end of the road. I stepped on the pedal, but nothing happened. It went straight down to the floor. I remember reaching for the emergency brake, but by then..."

She trailed off, and Sawyer nodded. "You're lucky it happened here."

She shrugged. "It could have been worse."

"Speaking of that..." Sawyer met her gaze, his voice gentle despite the worry gnawing at him. "When was the last time you had the brakes on your car checked?"

Her eyes narrowed. "Seriously? You really think this is the time for an interrogation?"

"I'm trying to figure out what happened, Bryn." He softened his tone, trying to reach her. "This isn't just about the car. It's about you."

She stared at him, her defenses still up, but he could see the flicker of doubt in her eyes. "I want to figure out what happened. Did anyone else drive it? Did you notice anything else strange over the past couple days?"

"No," she snapped, her voice tinged with frustration. "And I just got the car serviced a few months ago, so you can't blame me for not taking care of it. It was just an accident, so—"

"It wasn't an accident."

She paused her tirade and blinked at him. "What?"

Sawyer met her gaze, his expression serious. "Bryn, I had Mike over at Geiser's Garage take a look at the car. Your brake lines didn't fail—they were deliberately cut."

Brynlee's eyes widened in shock and fear. "They were... cut?"

He nodded slowly, and her face paled further. "Oh, my God."

He took her arm and led her to the couch, settling her in the corner before taking the seat next to her. "Do you have any idea who might be responsible?"

She wrapped her arms around her waist and shook her head emphatically. "N-no. I don't... I don't know."

"Think hard," Sawyer urged gently. "Anyone who might hold a grudge, anyone you've had issues with recently."

She glanced up at him, worry in her eyes. "Just you."

Irritation flickered through him, but he managed to suppress it. "I can assure you, it wasn't me. Seeing you like that took ten years off my life."

She stared up at him for a long moment, confusion tugging at the space between her brows. "What does that mean?"

He blew out a measured breath. "I know we fight sometimes, but trust me when I say this—I don't ever want to see you hurt."

She nodded and bit her lip, seemingly deep in thought. "I

mean... There's Jessica, but... you don't think she could do something like this, do you?"

"I stopped by the salon and spoke with Melanie today. She doesn't think Jessica could have caused the flooding in the salon. But..." He paused for a second. "We did find something strange under the car."

Her brows pulled together as she peered at him, and he elaborated. "There was a single, long dark hair." He held his hands up about a foot apart. "Do you know anyone who has dark hair like that?"

"Someone who would do this?" She shook her head. "No, I can't think of anyone. Jessica has brown hair, but last time I saw her the ends were dyed purple. You would definitely notice that."

He nodded his agreement. "I need you to think it over, Bryn. The salon, the accident—it's too much to be a coincidence."

For a moment, she just stared at him. Then, she shook her head, her voice low. "I can handle myself, Sawyer. I don't need you to protect me."

He brushed a stray lock of hair from her cheek. "I know you can. But you don't have to do it alone."

They sat there in silence, the weight of his words hanging between them. Brynlee looked away first, directing her gaze to the far wall, and he knew he'd pushed as far as she'd let him. Aggravation pooled in his gut, but he forced it down as he stood. "Just be careful," he said softly. "Please."

Turning, he headed for the door, pausing only long enough to add, "If you need anything, call me. Anytime."

Then he left, the door closing behind him with a quiet click. As he made his way back to his own side of the duplex, the worry gnawing at him didn't ease. Brynlee was stubborn, but he knew she was scared—more than she'd ever admit.

And that worried him more than anything else.

CHAPTER
THIRTY

Though the leads on the van were slowly going cold, he needed to speak with Fallon's mother again to see if she could recall anything new. Sawyer hoped she might remember something else—anything that could help.

He knocked on the door, and it wasn't long before Mrs. Ray answered, a strained smile on her face. "Detective Reed, good to see you again. Have you found something new?"

"Not yet, ma'am," Sawyer replied with a polite nod. "I was hoping you might've thought of anything unusual about Fallon recently. Anything new, or anyone she might've come into contact with?"

Mrs. Ray's expression turned pensive as she gestured for Sawyer to step inside. The cozy living room was as he remembered, filled with the scent of fresh flowers and a hint of nostalgia. She offered him a seat on the well-worn couch, but he remained standing, his focus on the task at hand.

"I've been trying to think if there was anything out of the ordinary," Mrs. Ray began, her brow furrowing. "But I can't seem to recall anything specific. Ever since the car accident, Fallon's been pretty reserved. She kept to herself more."

Immediately, Sawyer's mind conjured the image of Brynlee amidst the chaos this morning, her car mangled, her body trembling with fear. He shook the memory away and focused his attention on the woman in front of him. "What do you mean by 'car accident,' Mrs. Ray?"

"Oh, you didn't know?" Mrs. Ray's eyes widened slightly. "It happened about two months ago. Fallon and her ex-boyfriend, Mark Sullivan, were in an accident. They were arguing while Fallon was driving. She must've been distracted because she ran off the road and hit a telephone pole."

Sawyer's pulse quickened. "Were they hurt?"

"Thankfully, no. There wasn't too much damage, and they both walked away without any serious injuries. But they broke up after that. I suppose the accident was the last straw for them."

Sawyer filed that information away, a niggle of unease forming in the back of his mind. "Do you know where Fallon took the car to get it repaired?"

Mrs. Ray thought for a moment, then nodded. "I believe she took it to Leroy's Auto Shop, just a few miles from here. Leroy's been fixing cars around here for as long as I can remember."

"Do you remember how long it was in the shop?"

Mrs. Ray's mouth pursed as she thought back to the accident. "Oh, maybe a few days?"

Sawyer nodded. "And what did she do during that time? Did she hire a driving service?"

"No, she rented a car, I think."

"Do you by chance have that information?"

Mrs. Ray made a face. "I can't remember for sure, but I think she used the rental service right downtown."

Sawyer thanked Mrs. Ray and left her house with a couple new leads to follow. As he drove to Leroy's Auto Shop, his thoughts were swirling. The detail about the car accident felt important, but he couldn't yet piece together why.

The shop was a typical small-town garage, with a couple of cars parked out front and a strong smell of motor oil in the air. Inside, a wiry man in his fifties was bent over the engine of an old pickup truck. He straightened when he saw Sawyer, wiping his hands on a greasy rag.

"You Leroy?" Sawyer asked.

"That's me," the man replied, eyeing Sawyer warily. "What can I do for you?"

"I'm Detective Reed, Brookhaven Sheriff's Department." Sawyer showed his badge. "I'm looking into a car that was brought here a couple of months ago. Black 2015 Kia Forte, belonged to a woman named Fallon."

The man's head tipped to one side in contemplation. "Let me check."

Sawyer fell into step behind him as he led the wall to a desk at the back of the room, paperwork stacked haphazardly on the surface. "When did you say that was?"

Sawyer rattled off the date Mrs. Gill had given him, and Leroy dug through the filing cabinets for a moment before he extracted a piece of paper. He skimmed it, then nodded slowly, and passed it toward Sawyer for his inspection. "I remember that one. Not too much damage—just the front bumper and a busted headlight. She said she ran off the road and hit a pole."

Sawyer skimmed the invoice, looking for notes of any kind. "Do you remember anything unusual about the car? Anything that stood out?"

Leroy shook his head. "Nah, nothing out of the ordinary. I fixed it up and sent her on her way."

Sawyer frowned. "Did she mention anything about the accident or the argument she had with her ex-boyfriend, Mark Sullivan?"

"Not that I can remember," Leroy said with a shrug. "The name doesn't sound familiar."

Sawyer thanked Leroy and left the shop, his unease growing. He stopped by the rental agency and spoke with the manager next, who pulled Fallon's information. She'd rented a small sedan for two days, and Sawyer made a note of the manager's name as well as the attendants who'd been on duty the day she'd been issued the rental, and the day she'd returned it to the shop.

As he drove back to the station, he couldn't shake the feeling that there was more to the story. The car accident seemed like a small detail, but it nagged at him.

Lindsey Gill had also been in a car accident not long before she was killed. It could be a coincidence, but in his experience, coincidences often turned out to be something more.

If there was a pattern here, it might be the key to unraveling the mystery of Fallon's disappearance—and possibly the other cases as well. Something about those accidents didn't sit right with him, and he wasn't about to ignore his instincts.

He was starting to see the edges of a bigger picture, but the full image was still frustratingly out of reach. Whatever it was, he was determined to find out.

Pulling out his phone, he dialed Cam, who answered on the third ring. "Yeah?"

"I think I might have something for you." He explained what Mrs. Ray had told him. "Remember the Gills mentioning that Lindsey had been in an accident a few weeks prior to her abduction?"

"Yeah, but we questioned the mechanic and the Uber driver," Cam pointed out.

Sawyer ground his molars together. "I know, but for both women to be in accidents? Isn't that a little coincidental?"

On the other end, Cam scoffed. "Seriously? Do you know how many traffic accidents we deal with every week?"

Sawyer sighed and rubbed a hand over his forehead. Maybe Cam was right. They'd checked the mechanic and Uber driver Lindsey had hired and had come up empty handed. Fallon had used a completely different mechanic, and she'd rented a sedan from a popular establishment. He would run the men's information when he got back to the station, but he was beginning to doubt himself. Maybe he was looking for something that wasn't there.

"You're right. I'll run background anyway, but we probably won't get any hits."

"We'll keep digging," Cam promised. "If there's something there, we'll find it."

Sawyer hung up and steered the car back toward the station, tension sitting like a lead ball in his gut. The connection between Fallon and Lindsey's car accidents kept nagging at him the whole way back. He didn't believe in coincidences—not in cases like these.

CHAPTER
THIRTY-ONE

Unsurprisingly, none of the leads panned out. One of the employees from the rental agency had been charged with petty theft more than ten years ago when he was a teenager. Another had several moving violations, but nothing damning.

Sawyer stared at the crime scene photos spread out on his desk. Three women, three brutal murders, and a seemingly invisible thread tying them together. He turned his attention to the map pinned to the wall of his office. Red push pins marked the locations of the victims' homes, while blue pins indicated where their bodies had been found.

He picked up a marker and drew lines between the points. The web that formed looked almost random, but he knew there was a method to the madness; he just had to uncover it.

"Where are you, you bastard?" He murmured aloud, his eyes scanning the circle for potential hiding places. Industrial areas, remote farmhouses, and abandoned buildings—anywhere the killer could operate unnoticed.

Cam moved into the room and dropped into his chair. "Anything?"

Sawyer crossed his arms over his chest, then leaned back

against the desk and shook his head, eyes still glued to the map. "Not a damn thing."

"Maybe you were on to something with the accident reports," Cam said. "Why don't we go talk with Jayla and Hilary's parents again, see if they remember anything?"

Sawyer sighed, frustration coursing through him. "Let's split up, it'll be faster that way. I'll take the Simms, you take the Swansons."

* * *

Sawyer Reed stood at the end of the walkway leading to Mr. and Mrs. Simms's front door, his heart heavy with the task ahead. He'd been here before, more times than he cared to admit, but each visit only deepened his resolve to find Jayla's killer.

He straightened his shoulders and knocked. Mrs. Simms answered, her eyes dull with grief. "Detective Reed," she said softly, stepping aside to let him in.

"I'm sorry to bother you again, Mrs. Simms," Sawyer began, his voice laced with genuine regret. "I know how difficult this is, but I need to ask a few more questions. I want to make sure we haven't missed anything. I want to bring Jayla's killer to justice."

Mrs. Simms nodded, gesturing for him to sit in the living room. Mr. Simms was already there, staring blankly at the television. He acknowledged Sawyer with a slight nod, the exhaustion in his eyes mirrored in the deep lines that creased his face.

Sawyer settled into the armchair across from them, deciding it was best to jump right in. They'd been through enough; they didn't need to drag it out any more than necessary. "I know we've discussed this before, but I need to ask if anything unusual happened in the month or so before Jayla's abduction."

The room was silent for a moment, the only sound the

ticking of a clock on the mantel. Mrs. Simms furrowed her brow, thinking back. "I can't remember anything out of the ordinary," she said with a small shake of her head.

"Did she do anything different—jury duty, volunteer work, have anything fixed or replaced?"

Mrs. Simms started to shake her head again, then froze, her expression shifting. "Now that you mention it... A few months before she disappeared, Jayla was in a car accident. Nothing major, of course." She held up a hand in his direction. "Someone rear-ended her at a red light. "

Sawyer's interest piqued. "Do you remember where she had the car repaired? And did she rent a vehicle while it was being fixed?"

Mrs. Simms shook her head. "She took it to a mechanic not far from here—Riverside Auto Repair. It was a small job, just the bumper needed some work. It only took about a day, so she didn't need to rent a car or anything like that."

"Thank you for your help." He stood, and they rose with him. "Again, I'm sorry to bring this up. I know it can't be easy."

Mrs. Simms managed a weak smile. "We just want whoever did this to be caught. Thank you for not giving up."

Sawyer gave a tight nod, then made his way out to his car and headed toward Riverside Auto Repair. The small-town garage had seen more than its fair share of wear and tear. The exterior was a faded yellow, chipped paint clinging stubbornly to weathered wood. A rusty sign creaked in the breeze, proclaiming "Riverside Auto Repair" in peeling letters. The lot was littered with the carcasses of old cars, some stripped for parts, others seemingly forgotten by their owners.

Sawyer parked his car and stepped out, the sharp scent of oil and grease hitting him immediately. He could hear the faint clatter of tools from the open bay doors, where a mechanic was working on an old truck. Sawyer stepped inside the small office area and approached the front desk, where a burly man was hunched over an ancient computer.

"Excuse me," Sawyer said, pulling out his badge and holding it up. "I'm Detective Reed, investigating the murder of Jayla Simms. I understand her car was repaired here about a year ago."

The man looked up, his flicking to Sawyer's badge, then back up to his face. "What'd you say the name was?"

"Simms."

The man tapped at the keyboard for a moment, then paused, eyes glued to the screen, presumably reading. After a moment, he nodded. "Yeah, I remember her. Minor damage to the rear end. Fixed the bumper and sent her on her way."

Sawyer asked a few more routine questions, then thanked the man and headed back to his car. He climbed back inside and steered toward the station. He needed the accident report from the other precinct. It was a long shot, but if there was anything off about the driver, it might give him a lead.

As Sawyer made his way down the corridor inside the sheriff's department, he spotted Cam stepping out of Dare's office, a thick file in hand.

"Hey." Sawyer quickened his pace to catch up. "You got anything new?"

Cam shook his head. "I just got back from the Swansons. Hilary was never involved in a car accident—never even had a speeding ticket."

Sawyer felt his own frustration flare, a mix of anger and disappointment tightening his chest. "Damn it," he muttered under his breath, running a hand through his hair in agitation. The car accidents had seemed like a promising lead. "That means we're back to square one. I was hoping we'd found a pattern with these car troubles."

Cam nodded, his expression mirroring Sawyer's

frustration. "It was a good lead, but it looks like it was just a coincidence. Hilary's clean as a whistle."

Sawyer could feel the case slipping through his fingers again. He had been so close to thinking they might have something, a way to tie these women together beyond the gruesome fates they had met.

"Whoever this is can move through town completely undetected. He blends in, seems safe. Someone with access to information, making it look random but connected. Like..." Sawyer paused and glanced around the station. "A cop?"

Cam considered the possibility, his brow furrowing as he weighed the idea. "It's possible, but these incidents happened in different cities," he pointed out. "It'd be hard to coordinate, but not impossible."

Sawyer clenched his molars together. The thought of a rogue cop—or someone with access to police information—sent a chill down his spine. If that were the case, it meant their suspect was not only meticulous but also had resources at his disposal that most people didn't. "I need that accident report for Jayla," Sawyer said, his voice edged with determination. "Maybe it'll tell us something."

"Get it, and let's hope it gives us a direction," Cam replied, though he didn't sound particularly hopeful.

As Cam turned back to his office, Sawyer headed for his desk, already mentally drafting the request for the accident report. The precinct felt smaller today, the walls closing in as the pressure mounted. They were chasing a killer who was always one step ahead, and every dead end, every false lead, only added to the mounting tension.

Sawyer reached his desk and sat down heavily, the chair creaking under him. He quickly logged into his computer and pulled up the system to request the accident report. As his fingers moved across the keyboard, his mind raced.

The idea that the killer could be someone with insider

knowledge gnawed at him. It was a terrifying prospect, one that opened up a whole new set of questions. Who could it be? A cop, a mechanic, someone who worked in insurance, or just someone who knew how to exploit the system? The possibilities were endless, and that made it all the more dangerous.

The accident report request was submitted, but Sawyer knew it would take some time to process. He leaned back in his chair, his gaze unfocused as he stared at the wall, his thoughts spiraling. Every minute that passed was another minute the killer remained free, possibly planning his next move, possibly watching them as they scrambled to catch up.

The clock was ticking, and they were running out of time to stop a predator who was not only dangerous, but also smart —smart enough to stay ahead of them at every turn. And the worst part was, Sawyer couldn't shake the feeling that they were missing something, some crucial detail that could blow the case wide open.

CHAPTER
THIRTY-TWO

Brynlee pulled into the driveway and sighed heavily, the weight of exhaustion settling on her shoulders as she turned off the engine. The rental car was unfamiliar, and it felt strange as she gathered her belongings and climbed from the front seat. Her muscles protested the movement and she bit back a wince as agony ripped through her torso.

According to the scans, nothing had been broken, but her ribs were bruised, and every cell of her body felt tight, like her skin had shrunk two sizes. Today had been relatively easy, all things considered, but she'd declined to use the medication the doctor had prescribed for her. Once she got inside, she planned to take a long bath and relax.

She'd spent the morning making arrangements to rent a car for the next week or so. She'd called the sheriff's department—bypassing Sawyer completely—and spoke with Cam, who told her that her car was still being processed for evidence, but they hoped to get it released by tomorrow. After that, she would need to get it fixed.

The past week had been a huge blow to her bank account,

but at least Cam had promised to smooth the way with the insurance company.

She'd just reached the sidewalk when Sawyer exited his side of the duplex and headed straight for her, a box in his hands. "This was on my porch. Looks like it's for you. Must have been delivered to the wrong unit."

Her steps faltered, and her stomach dropped to her toes. He must have seen the look on her face, because he gave a small shake of his head. "It's not from Zane."

Her gaze shot upward, clashing with his, and Sawyer cleared his throat uncomfortably. "I forgot to tell you. I, uh... had a run-in with your ex yesterday."

The box in his hands momentarily forgotten, she stared at him. "What happened?"

His gaze slid away before meeting hers again. "I was sitting inside last night when I heard something outside. I looked out and caught him peeking in your windows."

Her mouth dropped open. "What?"

Sawyer nodded grimly. "I told him to stay the hell away from you. I think he got the message." He extended the box her way. "Besides, this actually has a return address."

A relieved sigh rushed from her lungs, and she juggled her purse before taking the box from Sawyer. "Thanks."

"Any time." He shoved his hands in his pockets and studied her, his gaze sweeping over her from head to toe.

Brynlee tensed under the scrutiny. She was still banged up from the car accident, and she knew she looked like hell. If he was going to judge the way she looked right now, she was going to throttle him.

But he surprised her when his eyes slid back up to hers, softer this time and full of concern. "How are you feeling?"

She blinked at him before slowly responding. "I'm... fine."

He stared at her. "How's the salon coming along? It looked really nice yesterday when I was there."

Her gaze narrowed. Why the hell was he being so nice to her? This was completely uncharacteristic of him. "Did you have a stroke?"

His eyes flew wide and he gave a startled laugh. "What?"

She held up a hand in his direction. "I'm trying to figure out what's happening right now. Are we actually having a civilized conversation?"

Sawyer's lips pressed together like he was holding back a laugh, and he tossed a quick wink her way. "Don't worry—I'm sure it won't last."

She couldn't help but smile, and she shook her head. "The salon is almost back to normal. Thanks for asking," she added as she took a step toward the duplex. "The massage room should be done by the end of the week."

Sawyer fell into step next to her as they headed up the sidewalk toward their respective porches. "I'm glad it's coming together."

"Me, too."

She paused near the bottom step, and Sawyer tipped his head her way. "Anyway, I'll let you get inside. Looks like you could use some rest. Yell if you need anything."

"Thanks." Brynlee shot him a small wave as she headed toward her front door. "See you later."

Inside, she made her way to the kitchen, then dumped her purse, and cell on the counter, setting the box next to them. She paused and glanced around. "Scooter! Here, kitty kitty!"

Silence hung heavily in the air.

That was odd. He always came out to greet her whenever she got home. Of course, after the last couple of days, maybe he was being extra cautious. Ainsley had stopped by to feed him and take care of him while she'd been in the hospital, and Ainsley reported that he'd hidden under the bed until she left.

She checked there first, but he was nowhere in sight. "Scoot! Here, kitty kitty!"

A twinge of worry pricked at her as she walked through the small house, checking all of his usual hiding spots. "Come on, Scooter. Where are you?"

The animal door immediately popped into her head, and she crossed the small kitchen, then bent down to check it. The wood was still firmly attached, so he couldn't have gotten out that way. Maybe Ainsley had come over again today and let him outside.

Pulling open the back door, she peered into the yard. "Scooter!"

But there was still no sign of him.

With a sigh, Brynlee returned to the kitchen, worry forming a cold ball of dread in her stomach. He was an expert at escaping, but she thought she'd fixed that. She grimaced. Hopefully he wasn't over at Sawyer's place wreaking havoc.

The box on the counter caught her attention as she closed the door behind her, and she moved toward the cutting block, where she pulled out a pair of scissors.

She glanced at the label, noting with relief that it wasn't Zane's handwriting. But... That was strange. The return address was for her salon. Maybe Melanie had sent her something?

Intrigued, she carefully cut through the tape, then lifted the flaps. For a moment, the dark, matted fur and lifeless eyes didn't register. Then, slowly, everything took shape.

Her stomach pitched and a scream tore from her throat.

CHAPTER
THIRTY-THREE

His ass had just hit the recliner when the scream pierced the air. Without a second thought, Sawyer bolted out of his chair and sprinted across the yard to Brynlee's back door.

He threw the door open and burst inside, his gaze already scanning the small space. "Bryn!"

Brynlee stood at the kitchen counter, an open box in front of her, tears streaming down her face. Fury immediately engulfed him as he strode forward. "What's wrong?"

"That son of a bitch!" She swiped at her tears, and a strangled sob escaped as she stormed toward the living room.

He grabbed her hand to stall her, but she struggled against him. "Let me go!"

He did as he asked but moved in front of her. "Talk to me, Bryn. What's going on?"

She ignored him, and he reached for her once more. "Brynlee, goddamn it, wait!"

She shrieked as his arm came around her waist, and he couldn't tell if it was more from pain or anger. She struggled against his hold, her hysteria making it impossible for her to calm down. Suddenly, her anger gave way to grief and she collapsed against him with a heart-wrenching sob.

He wrapped his arms around her more firmly, whispering words of comfort, gently rocking her back and forth. "Shh, it's okay. I'm right here. Breathe, Bryn. Just breathe. Everything's going to be okay."

Gradually, her struggles lessened, and her sobs turned into quiet, shuddering gasps. Sawyer loosened his grip slightly, giving her the space to breathe but keeping his hands on her hips.

His gaze raked over her, taking in her expression, tear-stained and full of grief and anger. The scream had been filled with a raw terror that had sent chills down his spine.

"Can you tell me what happened?" he asked gently.

Another tear slipped down her cheek, and she hastily swiped it away. "I... When I got home, I couldn't find Scooter. I looked everywhere."

Her voice cracked, and he gently rubbed her back, lending silent comfort. She drew in a shaky breath, glancing towards the kitchen where the box still sat open on the counter. "That box you got today... It's him, Sawyer. It's Scooter."

Her eyes, glassy with tears, met his, and his stomach flipped over. Jesus Christ. "Oh, Bryn. I'm so sorry."

Guilt assailed him. How had he not suspected something like this? He should have known that asshole would retaliate. He cupped her face in his hands and gently swiped away the trail of tears that clung to her skin. "I'm going to figure out what happened—I promise."

He leaned in and kissed her forehead before gently easing her in the direction of the couch. "I'm going to check it out, but I need you to stay here for a sec, okay?"

She looked like she wanted to protest for a moment but in the end, fear won out and she pressed her lips together and nodded. He lightly squeezed her shoulder. "I'll be right back."

Sawyer moved toward the kitchen. The box sat open, and anger coiled inside him at the sight of the lifeless cat inside. He closed his eyes for a moment, composing himself before turning back to Brynlee.

"Can I borrow your phone?"

She blinked uncomprehendingly for a moment before pointing toward the counter. "I think it's there... somewhere."

Sawyer rooted around for a moment and found the phone tucked out of sight behind the box, next to her keys and purse. He tapped the screen, and it immediately brought up the screen to enter the passcode. He started in her direction, but she anticipated his question and rattled off the numbers.

Sawyer typed in the digits, then brought up the phone app and dialed the sheriff's department, his stomach swooping violently. "This is Detective Sawyer Reed." He briefly explained the situation and directions to Brynlee's house. "I need a deputy over here as soon as possible."

He hung up and moved to her side. "We're going to find out who did this. I promise."

She gave a little shake of her head, the anguish from a few moments earlier replaced once more by anger. "Do you think it was Zane?"

Sawyer took her hand in his, anger boiling beneath his calm exterior. "I don't know, but I'm damn sure going to find out."

Brynlee blew out a deep breath. "Why? Why would he do something so hateful?"

He squeezed her hand, unable to answer the rhetorical question. "Come on. Let's go to my place and wait for them. You shouldn't be here right now."

She nodded, allowing him to help her up. He looped an arm around her waist, careful not to hurt her, as they made their way to his house next door. The late evening air was cool, and the silence of the neighborhood felt oppressive, as if the world had paused in the wake of the horror they had just discovered.

Inside, Sawyer gently pushed her in the direction of the couch. "You want some coffee?"

Brynlee shook her head and veered toward the kitchen. "I'll do it."

Sawyer lightly squeezed her waist. "I can—"

"Your coffee is terrible."

Sawyer bit back a smile as they moved to the kitchen. It wasn't a lie. He relinquished his hold on her but leaned on a cabinet nearby, watching as she worked.

"Besides," she continued quietly as she scooped grinds into the machine, "I need something to do."

He understood that. Brynlee pushed the button to begin the cycle, then settled against the counter next to him. Neither of them said a word. A minute later, the tantalizing aroma lifted on the air, and the brewer spit out the last of the liquid.

Without a word, Sawyer reached into the cabinet behind them and passed her a packet of sugar. She started to shake her head, but he pressed it into her hand. "It will help—I promise."

She nodded then dumped it into the dark liquid and took a fortifying sip. Sawyer curled one hand around the back of her neck and lightly massaged the tense muscles.

The minutes stretched into what felt like an eternity before the sound of tires on gravel reached their ears. "They're here," he said unnecessarily. "Why don't you stay here for a few while I go explain what happened. Okay?"

She gave a tentative nod, and he lightly squeezed her shoulder. "I'll be right back."

A faint glimmer of gratitude flickered in her eyes as she turned his way. "Thank you, Sawyer. I don't know what I'd do without you."

He squeezed her hand gently. "You don't have to worry about that. I'm here, and I'm not going anywhere."

Sawyer exited the front door and intercepted Deputy Duke Turner just as he climbed from the cruiser. "Not a great way to start your shift," Sawyer said as he tipped his head toward Brynlee's house. "It's in here."

Turner fell into step next to him as Sawyer led the way up the steps and into her house. "What happened?"

Sawyer gave him a quick rundown of the past week—Brynlee firing Jessica, the car accident, finding Zane outside her house, and now this.

Duke's expression darkened. "Someone really has it out for her."

Sawyer nodded. "I spoke with her ex. He seemed genuinely concerned, but—"

A knock on the door snapped Sawyer's attention to the front of the house. A moment later, Cam's voice floated his way.

"Hey," he said, his brows pulled low. "What's going on?"

"This." Sawyer pointed to the box on the counter and Cam drifted closer, his face pulling into an expression of disgust when he saw the contents.

"Jesus. What the fuck is wrong with people?"

He nodded to Turner. "We need this bagged and printed. See what you can find."

A memory niggled at the periphery of his brain. "Hold on a sec."

Sawyer slipped on a pair of gloves and turned the flap down, then glanced at Cam. "It didn't go through the mail service. No postage, no postmark. Someone had to hand-deliver it."

Turned nodded, his eyes narrowing. "Whoever did this wanted to create the illusion that it was mailed, but they were close enough to drop it off themselves."

Cam's jaw tightened. "So, someone grabbed Scooter during the day, killed him, and then left the box for Brynlee to find. That's sick."

Duke tossed a look his way. "We need to talk with Brynlee again."

"She already told me everything she knows," Sawyer argued. "She's been through enough; she doesn't need to deal with more of this tonight."

Cam paused midstep and turned to face him. "You know as well as I do that the faster we get her to talk, the faster we can find out who did this."

Sawyer growled. He knew Cam wasn't wrong, but still... "Fine. But go easy, would you?"

Cam studied him for a moment before nodding. "Of course." He glanced over at Duke. "You got this?"

The deputy nodded, and Sawyer led the way over to his place, knocking softly and calling out to Brynlee before pushing the door open. Brynlee sat on the couch, the mug of now-cold coffee still clutched in her hands.

He gently extracted it from her fingers and set it aside, then dropped into the seat next to her. "Cam wants to ask you a few questions."

She offered him a small smile that didn't reach her eyes, and Cam settled on the edge of the recliner. "Bryn, do you have any idea who might want to do this? Anyone with a grudge, someone who's been acting strange lately?"

Brynlee shook her head, tears welling up again. "I just... I can't imagine..." She fiddled with the hem of her shirt as she trailed off, her gaze sliding back to the floor.

Cam studied her. "What happened with Jessica?"

"She was mad at me for firing her." Brynlee lifted one shoulder. "She made a scene at the salon, said I'd regret it."

"Anyone else?" Sawyer pressed.

"Not really," Brynlee admitted. "I mean... You know about Zane."

Yeah, he did. That asshole was still on his list. Sawyer's expression tightened. "Tell me more about Jessica. Did she threaten you?"

"Not directly," Brynlee replied. "But she was angry, really angry. She said I'd pay for what I did, that I was ruining her life. I didn't take her seriously at the time, but now..."

Sawyer's mind raced. Jessica could be a potential suspect, but he needed more information. "Do you have any contact information for her? An address, phone number, anything?"

Brynlee nodded. "I have her address at the salon."

Sawyer placed a comforting hand on her shoulder. "We'll check into both of them."

Cam made a few more notes. "Do you mind if I take a look around?"

Brynlee shrugged. "Go ahead."

With one last smile, Cam pushed from the chair and headed toward the door. He paused and tossed a look at Sawyer, indicating he should follow. Sawyer dipped his chin a fraction, and Cam disappeared, closing the door behind him.

Sawyer turned back to Brynlee. "Bryn, do you remember anything unusual happening recently? Anything at all?"

Brynlee bit her lip, looking deep in thought. "I've been thinking about it all afternoon, but nothing stands out. We've just been trying to get back to normal after the damage."

Sawyer nodded, considering her words. "Whoever did this wanted to scare you, but it was more than that. They wanted to hurt you. The cat was a personal hit."

Brynlee's eyes filled with tears again, but she nodded resolutely. "I know. Scooter wasn't just a pet; he was family. I know you didn't like him, but—"

Sawyer took her hands in his and shook his head,

effectively cutting her off. "I'm sorry for that. I know he meant the world to you, and I promise I'll find who did this."

She nodded listlessly. "Thanks."

"I don't think you should stay here tonight," he ventured cautiously. "If you don't want to go to your parents' house or your sisters'..."

He trailed off, letting the unspoken offer hang in the air. Brynlee swallowed hard, her gaze fixed on the floor. Finally, she shook her head. "I'll go to Ainsley and Dare's tonight. I'm sure they won't care."

A zing of disappointment cursed through him but he shoved it away as he pushed from the couch and extended a hand her way. Brynlee remained silent as they moved to her bedroom and packed up enough clothes for a couple of nights, then fired off a text to Ainsley and let her know that she would be coming over.

Sawyer texted Dare, letting him know that he'd apprise him of the situation soon, then walked Brynlee out to her rental. "You sure you're good to drive?"

She offered a faint smile as she slid behind the wheel. "Yeah. Thanks."

Crouching down in the open space between the door and the cab, he reached inside and squeezed her hand. "If you need anything—doesn't matter what time it is—call me."

"I will."

She pulled away and started the car, then disappeared down the street. Sawyer watched her go, anxiety churning in his gut. She didn't deserve this. They would uncover the truth —and they would make damn sure justice was served.

CHAPTER
THIRTY-FOUR

Sawyer met Cam in Brynlee's kitchen. "Find anything?"

"Not yet." He shook his head. "Turner's next door questioning the neighbors. Hopefully someone saw something."

Sawyer nodded. "Have you checked out back yet?"

"That's next on my list."

Cam followed Sawyer as he stepped out into the small, fenced backyard that he and Brynlee shared.

"Looks like whoever it was came through this way," Cam stated as he inspected the back door.

Sawyer stepped closer and shook his head, his lips turned down when he saw the splintered wood of the doorjamb. How the hell had he missed that?

He scrubbed a hand over his face. "I was distracted. I heard her scream and I never even thought about it."

Cam nodded and began to pull equipment from his bag. "I'll print it."

Sawyer spun around, his gaze encompassing the small yard. If the person had entered through the back of the house, they most likely would have come through the backyard instead of parking out front. He began a slow circuit of the space, his eyes glued to the ground near the house. As he moved closer to the fence, he noticed several small impressions in the soft ground.

Footprints.

He leaned in, inspecting them closely. They were faint, but distinct enough to make out the shape. The prints were smaller than he expected, almost delicate. He had initially assumed a man was behind this—someone strong enough to snatch a cat and cruel enough to kill it. But these footprints, coupled with the long hair pulled from under her car, told a different story.

He straightened up, his mind racing. If these weren't Brynlee's, then they could belong to the person responsible. But if that person was a woman, it changed everything. He had been looking for someone who fit his preconceived notion of a male aggressor. This new possibility opened up a whole new set of questions.

He turned, gesturing for Cam to join him. "Come take a look at this."

He walked over, gaze immediately locking on the small footprints. "Are those Brynlee's?"

"I don't think so." Sawyer pointed to the prints. "I'll check her shoes to make sure the pattern doesn't fit. Besides," he continued, "nine times out of ten she's barefoot when she'd out here. Some shit about grounding herself or whatever."

Cam raised a brow, a smirk pulling at the corners of his lips. "Grounding?"

Sawyer waved a hand in the air. "Don't ask."

A half hour later, they'd checked each of Brynlee's shoes against the impression near the fence. The ground was still damp from the flooding the other morning, and the ground hadn't yet had a chance to dry out and shrink. Even so, the shoe print on the ground was nearly a half-inch larger than Brynlee's.

"It's not hers," Sawyer stated. "This is too big to be hers—and too small to be a man's."

Cam nodded slowly as he photographed the impression. "It would make sense. But why the hell would a woman do this?"

"I don't know," Sawyer admitted. "But think about it—the way they went about sabotaging her car, cutting every line underneath? A man would likely know which specific line to cut. It's like whoever did it was trying to make sure they got the right one but didn't know which it was."

Cam rubbed his chin thoughtfully. "And when that didn't work, they went after Scooter to send a personal message."

Sawyer frowned. What the hell had Brynlee gotten herself mixed up in? "But who? And why now?"

Cam leaned against the patio table and crossed his arms over his chest. "We know it's someone close to Brynlee, someone who knows her routines and has access. Maybe Jessica was pissed that Brynlee fired her and decided to retaliate." Cam raised an eyebrow. "What about her relationship with Brynlee? Any signs of tension before the firing?"

"Brynlee said Jessica was getting increasingly difficult to work with," Sawyer said. "Late to work, rude to clients, sloppy with her job. Brynlee gave her several chances, but she kept messing up."

"So Jessica felt she was being pushed out, maybe?" Cam suggested. "And when it finally happened, she snapped."

Sawyer nodded. "It fits. And a woman could come and go from the salon or Brynlee's house without anyone thinking twice. Less suspicious than a man."

Cam leaned back, crossing his arms. "We need to talk to

Jessica. Get a sense of where her head is at. If she's behind this, we need to catch her before she does something even worse."

"Agreed," Sawyer said, standing up. "But we need to be careful. If she's unstable, confronting her could be risky. We need a plan."

Cam nodded. "Let's get some backup. We'll approach her carefully, see if we can get her to talk without spooking her."

As they made their way to Jessica's apartment, the tension in the car was palpable. Sawyer's mind raced with possibilities, each one more troubling than the last. If Jessica was behind this, there was no telling what she might do next.

They arrived at the apartment complex a short while later and knocked on apartment 4D. After a moment, Jessica opened it, her eyes widening in surprise and worry. "What can I do for you?"

"We need to talk to you about Brynlee Layne," Sawyer said, keeping his tone calm but firm. "Can we come in?"

Jessica hesitated, her eyes darting nervously. "Uh, sure. Come in."

They stepped inside, and Sawyer took a moment to survey the room. It was cluttered, with clothes and personal items strewn about. Jessica seemed on edge, her hands fidgeting as she gestured for them to sit.

Sawyer took a seat, maintaining eye contact. "Jessica, we're investigating some incidents involving Brynlee. We need to ask you a few questions."

Jessica's eyes narrowed. "Incidents? What kind of incidents?"

"Someone's been trying to hurt her," Sawyer said bluntly. "Her car was tampered with, and her cat was killed. We're trying to find out who's responsible."

Jessica's face paled, her hands trembling. "You think I did it? I had nothing to do with that! Brynlee fired me, yeah, but I'm not a psychopath."

"We're not accusing you," Cam interjected calmly. "We're just gathering information. Can you tell us where you were today?"

Jessica's eyes flickered with anger. "I had an interview at 2:00 at a salon over in Danbury, but the rest of the time I was here. So I don't have an alibi if that's what you're asking. But I swear, I didn't do anything to Brynlee. I was mad, sure, but I wouldn't hurt her."

Sawyer studied her, looking for any signs of deception. "Jessica, if there's anything you know that could help us, now's the time to tell us. Even if it's something small."

Jessica shook her head, tears welling in her eyes. "I don't know anything, I swear. I'm not a bad person, Detective. I was just... upset. But I didn't do this."

Sawyer exchanged a glance with Cam, both of them sensing that Jessica was telling the truth. But there was still a nagging feeling that something was missing.

"All right, Jessica," Sawyer said finally. "We appreciate your cooperation. If you think of anything, anything at all, let us know."

Jessica nodded, wiping her eyes. "I will. I'm sorry."

As they left the apartment, Sawyer felt a mix of relief and frustration. Back in the car, Cam turned to Sawyer. "What do you think?"

Sawyer sighed. "I think Jessica's not our culprit. She's scared, but she's not lying. We need to keep digging. Someone out there has a reason to hurt Brynlee, and we need to find them before it's too late."

Sawyer and Cam exchanged a brief look as they approached Zane's apartment. The man was a wildcard, his past with

Brynlee making him a prime suspect, but something about the situation didn't add up.

Sawyer knocked on the door, his knuckles rapping sharply against the wood. A moment later, Zane answered, his expression a mix of irritation and wariness. "Detective Reed."

"We need to ask you a few more questions," Sawyer said, keeping his voice neutral.

Zane sighed, stepping aside to let them in, and Sawyer's gaze scanned the small space. The apartment was relatively clean; and empty can and a discarded fast food wrapper littered the coffee table, while a sweatshirt lay strewn over the back of the couch.

Once they were inside, Zane leaned against the arm of the couch and crossed his arms over his chest. "What's this about?"

Sawyer didn't waste time. "Brynlee's cat was killed earlier today. We're trying to piece together who might be responsible."

Zane's eyes widened slightly, then narrowed. "And you think I had something to do with that? Are you serious?"

"We're just covering all our bases," Cam interjected, his tone calm but firm. "We need to know where you were."

Zane scowled, his eyes flashing with anger. "I was at work, like I am every day. You can check with my boss."

Sawyer studied him, noting the tension in Zane's posture, the way his hands gripped the counter. "You got off at five, right? Where'd you go after that?"

Zane sighed. "I came home. Alone. Is that what you want to hear?"

"Did you see Brynlee at all?" Sawyer pressed.

"No, I didn't see Brynlee," Zane snapped, his temper flaring. "You made it pretty damn clear yesterday that the two of you are together. I told you I'd stay away from her, and I have."

Sawyer could feel Cam's gaze on him, but he ignored it. He felt zero compunction about lying to the man to keep Brynlee safe. "This isn't personal. It's about finding out who's behind this."

"It sure feels personal." Zane's fists clenched at his sides, his voice rising. "You think I'm the bad guy because she and I have a history?"

Cam stepped forward, trying to diffuse the situation. "No one's accusing you, Zane. We're just trying to get the facts straight."

But Zane wasn't having it. He pushed off the counter, his voice laced with bitterness. "You can play good cop all you want, but I know what this is. It's discrimination, plain and simple. You hate me because of my past with Brynlee, because I was with her before you even looked twice at her."

Sawyer tensed at the man's words, and he fought to kept his voice level. "This isn't about Brynlee's past. It's about her safety now."

"I told you—I didn't hurt her, and I didn't hurt her cat." Zane shook his head, his temper boiling over. "I'm done talking. Next time you want to question me, I'll have a lawyer present. Maybe then you'll stop treating me like a suspect just because I'm her ex."

With that, Zane turned and stalked toward the door, leaving Sawyer and Cam standing in the middle of his apartment, the tension in the room almost suffocating.

Zane threw the door wide and stared at them, unyielding, until Sawyer finally nodded. "Thanks for your time."

The door slammed behind them, and Cam made a small sound in the back of his throat. "I take it you two didn't get off on the right foot."

Sawyer snorted. "Not exactly."

Cam was quiet for a moment as they descended the stairs and started toward their car. "Is it true?"

Sawyer cleared his throat. "It's not a conflict of interest, if that's what you're asking."

Cam didn't say another word as he slid into the car and cranked the engine. Sawyer turned his gaze out the window, his mind spinning. Zane's defensiveness had struck a nerve, but it also raised more questions. If Zane was innocent, why react so strongly? And if he wasn't...

They had to dig deeper. Because if Zane was involved, Brynlee was in more danger than ever.

CHAPTER
THIRTY-FIVE

Brynlee stood in front of the mirror in Ainsley and Dare's guest suite, hands shaking slightly as she applied the finishing touches to her makeup. She studied her reflection, trying to recognize the woman staring back at her.

She'd spent last night cocooned in the safety of Ainsley and Dare's guest suite, the weight of recent events pressing down on her. The past few weeks had been a blur of stress and sorrow—the flooding at the salon, the car accident, and the loss of her cat had left her feeling adrift. The flooding at the salon had been bad enough, but then the accident and losing her cat on top of it all… it was as if the universe was trying to break her spirit.

Staying here at Ainsley's house had been a comfort, but tonight, she needed something more. She needed to feel like herself again, if only for a few hours. She'd talked with Melanie today at the salon, and they'd made plans to meet up at the local bar.

Brynlee grabbed her purse and glanced at her phone to check the time. The Uber should be here in five minutes. She stowed it in her back pocket and took a deep breath, mentally preparing herself for the night ahead. It wasn't that she didn't want to go out, but the idea of being around people, even Melanie, felt like a lot. Still, she'd promised her friend she'd be there, and she couldn't let her down.

Leaving the suite, Brynlee walked down the hallway to find her sister. Ainsley was in the living room, curled up on the couch with a book, but she looked up as soon as she heard Brynlee approach.

"Hey," Ainsley greeted with a warm smile. "You look great. Heading out?"

"Yeah," Brynlee nodded. "Meeting Melanie at the pub. I figured it was time to get out and do something normal."

Ainsley's smile softened with understanding. "I think that's a good idea. Do you want some company? I could tag along, keep you girls entertained."

Brynlee chuckled, shaking her head. "Thanks, but I think I need some time with just Melanie. It'll be good to catch up."

"All right, but you better call me if you need anything at all, okay?" Ainsley said, her tone serious. "I mean it, Bryn."

"I will, I promise."

Just then, the front door opened, and Dare walked in, the familiar jingle of his keys announcing his arrival. He set them down on the entryway table and made a beeline for Ainsley, pressing a kiss to her temple before turning his attention to Brynlee.

"Hey there, Bryn," Dare greeted, eyeing her outfit. "You're looking nice. Got plans?"

"Just meeting Melanie for a drink," Brynlee replied with a small smile.

Dare raised an eyebrow. "I could drive you if you want. It's no trouble."

Brynlee appreciated the offer, but the idea of being chauffeured around like a fragile package didn't sit right with her. She needed to do this on her own, prove to herself that she could still handle a simple night out.

"Thanks, Dare, but I've already got an Uber on the way," she said, holding up her phone.

As if on cue, her phone buzzed with a notification: **Your Uber has arrived.**

"See?" Brynlee smiled. "Already here."

Dare nodded, clearly still concerned but respecting her choice. "All right, but be careful, okay? And if you need anything, just call."

"I will," Brynlee assured him, slipping her phone into her purse. "I'll be back later."

Ainsley stood up to give her a quick hug. "Have fun tonight. You deserve it."

Brynlee hugged her sister back, feeling the comfort and love in the embrace. "Thanks, Ains. I'll see you later."

With that, Brynlee headed out the door. The Uber was waiting at the curb, and she walked over to it, feeling a mix of nerves and anticipation. Tonight wasn't about forgetting everything that had happened, but maybe it could be about finding a way to move forward.

As she settled into the back seat and the car pulled away, Brynlee took one last look at Ainsley and Dare's house, feeling a sense of gratitude for the haven it had been for her. But now, it was time to step out of that haven, if only for a little while, and remind herself that she was still capable of living her life.

The ride to the pub was quiet, with Brynlee staring out the window at the town she'd grown up in. Brookhaven was so familiar, yet everything felt different now. She leaned her head against the cool glass, her thoughts drifting to her cat. She still couldn't believe he was gone. The tears threatened to spill over, but she took a deep breath, blinking them away. Not tonight. She was determined to have a good time.

The Uber stopped in front of the pub, and Brynlee flashed the driver a smile. "Thanks."

As she climbed from the back seat the cool night air hit her face, and she breathed in deeply, savoring the moment. Tonight was exactly what she needed. The parking lot was crowded, and the sounds of laughter and music drifted outside as people came and went through the large front doors. Inside, Brynlee spotted Melanie seated at the bar, and she waved as she weaved through the people gathered on the floor.

"Hey, you," Melanie said as Brynlee slid onto the tall stool next to her. "I ordered us some drinks. "

Brynlee managed a small smile. "Thanks for this. I really needed it."

Melanie gave her a knowing look. "I know you do. And I'm here to make sure you have fun, okay? No sad talk, no stress. Just us, a few drinks, and maybe some bad karaoke if we're feeling brave."

"Sounds perfect," Brynlee said, genuinely meaning it.

As the night went on, Brynlee found herself relaxing more and more. Melanie had always been good at making her laugh, and tonight was no exception.

At some point in the evening, Melanie convinced Brynlee to get up and sing with her. It was a disaster—neither of them could carry a tune—but it felt good to be silly, to let go of everything weighing her down. For the first time in a long time, Brynlee felt something close to happiness.

As they sat back down, breathless from laughter, Melanie leaned over and squeezed Brynlee's hand. "You're going to be okay, you know that, right?"

Brynlee looked at her, feeling a lump form in her throat. "I don't know if I believe that yet."

"Well, I do," Melanie said firmly. "And until you believe it too, I'll keep reminding you."

Brynlee nodded, swallowing the lump in her throat. She

wasn't there yet, but she was starting to see a glimmer of hope, a tiny light at the end of the tunnel. Maybe Melanie was right. Maybe, just maybe, she would be okay.

Melanie downed the last of her cocktail and stood up, giving Brynlee a playful nudge. "I'm gonna hit the bathroom. Don't get into any trouble while I'm gone, okay?"

Brynlee smirked. "No promises."

As Melanie walked away, Brynlee turned back to her drink, lost in thought. She was trying to let the atmosphere of the pub distract her, but it was hard to fully escape the ache in her chest. Just as she was about to take another sip, she felt a light bump from behind. Startled, she turned around to see a dark-haired woman settling onto the stool next to her.

"Oh, I'm so sorry!" The woman grimaced apologetically. "I'm so clumsy sometimes."

"No problem." Brynlee offered a little smile. "It happens to the best of us."

"Some more often than others."

The woman rolled her eyes and Brynlee forced a laugh despite the sharp pain that ricocheted through her chest. She understood completely. She'd had enough bad luck of her own recently.

Brynlee's gaze flitted over the woman's face, taking in her high cheekbones and bright blue eyes. There was something oddly familiar about her, but Brynlee couldn't quite place it.

"You look familiar... Do I know you from somewhere?"

The woman stared at Brynlee for a moment before shaking her head. "I don't think so. I'm just visiting a friend. Maybe I've got one of those faces."

"That must be it," Brynlee said. "Enjoy your stay."

The woman shot her a warm smile. "I will, thanks."

Brynlee glanced around, checking to see if Melanie was back yet, when a voice from her left drew her attention.

"Hey there," the man said as he slid onto the stool two seats down. "You here alone, or can I keep you company?"

Brynlee turned to face him and offered a small smile. "Actually, I'm with a friend. She just stepped away."

"Well, I guess that gives me a few minutes to make an impression," he said, flashing a grin that was almost too perfect.

Brynlee couldn't help but laugh, the man's flirtatious energy pulling her out of her despondent mood. "Is that so?"

"Absolutely," he replied, leaning in just a bit closer. "So, what's a pretty woman like you doing in a place like this?"

Brynlee rolled her eyes at the cliché but played along. "Just needed a night out. What about you?"

"Same," he said with a shrug. "Needed a break from the usual. And now I'm glad I came out. I didn't expect to meet someone like you."

Brynlee felt a small thrill at his words, a welcome distraction from the heaviness she'd been carrying. The man smiled and held out a hand. "I'm Jamison."

Brynlee slipped her hand into his and shook. Her gaze traveled from his hands up to the man's torso. He was average height, a few inches shy of six feet, with a narrow build. His dark-blond hair was tied into a ponytail at the nape of his neck and his brown eyes looked almost black in the dim light of the bar.

She didn't feel a thing. No zing, no sparks, not even the tiniest little match-sized flame. Pulling her hand away, she pasted a polite smile on her face. "Brynlee Layne. Nice to meet you."

Her phone dinged, and she glanced at the message from Sawyer.

How's girl's night?

She set the phone down without responding and turned back to Jamison, determined to make more of an effort. He really was a good-looking guy, and he'd been a gentleman. She owed it to him to at least be pleasant.

She picked up her wine, sipping the sweet liquid and making idle chat with the man next to her, her mind all the while on the detective. Pushy, arrogant man. He seemed determined to upend her life and, so far, he was doing a good job of it. She couldn't even sit next to another man without thinking of Sawyer.

They continued to banter, his charm keeping her engaged and making her laugh. Just as the man was leaning in to say something else, Melanie returned, sliding back onto her stool with an exaggerated sigh. "Sorry, the line for the bathroom was insane."

Brynlee turned to Melanie with a grin. "No worries. I've just been making new friends."

Melanie raised an eyebrow as she took in the man on the other side of her. "I can see that."

The man gave Melanie a charming nod before turning back to Brynlee. "Well, I should probably let you two catch up. But if you find yourself wanting another drink later, you know where to find me."

Brynlee smiled. "Thanks. I'll keep that in mind."

As the man walked away, Melanie shot Brynlee a teasing look. "Well, well. Looks like someone's still got it."

Brynlee laughed, shaking her head. "He was just being friendly."

"Friendly, my ass," Melanie said with a grin. "But I'm glad to see you enjoying yourself. You deserve it."

Several minutes later, another text message came through and she leaned forward to glance at the screen. Sawyer again.

Hey. Everything okay?

She rolled her eyes. Seriously, the guy just wouldn't take a hint. She was a modern girl, after all, and she could take care of herself. Despite her declaration last night, she was perversely pleased that he actually cared enough to check on her.

Melanie noticed the movement and raised a brow. "Who's that?"

Brynlee rolled her eyes, a playful smirk tugging at the corner of her lips. "My neighbor from hell."

Melanie's brow furrowed in confusion. "I thought you hated each other. Why is he texting you?"

Heat crept up Brynlee's neck, and she hoped the dim lighting would hide the blush coloring her cheeks. "He just... wants to check on me, that's all."

Melanie's eyes flew wide, her voice a mix of shock and excitement. "You're sleeping together!"

"Shh!" Brynlee hissed, glancing around to see if anyone had overheard. She shook her head, trying to ignore the flutter in her chest at Melanie's assumption. "No, we're not. And it's not going to happen again."

Melanie's expression shifted to amusement. "So it did happen! And here I thought you hated each other. You're always fighting."

Brynlee huffed a small laugh. "We are. We do." She took another sip of her wine, trying to focus on the fruity flavor rather than the memory of Sawyer's lips on hers. "He makes me crazy, and we argue about everything, but... I can't explain it."

Melanie smirked, leaning in closer. "Sometimes that's the best kind of relationship, Bryn."

Brynlee laughed, lightly backhanding her friend on the arm. "Behave. It's not like that. He doesn't really care about me. He's just doing his job, looking out for me because he's a cop. It's his job to take care of people."

Even as she said the words, a pang of regret twisted in her chest. She tried to shake it off, but the feeling lingered, heavy and unsettling. She wanted to believe it—that Sawyer's concern was nothing more than professional courtesy—but deep down, she knew there was more to it. More than she was ready to admit.

Melanie watched her closely, her playful smile fading into something more thoughtful. "Maybe. But that doesn't mean he doesn't care, Bryn."

Brynlee shrugged, not trusting herself to say more. She picked up her glass, taking a long sip, wishing the wine could drown out the doubts in her mind. But the warmth in her chest wasn't just from the alcohol—it was from the memory of Sawyer's touch, the way he made her feel safe even when everything else was falling apart.

And that was exactly why she needed to keep her distance.

CHAPTER
THIRTY-SIX

What a clusterfuck. They were spread thin enough as it was with the current murder investigation. Adding Brynlee's issues on top of that damn near pushed him to the edge.

No matter how hard he tried, he couldn't get her out of his mind. He'd heard from Dare that she was out at the bar tonight with her friend, Melanie, enjoying a well-deserved break, but the thought of her being out there gnawed at him.

They weren't dating; he had no right to check up on her. Yet, here he was, pacing his living room, wrestling with the urge to make sure she was safe. The recent car accident had shaken him more than he cared to admit. Seeing her bruised and shaken had ignited a protectiveness he couldn't fully explain. And then there was the incident with her cat, the mutilation that had left him furious and helpless. Someone out there had targeted her, and he couldn't stand the thought of her being hurt again.

He pulled out his phone and stared at the recent string of messages. Well, his messages. Brynlee was ignoring him. Why? Was she deliberately trying to get under his skin? He knew he could be overbearing at times, but it was only because he cared

—more than he wanted to admit. He was a detective, trained to handle high-stress situations with a calm, analytical mind. But when it came to Brynlee, all logic seemed to fly out the window.

The memory of their last argument flashed through his mind. The way her eyes had sparked with anger, the fire in her voice. They bickered incessantly, yet, somewhere along the line, the animosity he used to feel had morphed into something far more complicated. Something he didn't want to examine too closely.

Sawyer glanced at the screen again, hoping for the telltale ping of a new message. Nothing. His frustration grew, and with it, a twinge of fear. What if something had happened to her? What if she was in trouble and couldn't reach out?

He shook his head, trying to dispel the worst-case scenarios playing out in his mind. He knew she was probably fine, just enjoying her night out.

He hated this feeling of helplessness, of not being able to control the situation. It wasn't just the cop in him that made him overprotective; it was the man who had grown to care deeply for Brynlee Layne, despite their constant clashes.

The minutes ticked by, each one feeling like an eternity. Still no response. He sighed, leaning back and closing his eyes, trying to calm the storm of emotions swirling inside him.

He exhaled deeply as he sat up straight and pushed from the chair. Fine. If she wouldn't respond to him, he would just go to her.

———

Her eyes had started to glaze over and she glanced at her phone. Just after ten o'clock.

Melanie chuckled. "Long day?"

Brynlee shot her an apologetic smile. "Actually, yes. I'm

going to go to the bathroom. Excuse me for a second." She picked up her phone and purse and slipped off the stool. Her vision blurred as she took a step, and she stumbled.

"Hey, you okay?" Mel was on her feet next to Brynlee a second later, concern etched deep in her expression.

"I'm good." Brynlee waved her off. "I didn't have much to eat today, so it must have snuck up on me. I'll be right back."

Brynlee made her way to the bathroom and sat down in one of the stalls. Leaning forward, she closed her eyes and put her head between her knees. She felt as if she was moving in slow motion, sluggish and unsteady, her surroundings distorted in her blurred vision. What in the world was wrong with her?

The familiar ring of her phone startled her and she dug through her purse, following the vibrations. The jaunty melody stopped before she could find it but started up again almost immediately. She blinked, trying to focus, and her hand finally curled around the device. Brynlee swiped a finger across the screen and lifted it to her ear.

"Hello?"

"Jesus, Brynlee, I've been trying to get ahold of you for the last hour. Where the hell are you?"

"Sawyer?"

"Why the hell couldn't you answer your phone?"

Brynlee let out an indignant huff. "I was talking to someone. Don't be such a jerk."

"A guy?"

She hesitated just long enough for Sawyer to interpret her response. "Goddamn it, Brynlee, I—"

The rest of his words were cut off as she hung up on him. Within seconds, the phone began to ring again. She rolled her eyes and slid her thumb across the screen. "What do you want?"

A heavy sigh filtered through the line. "How much have you had to drink?"

"I'm fine, Sawyer."

His voice was deadly calm. "How much?"

"Just one. But it was... really strong." Her mind spun and she couldn't focus on the words coming from the other end of the phone. "What?"

Sawyer was silent for a long moment and she heard a harsh exhalation on the other side. "Are you still at the bar?"

Brynlee looked around the stall as if it would magically answer his questions. "Um. Yeah. Mulligan's Pub."

"Is Melanie okay to drive or has she been drinking, too?"

She waved a dismissive hand in the air. "She's fine."

Another stretch of silence. "All right. I'll be right there."

"It's okay, I'm sure I'll be fine in a minute. I'll just call an Uber or something." Brynlee waited for a response but his end was silent. "Sawyer?"

She pulled the phone away from her ear and glared at the blank screen. Damn it, the man had hung up on her. With one last scowl, she dropped the phone in her bag and pushed open the door to the stall. Hoping it would help to sober her up, she took a few minutes to wash her hands and splash some cool water on her face. She touched up her makeup and took one last look in the mirror before heading back to the bar.

Loud music assaulted her ears as she made her way out of the bathroom, and she grimaced. Her head felt like it was swimming, a headache hovering right at the base of her skull as she made her way back to the bar. Catching sight of her, Melanie slid off the stool with a grin. "Let's dance!"

Grabbing Brynlee's hand, Melanie tugged her toward the dance floor in the corner. Brynlee bit back a grimace. In all honesty, she was ready to go home and curl up in bed. But she hated to let Mel down.

Closing her eyes, she allowed herself to get lost in the

rhythm of the heavy beat. Heat from the crush of bodies assaulted her, the scent of perfumes and colognes filling the air. She tuned it out, focusing on the music and lifting her arms high over her head.

A strong pair of hands landed on her hips, and a slow smile curved her face as the man moved in close behind her. His hips moved in perfect time with hers, and she sucked in a breath as he slid one hand around to her belly, sealing them together.

She glanced down at the dark hands gliding over her curves, then turned in his arms, her gaze slowly roving over him: strong hands and forearms, muscular torso, broad shoulders, chiseled chin... *Shit.*

Her gaze clashed with a pair of dark brown eyes and her mouth dropped open in shock. "Sawyer? What are you doing here? And how did you get here so fast?"

"I was already on my way here. Come on, I'm taking you home." He tugged on her hand but she resisted.

"No, I..." She teetered on her heels and Sawyer wrapped an arm around her waist, pulling her securely against him.

"You okay?"

"Yeah." Brynlee sounded breathless, even to her own ears.

Sawyer sighed and dropped his forehead to hers. "You've had too much to drink.

"I did not!" Brynlee reared back, stumbling in those godforsaken heels again. Thank God he hadn't let go yet or she'd be on her ass in the middle of the bar.

"Can you walk or do I need to carry you?"

The indignity of being drunk irked her but the thought of Sawyer having to carry her from the bar was too much. She shook her hand free of his and stomped toward the exit, pushing the door open and striding into the cool October night.

Brynlee stopped abruptly on the sidewalk, looking left and

right. She propped her hands on her hips before swinging around, right into a wall of solid muscle. Her hands came up to brace herself and wrapped around Sawyer's biceps. Her gaze met his hooded eyes and his arms tightened around her back, urging her even closer.

The tantalizing scent of cologne tickled her nose, and she leaned in slightly. "Why do you always smell so good? It's annoying. Actually..."

She tipped her head and peered up at him. "You're annoying. And arrogant."

"You mentioned that," he said, a wry smile pulling at his lips.

Was he laughing at her? She smacked his chest. "You're overbearing. And pushy. And..."

Her words halted as he dipped his head and kissed her shoulder. Her head suddenly felt too heavy to hold up, and she allowed it to drop to the side. Sawyer took advantage, kissing his way up the column of her neck. "Tell me all about it."

She jerked back and stared at him, eyes narrowed. "You think you can just barge in whenever you want, well you're wrong. You can't just kiss me and expect everything will be okay."

"Worth a try." He kissed her jaw, her cheek, and she felt herself melting into him.

"Sawyer..."

Brynlee's eyes dropped to his mouth and she swiped her tongue across her bottom lip. His head dipped to meet her halfway, the searing kiss stealing the breath from her lungs.

Breaking the kiss, Sawyer eased back and stared down at her, eyes glittering. He opened his mouth to speak just as a roiling sensation flared in her stomach.

"Oh, God!" She wrenched free of his grasp, frantically searching the area. "I'm going to be sick!"

CHAPTER
THIRTY-SEVEN

Sawyer quickly steered her toward the side of the building just as her stomach ejected its contents all over the alley.

"It's all right." He grasped her hair in a loose ponytail and rubbed her back in a soothing, circular motion. "You'll feel better if you get it all out."

She heaved several more times, her stomach clenching in knots. Shame swelled through her and hot tears sprang to her eyes, escaping before she could stop them. She swiped angrily at her cheeks and leaned against the brick wall, covering her face. Strong fingers circled her wrists and gently lowered her hands. She opened her eyes and peered up at Sawyer.

"Feel better?"

She dropped her gaze to the ground and nodded.

"Come on. I have water in the car." Sawyer braced one arm against her back and bent down, placing the other behind her knees. He scooped her into his arms and she struggled weakly against him.

Sawyer unlocked the car and swung open the passenger door before settling her in the seat. He reached into the back and retrieved a bottle of water. Unscrewing the cap, he handed the bottle to her.

"Drink. You need to rehydrate."

She took the proffered bottle and gulped greedily until half of it was gone. Brynlee took another small swig and swirled it around her mouth, then spit it onto the ground, carefully avoiding Sawyer's shoes.

Sawyer stroked her knee, the gentle brush of his fingertips sending goosebumps scattering over her bare skin. "You're lucky no one tried to take advantage of you."

She bristled at the clear admonishment. "I was perfectly fine."

"Obviously not, or I wouldn't be here." He glared at her.

"Whatever." Brynlee crossed her arms over her chest. "Just call me an Uber and I'll be out of your hair."

Sawyer laughed without mirth. "Oh, hell no. You're not leaving my sight."

He reached across her and snapped the seat belt into place before slamming the door on her protests. Brynlee fumbled with the clasp and had just managed to get the seat belt to release as he slid into the driver's seat and started the car. One hand on the wheel, the other hand deftly snatched the seatbelt out of her hands and clicked it back into place.

With a huff, Brynlee sulked back in the seat and stared out the window. Disgusted with herself and out of energy, she rested her head against the seat and closed her eyes, finally succumbing to the exhaustion pulling at her.

* * *

Light slowly invaded the darkness and she opened her eyes, blinking rapidly to dispel the last vestiges of sleep. Closing her eyes again, she turned onto her stomach and groaned into the pillow. Her head throbbed like someone had taken a tiny hammer to it and her mouth felt like it'd been stuffed with cotton.

Brynlee rolled over to her back, willing her head to stop pounding. She blinked up at the ceiling, watching the fan whirl lazily overhead. The motion was hypnotic and comforting, except... her room didn't have a fan.

Propping herself up on an elbow, she gazed blearily around the room. Oh, God.

She flopped to her back and flung one arm over her eyes. She knew exactly where she was. The question was—why?

Fragments of memory came back—sitting at the bar, talking with the man next to her, dancing with Mel, Sawyer showing up, and... Getting sick in the parking lot.

How humiliating.

She sat up, pulling the comforter with her. Her jeans and top had been replaced with a man's oversized shirt, and her cheeks heated. Fantastic. He'd not only watched her throw up, but he'd had to dress her like a toddler.

Sunlight filtered through a crack in the floor-length blackout curtains to her right, the panels parted just enough to keep the room partially bathed in darkness. Thank God for that. Her head throbbed just thinking of the bright light outside.

Suddenly a deep voice cut through the silence, and Sawyer strode through the doorway, a wide grin on his handsome face. "Hey, sleeping beauty."

"Oh, God." Brynlee dragged the comforter over her head.

Sawyer laughed out loud at Brynlee's obvious dismay. "Good morning to you too."

A moment later she felt his weight settle on the mattress next to his thighs. The comforter slowly slid down, exposing her to his view, and she peered up into his handsome face. "I hate you."

Sawyer tried to bite back a smile but failed. "Still so mean, even after everything we've been through."

"Ugh." She pushed her elbow. "If you could just forget all of that, that would be great."

"Sorry." He shook his head. "No can do."

Sawyer ran a finger along Brynlee's cheek and tucked a strand of hair behind her ear. "Honestly, though? You really worried me last night. What happened?"

She shivered then sat up, propping her back against the headboard. "It's weird. I was sitting at the bar when this guy came up and sat next to me."

Sawyer lifted a brow at her and she rolled her eyes.

"Don't start with me. He was nice, and we were just talking. It wasn't like I was going to go home with him. Anyway, I had a glass of wine while Mel and I talked. That was the only thing I had last night, but it really knocked me on my butt. Mel and I talked for a while, danced a little bit..." She shrugged a shoulder. "Then you showed up."

Sawyer stared at her. "Did you get up at all, leave your drink unattended?"

She glanced upward in thought for a moment before shaking her head. "No. I'd already finished it by the time we got up to dance."

Her gaze shot back to his. "Wait. You think someone slipped something in my drink?"

He nodded grimly. "That's exactly what I think. You were a mess. There's no way one drink would've done that, even to someone as small as you."

"But how...?" She gave her head a little shake. "I should have realized."

"I'm just glad I showed up when I did."

"I'm not a child," Brynlee snapped, feeling a sting of resentment. "I don't need you to play the hero."

Sawyer's smile faltered. "I wasn't trying to be a hero, Bryn. Shit could have gotten bad. Jesus, you're lucky someone didn't try to rape you."

"I was there with Melanie. It wasn't like I was going to go home with some random guy." She glared at him. "I can take care of myself."

"Obviously," he snapped.

"Whatever." Brynlee snatched held covers to her chest with one hand. "Just leave so I can get dressed and get out of your hair."

"Because I haven't seen you naked before?"

She smiled, the gesture cold. "Well, you don't have to worry about that again, either."

Sawyer sighed and scrubbed his hands over his face. "Goddamn it. That's not what I meant."

Brynlee bit her tongue, and silence fell between them for several long seconds before Sawyer spoke up. "Listen. I'm sorry. I know I can be a dick sometimes, but... I do care about you. I just want you to be safe."

Tears pricked Brynlee's eyes and she turned her gaze toward the window so he wouldn't see. One second they were fighting, the next he was telling her cared about her. Why was it always so damn complicated between them?

She could feel his gaze on her, but he didn't push any more as he pushed from the bed and stood. "I need to get to the station. Can you lock up behind you when you leave?"

Brynlee gave a curt nod, her gaze focused on the backyard through the window to her right. He hesitated for a minute before turning and striding out of the bedroom, closing the door softly behind him.

The moment the door closed behind him, the breath whooshed from her lungs. Asshole. Who the hell did he think he was?

A surge of defiance rose within her as Brynlee threw back the covers and slid from the bed. He thought he could tell her what to do, how to live her life? Hell, no.

Brynlee paced the bedroom for a few minutes, mind

churning furiously. When she thought enough time had passed, she crept toward the door, cracked it open, and peered out. The house was silent.

Slipping out of the bedroom, she padded softly toward the living room. Peeking outside, she checked the driveway to make sure he was gone. He was. Her smile started small then grew as she sashayed toward the kitchen.

She threw every cabinet door open wide, deciding to tackle the dishes first. The plates were stacked in a precise order, and the glasses were all aligned by size. Brynlee moved them around, placing the plates in the wrong spots and mixing up the glasses. She shuffled the cutlery in the drawers, swapping the forks and knives. It was small, subtle chaos, but enough to disrupt Sawyer's carefully curated order.

Nothing remained unscathed. She opened the fridge, gleefully rearranging each shelf and drawer before moving on to the bathroom. Sawyer's towels were always folded neatly, and just seeing the sharp corners made her lips curl with disdain. Brynlee shook them loose then re-folded them, rolling some into little cylinders, folding others in half, the rest into thirds, then stacked them haphazardly.

Feeling a surge of satisfaction, she moved to the bedroom where she pulled every article of clothing out of the dresser, mixing socks with shirts, boxers with sweats. The clothes hanging in his closet were organized by color, and she happily mixed up the hangers until the once orderly rainbow was beyond recognition.

Last came the living room. Sawyer's furniture was arranged in a half moon around the television. Brynlee shifted the sofa to the opposite wall, then dragged the chairs and tables into random places, facing them away from one another so there was no order to the room whatsoever.

Brynlee propped her hands on her hips and grinned as she

surveyed her handiwork. He was going to have a fit. She couldn't wait.

With everything in place, she took a final look around and headed for the door. She locked up, just as Sawyer had instructed, and left the house, feeling lighter than she had in days.

CHAPTER
THIRTY-EIGHT

Even though it was barely two o'clock in the afternoon, a handful of cars were already lined up in front of Mulligan's Pub when he pulled into the parking lot.

Sawyer climbed from the car and headed inside, his gaze sweeping the dim interior. Five men were seated at the bar while another two played pool in the room tucked off to the right side of the bar.

He nodded to the bartender who leaned her elbows on the bar and threw a smile his way. "What can I get ya?"

He waved off her offer. "I'm on the clock, Teagan, but thanks anyway. I'm here on business."

"Oh?" Her head tipped slightly to one side. "Usually I hear if things got out of control."

Mulligan's had seen its fair share of fights, but that wasn't why he was here today. "I was actually wondering if you remembered someone who was in here last night."

He pulled the paper from his pocket and unfolded it on the bar between them. The image of Brynlee had been pulled from her driver's license, and he watched Teagan study it for a moment before nodding. "I think I remember her, yeah. She was with another lady."

He nodded, then folded up the photo and stowed it away again. "Was she drinking?"

"Wine, I think, but I can't remember which one. I could check the computer system."

He waved off her offer. "Did she seem intoxicated?"

Teagan shook her head. "Not that I remember. I poured the wine for her, and she nursed that for a while. It was busy, but I'm pretty sure she left soon after that."

He flicked a glance at the ceiling where a tiny red light flickered sporadically inside a domed camera. He pointed upward. "That thing work?"

Teagan followed my gaze then nodded, brows drawn slightly together. "You need to see the footage?"

"If you've got it." He didn't want to get his hopes up, but maybe there was something on there that could help him figure out what had happened last night and if someone had, in fact, slipped something into Brynlee's drink.

"I'll need to check with Skye," she said, referring to the bar's manager.

"Whatever you need to do."

Teagan checked on her customers before ducking into the back room. Less than three minutes later she was back. "Skye is on her way in. She said she'll get the footage for you."

"No problem." Sawyer slid onto a barstool to wait, and his gaze slid over the length of the bar.

His thoughts were interrupted as Skye strode through the doorway that connected the kitchen into the bar.

"Detective?"

Sawyer turned to face a petite brunette, then tipped his chin her way and slid off the stool. "That's me."

"Come on back." She waved him around the bar, and he fell into step as she led the way through the kitchen to a small office. "Teagan said you wanted to review the footage from last night."

"That's right."

"Is there a specific time frame you're looking for?"

"Between eight and ten." Skye closed the door behind them, then took a seat behind her desk while Sawyer dropped into the seat opposite her. "Can you tell me if the camera above the register captures the entire bar?"

"Most of it," Skye replied. "Mind me asking exactly what you're looking for?"

"A young woman came in last night with a friend. They sat at the bar, had a glass of wine while they talked. She believes someone slipped something into her drink. I'm trying to figure out how it was administered."

Skye's lips flattened into a thin line. "Blonde?"

I nodded. "Do you remember her?"

"Yep. Stayed for about an hour and a half or so. Teagan poured their wine, and I checked on them again later, but they were already getting ready to leave."

Same story as Teagan, then. "Did she seem intoxicated at all?"

Skye mulled it over for a second, then shook her head. "No, not unless she hid it really well."

"Would you mind if I took a look at the footage?"

"Sure thing."

Skye was silent for a moment as she fiddled with the computer monitor, then swiveled the screen toward Sawyer. The timestamp in the lower right corner showed it was 8:17. The camera was situated over the bar, and it had a decent view of the cash register and drink well, as well as several seats around the bar top.

The clock read 8:21 when Brynlee arrived and slid onto a stool next to Melanie. Another two minutes passed before Teagan slid the first wine in front of her. Sawyer watched as

Melanie got up and casually walked away, presumably heading to the bathroom.

His eyes narrowed as a dark-haired woman, barely noticeable at first, slid onto the stool to Brynlee's right. Brynlee turned to her, smiling and exchanging a few words.

Suddenly, his attention was drawn to the man who suddenly appeared at Brynlee's left. Tall, broad-shouldered, and far too close for comfort. Brynlee turned to him, her smile widening, and they started talking, her body language open and relaxed.

Jealousy flared in Sawyer's chest, sharp and hot. He clenched his jaw, his hands tightening into fists as he watched the man lean in closer to Brynlee, their conversation seeming easy, almost intimate. He kept his eyes on the man, waiting for any sign that he was making a move, that he was the one responsible. But the man's focus seemed to be solely on Brynlee, his posture relaxed, casual.

Sawyer was so intent on watching their interaction that he almost missed the slight movement from the side. He jerked upright. "Skye, rewind that."

Skye quickly reached over, hitting the rewind button, and the footage rolled back to the moment just before the man appeared. Sawyer's gaze flicked back to the brunette sitting behind Brynlee. This time, he watched her more closely. She was sipping her drink, her posture casual. Then, as Brynlee's attention was on the man to her left, the woman's hand moved, just slightly.

Sawyer leaned in, his heart pounding. The woman's hand hovered over the bar, right near Brynlee's wine glass. It was a subtle movement, easy to miss if you weren't looking for it. She wasn't holding anything noticeable, but the way her hand lingered, just for a second, was enough to set off alarm bells in Sawyer's mind.

He watched as the woman's fingers barely grazed the rim

of the glass before she pulled back, sliding off the stool and disappearing into the crowd.

"Did you see that?" he asked, turning to Skye.

She frowned, replaying the footage again. "Yeah, but… I don't recognize her. She was only here for a few minutes. Paid in cash."

Sawyer cursed under his breath, frustration gnawing at him. He leaned forward, closer to the screen, trying to get a clearer look at the woman's face. Goddamn it. She had long, dark hair—just like the hair they'd found under Brynlee's car.

The woman had planned it out, making sure to leave no trace, no easy way to track her down. But at least now he had something, a new lead to follow.

He abruptly pushed from the chair, his mind already racing through possibilities. "Thanks, Skye," he said. "You've been a huge help."

She nodded, her eyes full of concern. "I hope you find her, Sawyer. Brynlee doesn't deserve this."

Sawyer gave a curt nod, his thoughts too tangled to respond properly. He turned and left the bar, the night air cool against his heated skin.

There was no time to waste—he had to find out who this woman was and what she had done to Brynlee. And he wouldn't rest until he had answers.

As soon as he slid inside, he yanked off his tie and tossed it onto the passenger seat. For a moment he sat there, drumming his fingers on the steering wheel, lost in thought. Frustration coursed through every cell of his body. He wanted answers, damn it. Who the hell was this woman, and what did she want with Brynlee?

After the day from hell all he wanted to do was go home and chill. No, that wasn't true. What he wanted was to see Brynlee. It made no sense, and yet… She'd somehow burrowed under his skin. She drove him crazy as much as she turned him on, and he could admit that his life might have taken a turn for the better when he'd moved in next to the crazy little hippie.

That was a stretch. She wasn't really a hippie. Just a little... eccentric. She was beautiful and smart, and she ran a successful business doing what she loved. He had to give her props for that. Not many people could pull it off, yet Brynlee managed to make it look easy.

He dug his phone from his pocket as he cranked the engine, then dialed up Bryn's favorite Chinese joint. Twenty-five minutes later he pulled into his driveway and glanced over at her sedan, parked in front of her duplex. Good. She was home. He'd been slightly concerned she might still be at the salon, especially since she had a lot of repairs to get caught up on.

There was a bottle of wine in the fridge. A little formal for Chinese takeout, but what the hell. Striding up the walkway, he headed into his side of the duplex—and froze.

CHAPTER
THIRTY-NINE

"What the—"

Everything had been moved. *Everything*.

He gaped at the living room furniture that, just this morning, had been arranged in a semi-circle. Now, it was pushed to the sides of the rooms, the side tables interspersed between them. He scowled. She'd even moved the damn plant.

Scooping up the potted plant, he carried it to a table out of direct sunlight and set it down, then dropped the bag of food on the kitchen counter and cocked his ears, listening for movement. He didn't hear anything, which meant Brynlee must be on her side of the duplex. Good thing, because he was going to throttle her ass.

He braced himself as he ventured deeper into the house to see what other destruction she'd wrought.

It was a lot.

Cup and plates had been mixed together, spices rearranged, his dish towels and small appliances mixed in with the pantry items. He propped his hands on his hips and scowled. Good God. How long had it taken her to do all this?

He grimaced as he padded cautiously down the hallway toward his bedroom, then paused outside the door and peeked inside. He shouldn't have. His eye began to twitch at the sight of the carefully organized clothes in the closet now hanging haphazardly. He turned away with a shake of his head. He couldn't bring himself to look anymore.

His dishes, the food in the refrigerator, first aid materials in the medicine cabinet... Apparently nothing was off limits for Brynlee.

Sawyer stomped toward the back door and threw it open, his blood thrumming rapidly in his veins. The moment he stepped outside, he saw her lounging in a chair, engrossed in a book.

She looked up as he approached, her face breaking into a mischievous grin, as if she'd been waiting for him. "Hello, darling. How was your day?"

He stopped next to her chair and crossed his arms over his chest, one brow arching toward his hairline. "Not nearly as productive as yours, apparently."

Brynlee affected a mock surprised expression, but she couldn't keep her smile from growing. "I don't know what you're talking about."

A snort escaped before he could stop it. "I'm not sure if I should be angry or impressed."

She lifted one shoulder, those wide, innocent eyes staring up at him. "Both?"

With a shake of his head, Sawyer pushed her legs aside, then dropped onto the chaise lounge next to her. "By the way, the plant doesn't belong in the sun."

"I know." She smiled cheekily. "I was just testing you."

Sawyer reached out and gave her hair a playful tug. "Brat. You gonna help clean up this mess?"

Brynlee swatted his hand away with a laugh. "Only if you ask nicely."

Sawyer smiled despite himself. The earlier tension and frustration had melted away, replaced by the familiar banter and camaraderie.

"Well, if you're done wreaking havoc, I picked up some dinner for us." He arched a brow her way. "I'd hate to see what you do to the kitchen next."

She let out a tinkling laugh as she pushed from the lounge chair. "I'm sure I could come up with something."

Sawyer shook his head and stood, then swatted her ass. "Get in there and find us some plates."

* * *

Brynlee was already on the patio, sitting at the table when Sawyer emerged from the kitchen with the bag of takeout and two sodas. She'd managed to find two plates and some napkins, and he felt another smile tug at his lips.

It was par for the course for them; they bickered, pushing one another's buttons until they were ready to break, then made up as if it had never happened.

Sawyer set a soda in front of each of their seats, then pulled out a small takeout box and placed it in front of her. "Your favorite."

Brynlee looked up, ready to thank him, but before she could say anything, Sawyer leaned in and gently grabbed her chin. His lips brushed against hers in a quick, hard kiss. Brynlee's eyes widened as she pulled back, her face turning a bright shade of pink.

Sawyer arched a brow her way. "That's the least I deserve."

Her mouth twitched as she fought back a smile, and Brynlee nodded, still flushed. "Fair enough."

Sawyer's grin widened as he took his own seat. It was nice to see her off balance for once. He started serving himself, making small talk to ease the tension and get to know Brynlee better.

"So," he began, his tone casual, "tell me more about your salon."

She threw a look his way as she cracked open the box and dipped her fork inside. "Why?"

"Why not?" he countered. Despite the fact that they'd lived next to one another for the better part of a year, he still didn't really know much about her. "How did you get into it?"

"You know Mel? She went to cosmetology school after we graduated. I thought about it, but I was no good with hair so that was out for me. I wanted something that would give me a little freedom in my schedule, so I ended up taking some classes for massage therapy and really loved it."

"Have you always had your own place?"

She shook her head. "No, I've only been in business for about a year and a half."

"Seems like you're doing well."

Brynlee swallowed a bite of food. "For the most part. It's stressful sometimes, but I love the challenge."

Sawyer leaned back in his chair and studied her. "You seem to have a real knack for connecting with people. Do you have any specific goals for the salon?"

Brynlee shrugged almost self-consciously. "I'd love to expand eventually, maybe add a few more services. But for now, I'm just focused on making sure everything runs smoothly and that my clients are happy."

Sawyer nodded. "That's a solid plan. It sounds like you've got a clear vision of what you want. It's impressive."

Brynlee blushed slightly, a shy smile tugging at her lips. "Thanks. I've put a lot of work into it."

"I can tell." Sawyer took a sip of his drink, his eyes never leaving her. "So, what about outside of work? What do you like to do for fun? Any hobbies or interests?"

Brynlee flashed a smile his way. "Yoga. Meditation."

He rolled his eyes. "Yeah, I got that."

Conversation lapsed as they finished their food, and Sawyer leaned back in his chair, trying to find the right words as he studied Brynlee's profile.

"I went to the bar," he finally said, his voice low, cutting through the quiet. Brynlee's head turned slightly, her eyes flicking to his. "To review the footage from the night you were there."

A flicker of worry crossed her features. "And?"

"There was a woman," Sawyer said, leaning forward, his elbows resting on his knees. "Dark hair, sat next to you after Melanie went to the bathroom. Do you remember her?"

Brynlee frowned, a small crease forming between her brows. "Yeah, why?"

Sawyer took a deep breath, trying to keep his voice steady despite his heart pounding in his chest. "Because she slipped something into your drink, Brynlee."

Her eyes flew wide, and she sucked in a sharp breath. "What? Are you sure?"

He nodded, his gaze unwavering. "I checked the footage this morning. It was quick, almost unnoticeable if you weren't looking for it. Her hand hovered over your glass for a second, then she slipped off the stool and disappeared."

"I... I had no idea." Brynlee shook her head. "I just remember feeling off after that, but I thought it was the wine, or maybe just the stress of everything."

Sawyer's jaw tightened as he continued, "I think this might be the same woman who cut the wires under your car. This wasn't random, Brynlee. Someone's targeting you, and we need to figure out who it is."

Brynlee's eyes grew distant as she struggled to remember. "I don't know... She looked familiar, but I couldn't place her. I can't think of where I've seen her."

Sawyer leaned in closer. "I need you to try. This woman is dangerous, and if she's not stopped…"

He didn't finish the sentence, but the implication hung heavy in the air. Brynlee swallowed hard, nodding slowly. "I'll think about it. I'll try to remember."

"Good."

He nodded, then stood. Brynlee followed suit, and they cleaned up, carrying the plates and trash into Sawyer's kitchen.

"Thanks for dinner." Brynlee flashed him a quick smile. "I guess I should head out."

She paused next to the back door, hand on the doorknob, looking indecisive. Sawyer watched her for a moment. Did her house feel empty without Scooter there to welcome her home?

Sawyer cleared his throat. "I think we had an agreement. You made the mess…"

Her eyes flicked his way, full of mirth, underscored by relief that she didn't have to be alone at the moment. "I get to clean it up?"

Sawyer pushed off the counter and extended a hand her way. Her eyes dropped, then met his again. After a moment, she slipped her palm into his and Sawyer tugged her close. "Later."

CHAPTER
FORTY

There wasn't a single damn connection between the women—not their jobs, their hobbies, or their history. Several of the women had been in car accidents, but there was no crossover with mechanics, car rental agencies, or the other drivers involved... What the hell were they missing?

Sawyer scrubbed a hand over his face. There was a loose thread somewhere, he just had to find it.

The day had been dragging on, and the relentless hum of activity at the station was beginning to wear on Sawyer Reed. He sat at his desk, tapping a pen against a stack of paperwork that seemed to be growing by the minute. Cam had stepped out for a moment, leaving Sawyer alone to field any calls that might come in. He barely noticed the phone ringing until the third chime.

"Reed," he answered, fatigue creeping into his tone.

"Uh, Detective Reed? This is Mr. Swanson," came the voice on the other end said. "I was trying to reach Detective McCoy. Is he around?"

Sawyer sat up a little straighter. "Cam's out at the

moment, but I can take a message or help if you need anything."

There was a brief pause, and Sawyer could almost hear Mr. Swanson weighing his next words. "Well, Detective McCoy stopped by a few days ago asking about any car accidents Hilary might have been in. I didn't think much of it at the time, but there's something that's been bothering me since then."

Sawyer's grip tightened on the phone. "What is it?"

"About a month before Hilary was abducted," Mr. Swanson began tentatively, "someone broke into her apartment near campus. They stole her laptop and some other things. She contacted both the campus police and the local precinct, filed a report, and even reported it to her insurance."

He hesitated for a long moment before continuing. "Insurance refused to pay out—said her door wasn't locked. She swears it was."

Sawyer's mind immediately jumped to Brynlee and the flood at her salon, a disaster that insurance likely wouldn't cover due to supposed negligence.

In his experience, insurance companies would do just about anything to avoid having to cover damages, but still... Something didn't feel quite right.

"They refused to pay because they claimed the door wasn't locked?"

"Yeah," Mr. Swanson confirmed. "It didn't make sense to me. Hilary was always careful, and something about the whole thing just felt off. I didn't think about it until now, but it's been bothering me, especially with everything that's happened."

"Mr. Swanson," Sawyer said, keeping his voice calm despite the rush of thoughts racing through his head, "do you happen to remember the name of Hilary's insurance company?"

"Yeah, it was Sterling Assurance," Mr. Swanson replied without hesitation.

"Sterling Assurance," Sawyer repeated, committing the name to memory. "Thank you, Mr. Swanson. I really appreciate your help."

After a few more words of reassurance, Sawyer hung up the phone, his heart beginning to pound in his chest. He quickly turned to his computer, pulling up Jayla Simms' file and scanning through her records. His breath caught when he saw it—Sterling Assurance, the same company.

Sawyer's fingers flew across the keyboard, pulling up Lindsey Gill's file next. He scrolled through the details until—

There it was. Sterling Assurance.

He leaned back in his chair, staring at the screen in disbelief. All three victims—Jayla, Hilary, and Lindsey—had used the same insurance company. This was no coincidence. His gut had been right; they'd finally found a connection, a lead that could crack the case wide open.

Sawyer's heart raced as he grabbed the phone again, this time dialing the number for Sterling Assurance. When the call connected, he quickly explained who he was and the urgency of the situation.

"I'm Detective Sawyer Reed with Brookhaven PD," he said, his tone leaving no room for doubt. "I'm investigating a series of murders, and I believe they may be connected through your company. I need all the information you have on these claims—anything you've got could be crucial."

The voice on the other end stammered for a moment before agreeing to process the request as quickly as possible. Sawyer could feel the tension coiling in his chest as he hung up.

He jumped up from his desk, his long stride carrying him swiftly across the station to where Dare Jensen sat in his office reviewing some files.

"Hey, I think we've got something. Jayla, Hilary, and Lindsey all used the same insurance company—Sterling Assurance. I just spoke with them, and they're pulling everything they've got."

Dare glanced up at him and nodded. "If that pans out, we might finally have a lead that connects these cases."

Cam walked by, looking curious. "What's going on?"

Sawyer quickly filled him in on the new discovery, the words tumbling out as he explained the link between the victims and the insurance company.

"This could be it." Cam nodded. "If we can trace this back to someone within the company—or someone with access to their data—we might be able to finally nail this guy."

Sawyer nodded, the adrenaline surging through him. They'd come so close to dead ends so many times, but this felt different. They had a direction now, a tangible lead that could lead them to the killer.

"Now we just need to wait for the information to come through," Sawyer said, glancing at the clock. Every second felt like an eternity, but they were closer than they'd ever been.

The station hummed with a renewed sense of purpose, the weight of the investigation heavy but manageable now that they had something concrete to hold on to. All they could do now was wait—and hope that this was the break that would finally bring justice to Jayla, Hilary, and Lindsey.

CHAPTER
FORTY-ONE

The hum of hairdryers filled the air, blending with the soft chatter of clients. It was all perfectly normal, yet Brynlee couldn't shake the sense of unease that settled over her.

Her mind kept drifting back to the night at the bar. She could see the woman's face so clearly in her mind—the sharp angles of her cheekbones, the way her lips curled into a smile that didn't quite reach her eyes. It was all so vivid, yet Brynlee couldn't place where she'd seen her before.

Mind drifting, she began her nightly routine of cleaning up while the stylists wrapped up their appointments and the clients filtered out one at a time, until only Jane remained at her station.

Brynlee straightened the stack of appointment cards, then glanced down at the appointment book. As she flipped through the pages, checking upcoming appointments, a sudden flash of memory struck her. A woman's face, so clear in her mind, seemed to overlay the name from last week—Elisa Travers.

Her breath caught in her throat. Jane's client, the one with the auburn hair and the bubbly smile—it had to be her. But her hair had been different that night at the bar, darker, and styled in loose waves. Still, the face was so similar it was uncanny.

Brynlee's heart pounded as she tried to remember every detail. She had thought nothing of the client at the time, just another appointment in a busy week. But now, with the memory of the bar superimposed on her thoughts, she felt a chill crawl up her spine.

Could it really be the same woman?

Her fingers tightened around the edge of the appointment book as she flipped back to the previous week and stared at the name. It wasn't unusual for clients to change their look, to experiment with different hair colors and styles. But the thought that this woman, Elisa Travers, might be connected to what happened that night sent goosebumps sprouting over her skin.

Why had Elisa come to the salon? Had she known who Brynlee was, or was it just a coincidence? And if it wasn't, what did that mean?

She looked around the salon, her gaze landing on Jane, who was laughing with her client as she worked. Everything seemed so ordinary, but Brynlee couldn't shake the feeling that something was terribly wrong.

She needed to tell someone—Sawyer, maybe. But even as she thought of him, she felt a pang of uncertainty. He had been so protective lately, so worried about her. She didn't want to add to his stress, not when he was already so consumed with his cases.

But if Elisa Travers was the woman from the bar, then Brynlee had to find out why she had been targeted. And if she was wrong, then at least she would know.

She reached for the phone and dialed the number listed. It rang twice before a robotic voice informed her that the number was disconnected. A chill swept down Brynlee's spine, and she felt the blood drain from her face. She lowered the phone slowly, her mind racing. It was as if the woman had vanished into thin air.

The moment Jane finished with her client, Brynlee waved her over. "Jane, can I talk to you for a minute?"

Jane locked the front door, then made her way to the front desk. "Sure, what's up?"

"Do you remember a client we had last week? Her name was Elisa—or at least that's what she went by. She had auburn hair, shoulder-length, came in for a trim."

Jane tilted her head, thinking for a moment. "Elisa... Yeah, I remember her. Really sweet. Why do you ask?"

Brynlee's heart pounded as she recounted the events of that night at the bar, how she'd been drugged, and how she now suspected that this Elisa Travers might be the same woman who had slipped something into her drink. "She used the bathroom right before she left that night—the same weekend it flooded."

As she spoke, Jane's expression shifted from confusion to concern. "You think she's responsible?"

Brynlee lifted her hands in supplication. "I can't be sure, but their faces... they're just so similar. The hair was different, but everything else matches."

Jane crossed her arms, her brow furrowing with worry. "That's creepy, Bryn. Did she say anything weird when she was here? Act suspicious?"

Brynlee shook her head, frustration gnawing at her. "No, nothing. That's what's so unsettling. She was just... normal. But now I can't shake this feeling that something's off."

"You should talk to the police," Jane suggested.

Brynlee nodded. "I will. Let's head out."

Together, they finished their tasks, locking up the salon for the night. Brynlee's hands shook as she went through the motions, her mind focused on one thing—getting out of there and telling Sawyer everything. Just as she was about to lock the door, she realized she had forgotten something.

"Damn it," she muttered, turning to Jane. "I forgot to check the laundry. You go on ahead, I'll just be a minute."

Jane hesitated, glancing back at the salon. "Are you sure? I can wait."

Brynlee shook her head, forcing a smile. "I'm fine. It's just towels. I'll be quick."

Reluctantly, Jane nodded and headed to her car. Brynlee watched her leave before turning back to the salon. The familiar space felt different now, shadows stretching longer, corners darker. She hurried inside, moving quickly to gather the towels from the laundry room. Her fingers fumbled as she stacked them, her senses on high alert.

With the towels in hand, she made her way back outside, the silence of the salon pressing down on her. She locked up, double-checking the door before turning to leave.

A sudden prickle of unease crawled up her neck. She needed to get home, to talk to Sawyer. Distracted, she didn't immediately hear the soft crunch of gravel behind her.

She turned to glance over her shoulder but a huge hand fisted in her hair, then yanked her backward. A soft cry ripped from her throat, but it was quickly extinguished when a brawny arm wrapped around her neck, constricting her air supply.

She fought against her assailant's hold, kicking at his legs and scratching at his arms and face. Her vision began to dim and her lungs burned from the exertion. The man uttered a muffled curse behind her, and something hard pressed into the nerve that ran along her neck. Her muscles spasmed and her legs gave out as everything around her disappeared into a fog of nothingness.

CHAPTER
FORTY-TWO

Sawyer pulled into his driveway, anticipation buzzing through his veins. They were so close. They just needed the last piece of the puzzle.

He turned off the engine, listening to the settling noises of his car, and looked over at Brynlee's house next door. Usually she beat him home, but tonight her place looked dark, her driveway empty.

A kernel of jealousy sat heavy in his gut. Was she out on a date? Shoving the thought aside, he grabbed his things and climbed from the car, then headed inside. He dragged himself toward the shower, exhaustion clinging to him, and ducked under the warm spray. It soothed his tired muscles and helped to clear his mind, despite the fact that his thoughts continued to flit toward the woman next door.

He finished showering, then headed to the kitchen to get something to eat. He couldn't help but detour past the living room windows, peering out to see if Brynlee was home yet. Her driveway remained infuriatingly empty, and he let out a low growl. Where the fuck was she?

Grabbing up his phone from where he'd left it on the

kitchen counter, he checked the screen. There were no texts, no missed calls. No surprise there. Tamping down his anger, he dialed Brynlee, and his heart rate increased when it rang over and over until her voicemail picked up.

His foot tapped an impatient rhythm on the floor, and he mentally scolded himself. She had no reason to report to him or keep him informed of every move she made. But damn it, didn't she realize she could be in danger? Someone had tampered with her car less than a week ago. What if something had happened?

Heart in his throat he grabbed his keys, then hopped in the car and headed toward town. As he drove, he used the Bluetooth function to try her again. When it too went unanswered, he immediately ended the call and dialed her again. Over and over it went to voicemail.

He pulled into the parking lot at Blissful Beauty, and his heart lurched in his throat. Thank God. There, in the far corner of the lot, sat Brynlee's rental car. A relieved sigh filtered from his lips, and he pulled in next to it, then parked. For a moment he sat there, willing his pulse to slow.

Shoving open the door, he clambered out of the car and strode up to the door of the salon. He tested the handle and found it locked, then knocked loudly. When no one answered, he knocked again, louder this time.

His heart rate kicked up as he cupped his hands over his face and peered through the darkened windows. Inside, the lights were off, everything seemingly locked up tight. But if that was the case, where the hell was Brynlee?

Impatiently, he glanced up and down the sidewalk, checking for any sign of her. It was always possible that she'd walked down to one of the local shops after work, but why wasn't she answering her phone?

Pulling out his phone, he called Brynlee again. A soft ringing filled the air, and the hairs on the backs of his arms stood on end. He turned in a circle, heart racing. Where the hell had that come from?

His worry only increased as her phone continued to ring in my ear, coinciding with the soft jangle nearby. Dread settled in his gut as he slowly approached the corner of the building and peered into the alley between the buildings.

A dumpster sat behind the building, and his stomach tumbled riotously as he dragged himself closer. He ended the call and the ringing stopped.

Hand shaking, he reached for the lid of the dumpster and cracked it open. Relief mingled with dread as he spied Brynlee's purse on top of a black trash bag. She wasn't here—thank God. But the fact that someone had tossed her phone and purse didn't bode well.

Oh, Christ. His stomach pitched violently as he dialed Dare's number, his hand shaking.

"Hey, Reed. What's up?"

It took him a moment to form the words, still not quite able to believe what he was seeing. Finally he managed to push them past his lips. "Bryn... She's gone."

* * *

Brynlee pushed through the fog that penetrated her brain, shoving the darkness aside. She blinked hard once. Twice. Finally, she managed to crack her eyes open. She stared at her surroundings, blurry and unfocused. Nothing looked right. Then she realized why: everything was upside down and moving.

Her body swung gently, like a pendulum, and panic surged through her as she realized she was draped over someone's shoulder, her hands bound tightly behind her back.

Fragmented memories assaulted her—leaving the salon, a man coming up behind her, the squeeze of her lungs as they fought to draw in air...

She twisted her head from side to side, trying to see her

captor, but the world spun dizzily. The ground was too close, the ceiling above too far, and everything was tilted at a nauseating angle. She could make out the shape of a man's legs and back, his movements steady as he crossed the darkened room.

Where the hell was she? She tried to cry out, but her throat was dry, and her voice came out as a hoarse whisper.

Fear gripped her chest, squeezing tighter with each passing second. She started to thrash, kicking her legs wildly, her bound hands straining against the ties. The man grunted, struggling to keep his balance.

"Just relax," the man said, his voice calm and measured.

Relax? How the hell was she supposed to relax? His ambivalence served only to spur her fear, and Brynlee kicked harder, bucking wildly against his shoulder. She felt her feet connect with something solid and the man stumbled, his grip on her legs loosening the tiniest bit. With a final desperate thrash, she managed to break free, and all of a sudden she was falling.

The ground rushed up to meet her, and the air rushed from her lungs in a painful whoosh. Agony shot through her arms and shoulders as she hit the hard ground, but adrenaline coursed through her, forcing her to move. Awkwardly she rolled to her knees and lurched forward, her movements jerky and uncoordinated.

She didn't get far. The man lunged after her, grabbing her by the waist and yanking her back. She screamed, kicking and struggling against his hold with all her might. He was stronger, though, and she felt herself being lifted off the ground again, her frantic movements doing little to slow him down.

"Help!" she screamed, her voice breaking with fear and frustration. "Somebody, please help!"

The man threw her to the ground again, this time harder, knocking the wind out of her. She gasped, trying to catch her breath, her vision swimming with tears. The man loomed over her, his face twisted with anger, and her blood ran cold.

She froze, momentarily caught off guard. She knew that face—she'd seen it just a couple of weeks ago when he'd inspected the salon. Her mouth parted but nothing came out.

"Listen to me," he growled, his voice low and menacing. "You try that again, and I'll make sure you regret it. Understand?"

Brynlee nodded, tears streaming down her face. She had to stay calm, had to think. Panic would only make things worse. She needed to find a way out, a way to survive.

The man grabbed her by the arm and hauled her to her feet. "Now, move," he ordered, shoving her forward.

She took in her surroundings, looking for anything that could help her. The dim light overhead flickered, casting eerie shadows on the rough stone walls. She realized with a sickening jolt that she was in a basement, far from any chance of immediate rescue.

Something came into sight up ahead, and she squinted against the dim light. The object was large and white, and—

Brynlee froze, her heart jumping into her throat at the sight of the stained mattress on the floor beneath the halo of light. Worse, several feet away lay a second mattress, its occupant sleeping, or...

She didn't want to consider the alternative. Brynlee tried to backpedal, digging in her heels. She bumped into the man behind her, but he shoved her forward and she stumbled, her legs collapsing as he forced her downward.

Brynlee could do nothing to stop herself as fell face-first onto the revolting mattress, the putrid scent of filth filling her nostrils and tainting her tongue. She struggled to move her bound hands, but they were tied too tightly. She kicked out with her feet, desperate to fight back, but he was too strong, too big. His weight pressed down on her, pinning her in place.

Terror surged through her as she heard him fumbling with something. She twisted her head to see, catching a glimpse of a small bottle and a cloth. The realization sent a wave of panic crashing over her.

Oh, God.

She couldn't let him knock her out again. Summoning all her strength, she thrashed violently, managing to lift her head just enough to headbutt him with all her might.

"Damn it!" he swore, recoiling in pain.

But her victory was short-lived. Enraged, he wrapped a hand around her throat, squeezing tightly. Brynlee gasped, her vision blurring as her airway constricted.

Black spots danced in front of her eyes, and the room spun, the shadows growing darker. Her last thought was a desperate plea for Sawyer to find her, for anyone to save her, as everything faded to black.

CHAPTER
FORTY-THREE

His heart felt like it was beating right out of his chest, and his lungs felt tight, like he couldn't draw in enough oxygen. Brynlee's face flashed before his eyes—that bright smile, her huge blue eyes that tempted him and pushed him over the edge.

No. She couldn't be gone—she just couldn't. His throat tightened, his stomach clenching into a tight knot.

"Start from the beginning," Dare ordered. "Who's missing?"

"Brynlee." Sawyer choked out her name, pain like he'd never known shooting through his chest. Where could she be? Who would have any reason to take her? Why—?

"Where are you?"

Sawyer forced himself to focus. "At the salon. Her car is here, but her purse and phone were tossed in the dumpster. Whoever—"

A face materialized in the back of his mind, and he immediately cut off. Zane. He'd been so furious the night Sawyer had found him sneaking around the house. What if he was stupid and vindictive enough to come after her?

"That motherfucker!"

He was already striding toward his car before Dare's words registered. "Reed! What's going on?"

"Her ex," I ground out as I threw open the car door. "I found him snooping around her house. He said he wanted her back—He thinks he's going to get her."

If Zane had something to do with Brynlee's disappearance, Sawyer was going to rip the man apart with his bare hands. He hung up and stomped on the gas, navigating toward Zane's house, sending up a silent prayer as he drove. His phone rang incessantly, vibrating against the passenger seat where he'd tossed it earlier. I knew it was my brother calling again, just as I knew he would try to stop me from going to Zane's. But that wasn't going to happen.

His heart beat hard and fast in his chest, his pulse kicking up as each mile brought me closer. His fury grew as he drove, billowing up inside me until it was all he could focus on. Zane's small SUV came into view as Sawyer turned onto the street, and his vision went red.

He slid to a stop at the curb in front of the house then threw open the door. He didn't bother to kill the engine before charging up the walkway and pounding on the front door. "Open up!"

Over and over he slammed the side of his fist against the steel door until the rapid shuffle of footsteps grew closer. "I'm coming!"

The door started to swing inward, and Sawyer shoved it the rest of the way open, already reaching for him. "Where is she?"

"Wh—?"

He wrapped one hand around Zane's neck and slammed him into the wall. "What did you do to her?"

A feminine scream echoed behind them, but Sawyer paid

the woman no mind. Zane's eyes were wide with fear and surprise. "What the hell are you talking about?"

"Brynlee!" Sawyer tightened his grip and shoved the man against the wall again. "Where is she?"

He clawed at Sawyer's hand in an attempt to get free. "I don't know what the hell you're talking about!"

"Don't lie to me, motherfucker!"

A cacophony of raised voices lilted on the air, the sound dim beneath the force of his rage.

"Reed, stop!" Dare's voice filtered over Sawyer's shoulder a moment before two strong arms wrapped around his torso and yanked him away from Zane.

The screech of tires from the direction of the street dimly penetrated my brain, and all of a sudden Tony and Evan were there. I was furious that they'd intervened, but at the same time I was immensely relieved. I knew they would have my back.

Sawyer fought Dare's hold, reaching once more for Zane. "That piece of shit knows where she is, I know he does!"

"I didn't do shit." Zane sneered. "You're just jealous."

Tony stepped in front of Zane. "Let's all calm down."

Sawyer glared at the man. "If you hurt her, I swear to God I'll kill you!"

"I'm pressing charges," Zane yelled at Dare. "Get him out of here!"

Sawyer whipped around, but his attention snagged on the woman standing just a few feet away. He paused midstep, his gaze zeroing in on her face. "You!"

Her eyes flew wide. "W-what?"

Sawyer took a step forward. "You're the one from the bar—the one who drugged Brynlee."

Her eyes flitted around the room, looking at everyone but Sawyer. "I—I don't know what you're talking about. I didn't do anything."

"What are you talking about?" Zane's brows pulled together. "Elisa didn't do anything. She—"

"It was her." Sawyer whirled toward Dare. "She's the one from the video. Her hair was longer an darker, but that's her face."

The woman's face went deathly pale, and she shook her head emphatically. "I didn't do anything."

"Tell them the truth!" A low snarl ripped from his throat. "You drugged her... Cut the lines under her car... Didn't you?"

The woman's mouth parted, and she dropped her face into her hands, the sound of harsh sobs filling the air.

Dare grabbed Sawyer's arm and hustled him out of the house. "You need to calm down," he commanded. "We're not going to accomplish anything by screaming at her."

"It was her," Sawyer insisted. "I know it was."

"We'll figure it out." Dare didn't try to comfort him this time. "We'll check the house, but do you really think they would keep her here?"

Christ. Dare was right. Sawyer scrubbed a hand over his face. "Then where the hell is she? She knows something—I know she does."

A muscle in his jaw ticked as Dare glanced toward the house. "I'll have a couple deputies start looking into her, check her alibi. Is there anywhere else Bryn would have gone?"

"Absolutely not." Sawyer shook his head. "She always comes straight home."

"All right." Dare flicked a look toward Evan and Tony, who had separated Elisa from Zane, and were currently questioning them separately. "They've got this under control. Let's head into the station and see what we can find."

He didn't like it, but Sawyer nodded regardless. He moved toward my car, but Dare stopped me with a hand on his arm. "I'll drive."

Anger simmered in his veins. What the hell did he think he was going to do? "What the fuck, Dare?"

He shook his head. "You're upset right now and not thinking clearly."

He was thinking more clearly than he ever had. He knew what was important, and the only thing that mattered was finding Brynlee. But Sawyer was also smart enough to pick his battles. No matter how much he hated to admit it, he knew he couldn't find her by himself. At this point, he didn't even know where to start.

His stomach twisted into a knot as he slid into the passenger seat of Dare's cruiser. Silence fell as they drove toward the station, and he was grateful for the reprieve. His head pounded, and his heart felt like it'd been shredded. If Elisa truly wasn't involved, then where the hell could Brynlee be?

Burt Johnson adjusted the rearview mirror as he pulled out of his driveway, catching a glimpse of his own reflection. His grin stretched wide, almost too wide, as he turned onto the quiet suburban street. The sun was low on the horizon, casting long shadows across the pavement, but the heat of the day still lingered in the air.

As he drove slowly past his neighbor's house, he noticed Carl Jenkins standing in the front yard, leaning on a cane while his small terrier sniffed around the flower beds. The large white van that Burt had borrowed sat parked in Carl's driveway, its imposing bulk out of place in the tidy neighborhood. Burt felt a surge of satisfaction, the thrill of his plan coming together almost intoxicating.

He slowed the car to a crawl and rolled down the

passenger-side window. "Hey, Carl!" he called out, waving enthusiastically.

Carl looked up, squinting against the sun. "Hey, Burt! You get what you needed?"

Burt's grin widened, his heart pounding with a mix of excitement and anticipation. He couldn't help but think of Brynlee Layne, and how everything he had worked for was about to come to fruition. She would be the one. He had no doubt.

CHAPTER
FORTY-FOUR

Brynlee's eyes fluttered open once more, and she blinked at her surroundings, her mind still groggy from the lingering effects of the drug her captor had used to subdue her. A bitter taste clung to her tongue and a dull ache pulsed behind her temples, but the pain was nothing compared to the horror that surrounded her.

She lay in the middle of the stained, dirty mattress that reeked of mildew and decay, her wrists tethered to the wall behind her by thick leather cuffs. Panic surged through her, and she struggled against the restraints, the leather biting into her skin as she fought to free herself. The more she struggled, the more the cuffs seemed to tighten, and her breath came in short, panicked gasps.

A movement across the room caught her eye, and she turned her head sharply, wincing as the motion sent a fresh wave of pain through her skull. In the corner, huddled on a second filthy mattress, was a woman. Her blonde hair was a tangled mess, her clothes torn and dirty, her eyes dull and tired.

"Who… Who are you?" Brynlee's voice was hoarse, her throat dry and scratchy.

The woman hesitated, glancing nervously at the stairs before answering in a whisper, "Fallon."

The name hit Brynlee like a punch to the gut. Fallon's name had been all over the news, the woman the sheriff's department had been searching for. The realization struck her hard—this man had captured Fallon, too. Her heart pounded, a relentless drumbeat echoing in her chest, as the full weight of their situation sank in. This man had already taken other women. She and Fallon were just the latest in a line of victims. And if they didn't find a way out, they would be next.

Sweat beaded on her forehead, dripping down the sides of her face despite the damp chill that clung to the basement air. She felt her pulse quicken, fear threatening to overwhelm her, but she forced herself to focus. There had to be a way out. They couldn't stay here, waiting for the inevitable.

"We need to get out of here," Brynlee whispered. "He's going to kill us."

Fallon's eyes filled with tears, but she nodded, her jaw set with grim determination. "I know," she whispered back. "But these cuffs… I've tried everything. They won't budge."

Brynlee tugged at her own restraints again, trying to slip her wrists free, but the leather held fast. The wall behind her was solid stone, cold and unyielding. She bit down on her lip, thinking hard. There had to be something they could use, some way to loosen the cuffs or break the chains that held them.

Her gaze swept the room, taking in the bare, damp walls, the dirty floor, and the scattered debris. There was nothing useful in sight, nothing they could use to cut through the leather or pry the cuffs open. Despair gnawed at the edges of her mind, but she shoved it aside. She couldn't afford to give up. Not now.

"Maybe there's something... something sharp?" Brynlee suggested, her voice trembling with the effort to stay calm. "We have to find something."

Fallon shook her head, defeated. "There's nothing. Trust me—I've looked."

Brynlee let out a shaky breath, trying to think. The basement was too clean, too empty—like he had planned for this, made sure they wouldn't have anything to use against him.

Her mind raced, trying to come up with a plan, anything that could get them out of this nightmare. The man knew what he was doing. But there had to be a way. There was always a way.

Brynlee had been working at the cuffs for what felt like hours, her wrists raw and bruised from the relentless tugging. The leather dug into her skin, unforgiving, as she tried to twist her hands free. But no matter how much she struggled, the cuffs remained tight, binding her to the cold, damp wall. Her heart pounded in her chest, each beat echoing in her ears like a drum.

The basement was silent, save for the occasional creak of the house above. The darkness seemed to press in on her, suffocating, but she kept going, desperation fueling her efforts. She couldn't stay here, trapped and helpless, waiting for whatever horror he had planned. She had to get out. She had to—

A sound broke through her thoughts, and she froze, every muscle tensing as she listened. The basement door creaked open, the hinges groaning in protest, spilling harsh light down the narrow stairs. Her breath caught in her throat, and her pulse spiked, fear surging through her veins like ice water.

The man stood in the doorway, his silhouette dark against the brightness behind him. He descended the steps slowly, deliberately, the floorboards groaning under his weight with each step. Another footstep, closer now, then another.

As he approached, Brynlee could see his face clearly now—the same face that had smiled at her in the salon, the face she had trusted. Now it was twisted into something far more sinister.

As Burt approached, Brynlee instinctively scuttled backward, shrinking against the wall, her body curling inward as if she could somehow make herself smaller, less noticeable. But it was no use—he was already focused on her as he stopped a few feet away.

His gaze slid from Brynlee to Fallon, then back again, and his mouth curved into a smile. "I see you've met," he said, his voice smooth, almost pleasant.

He took a step closer, looming over her, and Brynlee's breath caught in her throat, her body going rigid with fear. She forced herself not to recoil as he leaned down, inspecting the cuffs around her wrists.

"Don't worry, everything will be okay," he murmured, his voice deceptively soft. "I'll take good care of you,"

She wanted to scream at him, to tell him to stay away, but the words caught in her throat, strangled by fear. Her hands clenched into fists, the leather cuffs biting deeper into her wrists as she tried to inch away from him, but there was nowhere to go. The wall behind her was solid, unyielding.

She was trapped.

He reached out and trailed his fingers down her arm, and she flinched, her skin crawling at his touch.

"Shh," he soothed, his voice still soft, almost gentle. "You're exactly what I've been looking for."

Brynlee's breath came in short, panicked gasps, her chest

heaving rapidly as terror unlike anything she had ever known coursed through her. She wanted to scream, to kick, to claw at him, but her body refused to obey, paralyzed by fear.

The man's hands moved to her ankles, and she felt the panic rising, a wave of pure, unadulterated fear crashing over her. He gripped her ankles firmly, dragging them toward the metal cuffs bolted into the ground at the foot of the mattress.

"No, please—" Brynlee's voice was a choked whisper, barely audible, but it didn't matter. He wasn't listening.

She kicked weakly, the last vestiges of her strength draining away with each futile attempt. He shook his head in disapproval. "Don't fight it. I'll make you happy, Brynlee. You'll see."

The words sent a shiver of revulsion through her. She bit back a sob, trying to keep her emotions in check, but the panic was like a wave, crashing over her, dragging her under. His hands moved with methodical precision, yanking her jeans down past her hips. She writhed in his grasp, but it was useless. He was stronger—so much stronger.

He leaned over her, his face inches from hers, and she felt his breath hot against her cheek. His hand wrapped around her throat, not tight enough to choke her, but just enough to make his dominance clear. "You'll be happier if you stop fighting," he whispered, his lips curling into a cruel smile. "You'll be mine. I'll take care of you."

Brynlee's vision blurred with tears. She felt herself sinking, the fear swallowing her whole. Every muscle in her body screamed at her to fight, to resist, but her mind was trapped in a suffocating fog. She lay still, allowing him to strip her, the humiliation and terror mixing into a toxic brew that paralyzed her.

"There we go," he cooed, his voice dripping with false tenderness. He smoothed his hand over her bare skin, and she fought back the bile rising in her throat. "That's better, sweetheart. See? Isn't it easier when you don't fight?"

The praise ignited something in her, a spark of anger that flickered weakly in the darkness. His touch, his words—they were a violation of everything she was, everything she had fought to hold on to. That spark flared, and her teeth clenched.

Burt leaned back, resting on his knees, his hands fumbling with his belt. The sound of the leather sliding through the loops echoed in the confined space, and Brynlee's heart pounded in her chest. She had to escape—had to get away—but how?

The soft rustle of fabric filled the air as he unzipped his pants, then shoved the material down.

And then, without thinking, Brynlee laughed.

It was a bitter, hollow sound, but it was the only weapon she had left. It burst out of her in a broken, jagged laugh that echoed off the walls. Burt Johnson froze, his eyes narrowing in confusion and anger. The look on his face only made her laugh harder.

"What the hell are you laughing at?" he hissed, his voice thick with rage.

Brynlee kept laughing, the sound spilling from her lips uncontrollably. It was the only way she knew how to fight back, the only way to push back against the overwhelming fear. She knew it wasn't real courage—it was a defense mechanism, a desperate attempt to distance herself from the horror unfolding around her. But it was all she had.

Johnson's face twisted in fury. "Shut up!" he barked, but she couldn't stop. The laughter poured out of her, mingling with tears, turning into something wild and unhinged. She could see the fury building in his eyes, the way his muscles tensed with the effort to contain it.

And then he snapped.

He lashed out, his fist connecting with her jaw. The force of the blow sent her head snapping to the side, pain exploding in her skull. Her laughter died instantly, replaced by a cry of pain as the taste of blood filled her mouth. He hit her again and again, each punch more vicious than the last. He was shouting something, but the words were a blur, lost in the ringing in her ears.

"Why are you doing this?" he screamed, his voice cracking with emotion. "Why are you always like this? Why am I never good enough?"

He kept hitting her, his fists pounding into her with a frenzied desperation, calling her by a name that wasn't hers, venting years of pent-up rage on her battered body. Brynlee felt her teeth rattle in her skull, the metallic taste of blood flooding her mouth. The world began to spin, her vision dimming at the edges. She was on the verge of losing consciousness when, suddenly, he stopped.

Burt stood over her, panting, his fists still clenched. He stared down at her, his face contorted with a mixture of satisfaction and disgust. "You'll learn," he muttered, his voice shaking. "You'll learn to be what I need."

He turned and stormed out of the basement, the heavy door slamming shut behind him. The sound echoed in the silence that followed, leaving Brynlee alone, her body throbbing with pain.

Relief washed over her in waves, mingling with the agony that wracked her frame. He was gone. For now, at least, she was safe. But she knew it wouldn't last. He would come back, and next time, she might not survive.

She had to escape.

With a groan, Brynlee forced herself to move, her limbs trembling with the effort. She couldn't let the fear control her

—not anymore. There had to be a way out, something she could use to free herself. She scanned the basement, her eyes searching for anything that could help.

She couldn't give up. Not now, not ever. She would find a way out. She had to. Her life depended on it.

CHAPTER
FORTY-FIVE

Tears coursed down her cheeks as she held her hands over her ears, desperately trying to block out the sounds of the man's grunts mingled with Fallon's soft cries.

Bile rose in her throat, and her stomach heaved, threatening to expel the contents of her stomach. She tamped down the urge, swallowing hard and turning her mind toward something—anything—else. Another shiver racked her body, and she imagined herself far away from here, where the sun warmed her skin.

Finally, after what felt like hours, the sounds just a few feet away subsided. Brynlee kept her head down, eyes closed. She couldn't bear to look. Not yet.

The soft scuffle of movement filled the air, the ancient springs of the mattress creaking as the man lifted himself away, then stood. She heard the soft purr of a zipper, and her stomach flipped once more. She had to get out of here. She had to save herself and Fallon before it was too late.

Suddenly, a low buzzing noise broke the quiet stillness of the basement. Brynlee peeked up at the man who paused, a frown creasing his brow as he pulled the phone from his pocket. Brynlee watched him, her heart hammering against her ribs, every nerve on edge.

The screen lit up, casting a bluish glow over his face, and surprise flickered across his features before it settled into something more guarded.

"Looks like we have visitors," he murmured quietly, almost to himself. His gaze drifted to Fallon, who was curled in a ball on the mattress, then over to Brynlee. For a moment, he seemed to be weighing his options, his lips pressed into a thin line.

Her stomach churned, a mixture of dread and hope washing over her. Who was here? Were they here to help? Did they suspect she was down here? She tried to keep her breathing steady, but the tightness in her chest made it difficult.

Without another word, Mr. Johnson moved swiftly, walking toward the large metal storage unit and grabbing an object from the rusty surface. As he drew closer, Brynlee saw that a strip of fabric dangled from his fingers. Before she could react, he shoved it into her mouth, the rough material scratching against her tongue as he gagged her. She tried to pull away, but the restraints held her fast, and she could only manage a muffled whimper as he secured the gag tightly around the back of her head.

"Not a sound," he whispered, his voice low and menacing. He moved to Fallon next, repeating the same action, gagging her with a practiced efficiency that sent a chill through Brynlee.

Mr. Johnson stepped back, surveying his work with a critical eye. Satisfied, he glanced at the stairs, his posture tense. "If either of you makes a noise," he warned, his tone deadly serious, "I'll kill you."

Brynlee's breath hitched, panic clawing at her insides. He didn't linger, didn't give her time to process his threat. He was already moving toward the stairs, his footsteps eerily quiet on the concrete floor. He climbed the steps quickly, then was gone, the basement door creaking shut behind him.

The sound of the bolt sliding into place echoed in Brynlee's ears, sealing their fate. But as the silence settled in once more, Brynlee's fear was slowly replaced by a burning determination. She wouldn't let him win. They had to get out of here. And somehow, she would find a way.

She began to thrash against the restraints, her body writhing as she tried to free herself. The leather cuffs bit into her skin, but she didn't care, her desperation giving her strength she didn't know she had. The gag muffled her screams, but she screamed anyway, a raw, frantic sound that tore from her throat as she struggled.

She kicked out with her legs, her movements wild and uncontrolled, and her foot collided with something solid. The bucket by the side of the mattress tipped over, clattering loudly as it hit the floor. Brynlee's heart leaped in her chest, hope flaring to life. Someone upstairs had to have heard that. They had to.

She stilled, her breath coming in harsh, ragged gasps behind the gag, and strained to listen. The silence was deafening, pressing in on her from all sides. She waited, every muscle tensed, hoping—praying—that there would be some response, some sign that whoever was upstairs had heard the noise.

But there was nothing. Just the oppressive silence and the faint hum of the house settling above her. No footsteps, no voices, no indication that anyone had noticed.

Despair crashed over her, dousing the fragile spark of hope she'd felt. She was still trapped, still helpless, and no one was coming to save her. Tears welled in her eyes, and she bit down hard on the gag, trying to hold back the sobs that threatened to overwhelm her. She couldn't afford to lose control, not now. She had to think, had to find another way.

Brynlee's mind raced, grasping for some plan, some way to signal for help, but the restraints held her in place, unyielding. She was running out of time, and the clock was ticking down with each passing second.

But then, in the distance, she heard something—faint, almost imperceptible. Footsteps? A muffled voice? Brynlee's breath hitched, and she strained to hear more, her ears pricked for any sign that someone was coming.

Her heart pounded in her chest, a frantic rhythm that echoed in her ears. Was it Mr. Johnson? Or had someone else come?

Her body trembled, every muscle quivering with tension, as she waited, poised on the edge of hope and despair. She had one chance. If someone was upstairs, if they could hear her, she had to make them realize something was wrong.

She began to kick again, her movements more calculated this time. She aimed for the bucket, trying to knock it against the wall, anything to make more noise. But her legs were tiring, the fight draining out of her with each failed attempt.

The basement door suddenly creaked open, and Brynlee froze, her blood turning to ice. Had they heard her? Or was it Mr. Johnson, returning to finish what he'd started?

She waited, her heart in her throat, as the footsteps descended the stairs. Her breath came in shallow, rapid gasps, her eyes wide with terror as she braced herself for what was coming. Would it be salvation, or another nightmare?

She was about to find out.

CHAPTER
FORTY-SIX

Dare glanced over at Sawyer as they entered the dimly lit office. "Tell me everything you know."

"Not much." Sawyer shook his head, but his heart and mind raced with fear. "I know she went to the salon today, just like she always does. I was surprised that she wasn't home, because—"

He trailed off, a sudden realization creeping up on him. His pulse quickened, and he straightened, his mind zeroing in on a detail he'd almost overlooked. "The salon," he said slowly. "There was that leak..."

Dare tipped his head in question, his brow furrowing. "Yeah, she mentioned it. But what does that have to do with her disappearance?"

Sawyer's thoughts were moving faster than his words could keep up. "The insurance claim," he said, the pieces falling into place. "She said she'd spoken with an insurance agent to assess the damage."

Dare's eyes narrowed as he caught on. "And she fits the profile of the other victims. Blonde hair, blue eyes..."

Sawyer didn't need any more prompting. He rushed over

to the nearest computer, his fingers flying over the keyboard as he accessed the insurance records. His heart pounded in his chest, the dread building with each passing second. He had to know who that agent was—had to find out if there was a connection.

Cam appeared in the doorway, and Dare turned his way. "What are you doing back here?"

"I heard something happened with Brynlee, so I told Kins I would come check it out." His brows pulled together as he glanced at Sawyer. "What's going on?"

Dare gave him a quick rundown, and Cam swore under his breath. "We think it's the same guy?"

"We're still waiting on Sterling to send over the info, so I can't be sure." Sawyer shook his head. "She stopped by one day, said she wanted to file a report because she thought the valve had been tampered with. She'd just spoken with the insurance adjuster, who said it was likely she wouldn't be covered, but I took down the info anyway, just in case."

The screen flickered, and the details of the insurance claim filled the screen. He scanned the document quickly, searching for the name. When he found it, a cold chill ran down his spine.

"Burt Johnson," he read aloud, his voice grim. "From Sterling Assurance."

Dare's face darkened at the name. "Check vehicle registrations."

He pulled up the database and typed in Johnson's information, and his breath caught as the screen loaded. He slid a look Dare's way. "He drives a 2012 Honda Civic—navy."

Cam arched a brow. "What do you want to bet we find a decal in the back window?"

"We need to talk to him—now."

Dare shook his head. "We need a warrant. If this guy is responsible, I don't want to tip him off."

Sawyer hopped up from the chair, anger and worry coursing through him. "I can't just leave her out there! What if he has her right now?"

Dare held up a hand. "I get it, I do. But we're still waiting on the insurance company to send over the claims from the other victims. We need more than this."

"He drives the same car that was seen at two different scenes," Sawyer fumed. "That should justify the warrant right there."

"And you think you're going to get the judge to sign off this time of night?" Dare's gaze flicked to the clock. "We need all the information we can get. We can't afford to let him slip through our fingers."

"He's right," Cam said softly. "If this is the guy…"

He trailed off, and Sawyer ran a hand through his hair. "We need to at least talk to him. Please. I need to see him."

Dare stared at him for a long minute, his expression implacable. "You understand what can happen."

It wasn't a question, and Sawyer's stomach tumbled. If Johnson got spooked, there was a good chance he would kill Brynlee to get rid of any evidence. But if she was there…

Sawyer swallowed hard and nodded. "We'll tell him it's routine, that we're just checking recent contacts."

Dare blew out a harsh breath. "Ainsley will have my fucking balls if anything happens to Brynlee."

"Same with Kins," Cam chimed in. "I'll get the warrant rolling. If too many of us show up, it's going to look suspicious. Just don't do anything stupid," he warned.

Sawyer shook his head. "I won't let anything happen to her—I promise."

Finally, after what seemed like forever, Dare nodded. "Let's go."

There was no time to waste. Sawyer grabbed his jacket, and they headed to the cruiser. The drive to Johnson's house felt like an eternity, the silence in the car heavy with tension. They arrived at the house just as dusk was settling in, the sky a deep shade of blue.

The house was unremarkable, a modest single-story home in a quiet neighborhood. But there was something about it that set Sawyer's nerves on edge. He couldn't shake the feeling that they were on the edge of something dark, something dangerous.

Dare knocked on the door, the sound echoing in the stillness. They waited, each second dragging on interminably, until finally, the door creaked open.

Burt Johnson stood in the doorway, and he offered them a politely curious smile. "Officers. What can I do for you?"

Sawyer stepped forward, his assessing gaze sweeping over the man in front of him. He guessed the man to be in his mid-forties, with thinning hair and a slight paunch. Three pale pink lines stood out against the pale flesh of his cheek. "Mr. Johnson, we're investigating a missing persons case, and we'd like to ask you a few questions."

Johnson didn't hesitate. "Of course, come in," he said, stepping aside to let them in. "I'm happy to help in any way I can."

The interior of the house was neat, almost sterile in its cleanliness. Sawyer's unease deepened, but he kept his expression neutral as they all took seats in the living room.

"Mr. Johnson," Dare began, his tone measured, "I believe you were recently in contact with a woman named Brynlee Layne."

Johnson's brow furrowed in apparent concern. "Yes, I remember Ms. Layne. A very unfortunate situation with her salon. I spoke with her about the damage a few weeks ago. Is she all right?"

Sawyer watched him carefully, looking for any signs of deception. But Johnson seemed genuinely concerned, his eyes reflecting a sincere sympathy. "I'm afraid she's gone missing," Dare said.

Johnson's expression shifted to one of shock. "Missing? That's terrible. I hope she's found safe."

"We're questioning everyone who's been in contact with her for the past several weeks," Dare continued. "Did you notice anything unusual at the salon?"

Johnson shook his head slowly, his gaze thoughtful. "Not really. She was understandably upset about the damage, but there was nothing out of the ordinary in our conversation. I filed the claim and moved on to the next case."

Sawyer felt a gnawing doubt in his gut. Johnson was too composed, too cooperative. But there was nothing concrete, nothing that screamed guilt. He exchanged a glance with Dare, whose gaze flicked to the fireplace.

Sawyer shifted so he could see better, then froze. There on the mantle were a handful of framed photographs. One in particular jumped out at him: a young girl, no more than three, with cerulean eyes and pale blonde hair.

Sawyer's mind spun as he listened to the conversation around him.

"We believe her disappearance might be connected to a few other women who were murdered recently. Can you tell me if you saw anyone hanging around?"

Johnson shook his head again, a somber expression on his face. "It's heartbreaking what happened to them. I wish I could offer more help, but I interacted with Ms. Layne only briefly. I didn't notice anything out of the ordinary that I remember."

"We appreciate your cooperation. And if you remember anything at all, please don't hesitate to reach out," Dare said as he pushed to his feet. "This is all routine, of course, but we might need to speak with you again as we continue our investigation."

"Of course," Johnson replied smoothly. "I'll do whatever I can to assist."

"Thank you for your time." Sawyer stood, then tipped his head toward the mantle. "Is that your daughter?"

Burt Johnson stared at the photo for a long moment, myriad emotions flickering across his face before he nodded. "Kyra. She was the light of my life." He glanced over at Sawyer. "She was killed by a drunk driver almost four years ago now."

Sawyer felt a twinge of sympathy move through his heart. "I'm so sorry for your loss."

"Thank you." Johnson led them toward the door. "The pain never really goes away, you know?"

"I'm sure," Sawyer murmured. He paused near the front door and turned toward the man. "I know a good grief counselor if you ever need one."

Johnson smiled, but it didn't reach his eyes. "Thank you, but... We all have our own ways of coping."

The man's words sent a chill down his spine. As they left the house, Sawyer's mind was a storm of conflicting thoughts. He seemed genuinely sympathetic, but something about the man didn't sit right with him.

"He's hiding something," Sawyer muttered as they walked back to the car. "Did you see those scratches on his face?"

Dare nodded slowly. "Lindsey?"

Sawyer's gut twisted. Now it all made sense. The killer had removed Lindsey's fingers posthumously because he couldn't risk them finding his DNA.

They were close—he could feel it. And he wasn't going to stop until he found Brynlee and put an end to whatever twisted game Johnson was playing.

CHAPTER
FORTY-SEVEN

Shivers racked Brynlee's body, each one sending a fresh wave of dread through her. The air in the basement was damp and cold, seeping into her bones and exacerbating the ache in her muscles from hours of captivity. She had lost track of time down here, in this hellish place where the darkness felt like a living thing, pressing in on her from all sides.

Her hands were bound with a thick nylon rope, the rough fibers digging into her skin with every slight movement. The rope was tethered to a metal ring bolted into the wall, giving her just enough slack to sit or lie down on the dirty mattress in the corner. She'd tested the strength of the tether several times, pulling with every ounce of strength she had left, but it held firm. Her captor had made sure there was no easy escape.

There was a small rectangular window high in the wall to her right, but it was too far away for her to reach. She hadn't even realized it was there until the first gray rays of dawn broke through the filthy, dirt-encrusted glass. She stared longingly at it, so close to freedom, yet still so far away.

She couldn't keep sitting here, waiting for whatever horrific fate awaited her. The fear that had initially paralyzed her had morphed into something sharper, more desperate. She had to get out. Brynlee forced herself to focus, her mind racing as she scanned the basement for anything she could use to her advantage.

She turned her gaze back to the tray of food beside the mattress, and her lip curled. Johnson had brought it down not long ago, the same time he'd removed their gags. He'd given Brynlee a hard look, then picked up the bucket she'd kicked over and moved it far away. With a final warning, he'd told them he had errands to run, and that he would be back later.

Her eyes fell on the spoon lying on the tray next to a lumpy bowl of oatmeal. The bowl was styrofoam, but the spoon was metal. She rolled her eyes. Probably so she couldn't break a plastic one and try to stab him with it. Because she absolutely would have.

As she stared at it, her mind began to whirl. She shuffled toward the edge of the mattress, her bound hands making the movement awkward and slow. When she finally reached it, she grabbed up the spoon, the cool weight of it in her palm sparking a tiny flicker of hope.

With a grunt of effort, she hurled the spoon at the window, aiming for the center of the glass. It pinged off, not even scratching the surface, then clattered to the floor next to Fallon's mattress.

Fallon sent a panicked look her way. "What are you doing? He'll hear you!"

"Do you really want to stay here and wait for him to come back?"

Fallon flinched at Brynlee's harsh words, but she couldn't tamp down the urgency that coursed through her. "He's never going to let you go, you know that. Whatever happens next will be worse. We have to try."

Fallon bit her lip, and Brynlee pressed on. "Please, Fallon. We need to get out of here. Give me the spoon."

Reluctantly, Fallon picked up the spoon and tossed it toward Brynlee. It landed on the mattress a few feet away, and she grabbed it up, then took aim again.

She threw it again, harder this time, using the rage and fear that boiled within her to fuel the throw. The spoon struck the glass with a sharp crack, and a small fissure appeared at the point of impact.

Hope exploded through her chest. "Again!"

Fallon passed her the spoon once more, and Brynlee gripped it hard as she scrambled to her feet, straining against the rope as she readied herself for another throw.

This time, she threw the spoon with everything she had. It hit the window dead center, and the glass shattered with a satisfying crash. Shards of glass rained down, a few pieces clattering to the basement floor, glittering like tiny diamonds in the dim light.

Fallon whipped her head toward Brynlee. "What do we do now?"

Brynlee didn't waste a second. She yanked up the threadbare sheet that had been tossed carelessly over the mattress, her breath coming in ragged gasps. Gripping the sheet tightly, she pulled it so it was taut, then threw it toward the broken window, using it to drag the shards of glass closer to her. She had to be careful; one wrong move and the glass could slice her open, but she was beyond caring. This was her only chance to free herself.

Slowly, painstakingly, she managed to pull a small shard of glass within reach. She picked it up, then tossed it toward Fallon. "Start cutting!"

She picked up another shard, the jagged edge biting into her palm as she positioned it against the rope binding her hands. She sawed at the rope with the glass, her hands trembling with the effort. Sweat mingled with the grime on her skin, her breath coming in harsh pants as she worked.

"Ow!" Fallon cried out and tears slipped down her cheeks as a rivulet of blood trickled down her arm. "I can't do it!"

"Yes, you can. I know it hurts," Brynlee said sharply, "but this is our only chance. Keep going."

Brynlee bit back her own cry of pain as the shard slipped and sliced her skin. Blood mingled with fluid as the ropes cut into her flesh, but she didn't dare stop.

Minutes felt like hours as she sawed, the sharp glass gradually cutting through the thick rope. Her hands were raw, her muscles screaming in protest, but the fear of being caught, of her captor returning before she was free, spurred her on. She couldn't let herself think about what would happen if she failed.

Finally, with one last desperate effort, the rope began to give way. The fibers frayed and snapped under the relentless assault of the glass shard, and with a final tug, the rope fell away from her wrists. Brynlee let out a choked sob of relief, tears blurring her vision as she flexed her hands, the circulation returning in painful tingles.

But she couldn't rest, not yet. She still needed to get out of the basement, out of this nightmare. Wiping her tears on the back of her hand, Brynlee clutched the shard of glass like a lifeline. Her hands might be free, but she was far from safe. She glanced up at the broken window, gauging the distance, the escape it promised.

She just had to figure out how to reach it before it was too late.

CHAPTER
FORTY-EIGHT

Everyone had come out in full force to join the search. Brynlee's friends and family had been questioned, but no one knew where she was. For the past several hours they'd been searching every part of town looking for her. Dare had explained to the Laynes that they had a person of interest, but it was better to be safe than sorry. Plus, it took the heat off Johnson for the time being.

Sawyer hoped like hell the distraction worked and lulled him into a false sense of security. He had a feeling Johnson was exactly the man they'd been looking for—they just needed a little more evidence.

Sawyer scrubbed a hand over his face and momentarily closed his eyes. They burned with fatigue, but he didn't dare give up. Not when it was Brynlee's life on the line. He'd spent hours going over every piece of information they had on Johnson—his work history, financial records, and even his social media activity—but nothing stood out as overtly suspicious.

Johnson was clean—too clean. But Sawyer knew better than to trust appearances; he had a gut feeling there was something buried in Johnson's past, something that could explain the connection between him and the missing women.

Sawyer dug deeper, searching for anything that might shed light on Johnson's life. It didn't take long before something caught his eye—a court record, dated almost five years ago. Sawyer clicked on the link, his pulse quickening as the document loaded.

It was a custody hearing.

The details of the case unfolded before him. Johnson had been married once, years ago. His wife, Rebecca, had filed for divorce after the death of their child—a daughter who had died in a tragic accident when she was only three years old. The loss had shattered their marriage, and within a year, Rebecca had moved on, remarried, and started a new family.

Sawyer's eyes narrowed as he continued reading. Rebecca had given birth to a child, another little girl, with her new husband just over a year ago—right around the same time that Jayla Simms had gone missing.

Sawyer leaned back in his chair, the pieces starting to come together in his mind. Johnson had lost everything—his child, his wife, his family. Rebecca had moved on, but Johnson hadn't. He'd been left alone, his life unraveling while she rebuilt hers. And then, women with a certain look—blonde hair, blue eyes, young—had started to disappear.

They all looked eerily similar to Johnson's ex-wife, Rebecca.

Sawyer's heart raced as the implications of his discovery sank in. What if Johnson had been trying to recreate the family he'd lost? What if he was targeting women who reminded him of Rebecca, trying to make them fit the mold of the life he'd once had? The thought was chilling, but it made a twisted kind of sense.

His mind flashed to the autopsy reports. Lindsey Gill had a birth control implant removed from her arm—carefully, almost surgically. At the time, it had struck the medical examiner as strange, but without context, it hadn't made much sense. But now, with what Sawyer had learned, it painted a horrifying picture.

Had Johnson been trying to get Lindsey pregnant? Was he trying to recreate the family he lost by forcing these women into roles they didn't want, roles they couldn't fill?

Sawyer's stomach turned as he thought about Hilary Swanson. She'd been pregnant when she died, supposedly miscarried due to the stress her captor had put her through. Had she been another attempt? Another failed attempt at Johnson's twisted dream?

And what about Jayla Simms? Her autopsy hadn't shown anything indicative of pregnancy, but maybe she hadn't lived up to Johnson's delusion either. Maybe when the women didn't fulfill his expectations, when they couldn't be the perfect wife and mother he was trying to force them to be, he eliminated them.

Sawyer pushed back from the desk, pacing the small office as the pieces of the puzzle clicked into place. They needed to act, and fast. If Johnson was indeed the man behind these murders, there was no telling what he might do next—especially with Brynlee's life hanging in the balance.

He tapped the button to print off the paperwork, then grabbed it up and moved toward Dare's office. Cam had gone home to be with Kinley and get some rest, but he'd seen Dare prowling restlessly through the station several times over the course of the night.

Sawyer jerked to a stop when he saw Ainsley curled up in a chair next to Dare's. Her eyes, drowsy with exhaustion, flew wide at the sight of him. "Did you find something?"

"Maybe." He flicked a look at Dare, who took his cue to excuse himself.

Dare pushed from the chair and dropped a kiss on Ainsley's head. "I'll be right back, sweetheart."

Ainsley watched them intently as Dare crossed the room, and they made their way to the interview room next door. Dare closed the door and turned to him. "What did you find?"

Sawyer spread the papers on the table. "Remember that photo on the mantle? Johnson lost his daughter to a drunk driver almost five years ago. His wife left him, remarried, had another kid—another little girl. The women he's been targeting—they all look like his ex-wife and the daughter he lost. I think he's trying to recreate his family."

Dare's face twisted. "That's... sick. But it makes sense. It explains the removal of Lindsey Gill's birth control implant."

Sawyer nodded. "Exactly. He removed it—probably to try and get her pregnant. Hilary was already pregnant when she died. Maybe the others didn't live up to his delusion, and he—"

"Eliminated them," Dare finished, his voice cold. "Fuck. We need the damn list from the insurance company."

Sawyer flicked a look at the clock. Dawn was fast approaching. "We don't have time. I'll go see if we can get the search warrant rolling."

He snatched up his keys and headed for the door, his blood thrumming in his veins. He could only hope they weren't too late.

CHAPTER
FORTY-NINE

The glass shard finally sliced through the last strand of the rope, and Brynlee's wrists fell free. A gasp of disbelief escaped her lips, quickly followed by a surge of hope that felt like a wildfire igniting in her chest. She stared at her raw, trembling hands, barely able to believe she'd done it. But there was no time to savor the victory. She had to move. Now.

She cast a quick glance at the broken window, the only possible escape from this nightmare. It was a tight, rectangular opening, barely wide enough for her to squeeze through, but it was her only chance. Brynlee knew she couldn't afford to waste a second.

Wincing at the pain in her hands, she picked up the threadbare sheet she had used earlier. Carefully, she folded it over and began sweeping the shards of glass from the floor beneath the window, pushing them into the corner as best as she could.

Fallon glanced over at her, eyes large and full of tears. "Wait! I'm not ready yet!"

"Keep going," Brynlee urged. "I'm going to get the glass out of the way, then we need to get out of here."

With the glass mostly out of the way, she turned her attention to the window itself. The broken glass was still embedded in the frame, jagged edges waiting to tear into her flesh if she wasn't careful. Grabbing up the bucket, she turned it upside down and placed it beneath the window, then climbed on top. She used the sheet to knock out as many pieces as she could, wincing as a few larger shards clattered to the floor beneath her.

"Come on, Fallon!"

Brynlee folded the sheet several times and draped it over the windowsill. The fabric was thin, but it would cushion the sharp edges and give them something to grip onto as they climbed. The window was high up, and the concrete block wall was smooth and unyielding, but she couldn't let that stop her.

"Almost there!" Fallon called, her voice cracking with fear. "Don't leave me!"

"I won't. I'll go first, then help pull you out."

Taking a deep breath, Brynlee braced herself and jumped, fingers grabbing the outside edge of the windowsill. The muscles in her arms screamed in protest as she pulled herself up, her feet scrabbling against the wall for purchase. She managed to hook one leg over the sill, then the other, her breath coming in short, panicked gasps as she squeezed her body through the narrow opening.

She could feel the cold early morning air on her face, and goosebumps broke out over her skin, but a smile split her face. She was almost there!

Suddenly, the sound of a door slamming open, followed by the heavy tread of footsteps pounding on the stairs reached her ears.

"Brynlee!"

Fallon's panicked cry was right behind her, and her blood ran cold, panic surging through her veins as she twisted her body, trying to wriggle through the rest of the way before he reached her.

"Get back here!" The man's voice was a harsh growl as he grabbed her hips, his fingers digging in like claws.

Pain and fear exploded outward, and she screamed. "Help! Somebody, please!"

She kicked wildly, trying to push herself out the window, but her body was wedged in tight, her hips caught in the narrow frame. She felt his hands on her legs, strong and unforgiving as they yanked her back.

"No!" Brynlee shrieked, thrashing against him with every ounce of strength she had left. "Help!"

But it was no use. He was too strong, his grip like iron as he dragged her back inside, the stars disappearing from view as her head was pulled through the window.

He threw her to the floor with a vicious force, her body hitting the ground with a thud that knocked the breath from her lungs. She barely had time to catch her breath before he was on her, his fists raining down on her in a flurry of blows. Pain exploded in her head, her vision going white with each strike.

"Stupid bitch!" he snarled, his voice a low, dangerous rumble. "You think you can just leave me? After everything I've done for you?"

Brynnlee tried to curl into a ball, to protect herself from the onslaught, but the blows kept coming, relentless and brutal. She could taste blood in her mouth, feel it trickling down her face. Her body screamed in agony, every nerve ending alight with pain. She could feel her strength fading, her consciousness slipping as her vision blurred at the edges.

"You're just like the others," he hissed, his voice full of venom. "But you won't get away from me. None of you ever do."

The last thing Brynlee saw before the darkness claimed her

was his face, twisted in rage and something else—something almost like despair. Then, with one final, brutal blow, everything went black.

CHAPTER
FIFTY

Sawyer gripped the warrant in his hand, his knuckles white with tension. The ink on the paper was still fresh, the official stamp barely dry. He glanced at Cam and Dare, their grim expressions mirroring his own. They all knew time was running out.

Without a word, the three men climbed into Sawyer's car, the engine roaring to life as they pulled out of the station parking lot. The drive to Burt Johnson's house felt both too long and too short, every second ticking away like a countdown in Sawyer's head. The implications of what they might find weighed heavily on them. Brynlee's face flashed in Sawyer's mind, her smile, her laughter—memories now tainted with the stark reality of her abduction.

As they sped down the road, Dare's phone rang, the sharp sound slicing through the tense silence. He hit the Bluetooth button to answer.

"Jenson.

"Sheriff, we just got a call from a neighbor near the Johnson place," the dispatcher's voice crackled through the speaker. "They reported hearing screaming coming from his house. We're sending units, but you're closest. You need to get there, now."

The engine roared as Dare pressed down on the accelerator and the cruiser lurched forward. The drive was a blur of lights and speed, and every second that passed felt like an eternity, the fear clawing at Sawyer's gut.

They screeched to a halt outside Johnson's house, tires skidding on the gravel. The place was dark, the curtains drawn, but the air was thick with the oppressive silence that spoke of something horribly wrong. Sawyer's pulse pounded in his ears as he jumped out of the car, his eyes scanning the house for any sign of movement.

"I've got the back." He didn't wait for a response as he took off around the house. A broken window low to the ground caught his attention, and he cautiously skirted it, pistol aimed at the black space.

He hopped up the two steps that led to the back door, waiting for Dare's call.

"Johnson!" Dare bellowed, his fist pounding against the wood. "Sheriff's department! Open up!"

There was no answer. The only sound was the creaking of the porch under their feet and the distant chirping of crickets. Sawyer's heart raced as a muffled sound lilted on the air.

"Going in," cam Dare's voice.

Sawyer tested the doorknob. Locked.

He dropped back, then kicked the door with all the force he could muster. The wood splintered under the impact, the door flying open with a loud crack.

They stormed inside, weapons drawn, the beam of their flashlights cutting through the darkness as they cleared the house. The interior was eerily quiet, the only sound their heavy breathing and the distant hum of the refrigerator. But Sawyer could feel it—the wrongness, the sense of something sinister lurking just beneath the surface.

"Basement," Cam muttered, nodding toward a door at the end of the hallway. There was a faint sound, almost imperceptible, but enough to set their instincts on edge.

Sawyer led the way, his grip tight on his weapon as they descended the narrow staircase. The air grew colder as they went deeper, the scent of damp earth and something metallic filling their nostrils.

As they reached the bottom, the scene that met their eyes was a nightmare made real.

Burt Johnson stood in the middle of the basement, his back to them, his hands still clenched in fists. In front of him, two women lay crumpled on the floor, their bodies bruised and broken. One was Brynlee, her blonde hair matted with blood, her face pale and lifeless. The other was a woman they hadn't expected to find—Fallon, the missing woman they'd been searching for.

Dare moved with a speed that belied his size, tackling Johnson to the ground before the man could even react. The struggle was brief, Dare's years of training overpowering Johnson's deranged strength. Cam snapped the cuffs around the man's wrists, then they hauled him to his feet as Dare read him his rights, the words barely registering in the chaos.

But Sawyer had eyes only for Brynlee. He dropped to his knees beside her, his hands shaking as he checked for a pulse. Relief washed over him when he felt the faint throb beneath her skin, but it was weak—too weak. Her breathing was shallow, each breath a struggle.

"Bryn," he whispered, his voice thick with emotion. "Hang on, okay? Just hang on."

Gently, but with an urgency that bordered on desperation, Sawyer scooped Brynlee into his arms. Her body was limp, her head lolling against his chest as he carried her out of the basement, his heart breaking with every step. She was so light, so fragile—nothing like the vibrant, strong woman he knew.

Behind him, Cam was doing the same with Fallon, his face a mask of grim determination. They had to get them out of here, had to get them to safety before it was too late.

"Medic!" Sawyer shouted as they emerged from the house, his voice carrying across the yard. The wail of sirens grew louder as the ambulance skidded to a stop, EMTs rushing to meet them.

"Over here!" Cam called out, laying Fallon down on a stretcher as the medics took over. Sawyer did the same with Brynlee, his hands lingering on her for a moment longer before he was forced to let go.

"She's got a pulse, but it's weak," one of the medics said, checking Brynlee's vitals. "We need to move, now!"

Sawyer didn't hesitate, climbing into the back of the ambulance beside her. He couldn't let her out of his sight, not after everything that had happened. Cam climbed into the other ambulance with Fallon, his expression grim.

As the doors slammed shut and the ambulance sped toward the hospital, Sawyer kept his eyes on Brynlee, praying she would pull through. The ride was a blur of flashing lights and frantic voices, every bump in the road sending a jolt of fear through him. He held her hand, willing her to hold on, to fight.

They reached the hospital in record time, the medics rushing Brynlee and Fallon into the ER as doctors and nurses descended on them. Sawyer was forced to stay behind, pacing the waiting room, every minute that passed feeling like an eternity. Cam joined him, his face ashen, but they didn't speak. There was nothing to say.

All they could do was wait, and hope that they hadn't been too late.

CHAPTER
FIFTY-ONE

Sawyer stood outside Brynlee's hospital room, the fluorescent lights casting a harsh glow on the linoleum floor. He could hear the faint hum of the machines inside, the steady beep of monitors tracking her vitals.

But each time he reached for the door, her family blocked his way with gentle, pitying expressions that made his stomach twist.

"Thank you for coming, Sawyer," Mrs. Layne had said the first time, her voice kind but tinged with regret. "But Brynlee's not ready yet. She needs more time."

Time. It was always the same. Every visit, every attempt to see her, was met with the same soft apologies, the same promises that she just needed a little longer. But the hurt in Sawyer's chest only deepened, each rejection feeling like a knife twisting in his heart. Why the hell wouldn't she see him?

He had spent every waking moment thinking about her, worrying over her, reliving the horror of finding her bruised and broken in that basement. He had carried her out, held her in his arms as he begged her to stay with him, to keep fighting. And now, when she was safe, when he needed to see for himself that she was going to be okay, she wouldn't even look at him.

Sawyer clenched his fists, his jaw tightening with frustration. He understood trauma, understood that she'd been through hell, but it didn't make it any easier to swallow. Every time he was turned away, it felt like she was slipping further away from him, like he was losing her all over again.

The last few days had been a whirlwind, a chaotic blur of interrogations, arrests, and reports. Elisa Travers had finally cracked, admitting to every vile act she had committed against Brynlee. She had sabotaged Brynlee's salon, tampered with her car, drugged her at the bar, and even killed her cat—all out of jealousy.

During the interview, Elisa had ranted about how Zane was always comparing her to Brynlee, how he still wanted Brynlee back. Her jealousy had consumed her, turned her into someone capable of unspeakable acts. And for what? Sawyer couldn't wrap his head around the sheer madness of it.

Burt Johnson, on the other hand, had been a tougher nut to crack. He hadn't admitted a thing, not that he needed to. The evidence was overwhelming. DNA from all of the victims had been found in the basement of his home, and Fallon had provided a detailed statement that left little room for doubt. Johnson was done for, his sick fantasies and twisted desires finally exposed for the world to see.

Brookhaven was at peace, the storm that had wreaked havoc on the small town finally dissipating. People were moving on, trying to forget the horrors that had unfolded in their own backyard. But Sawyer couldn't move on. Not without seeing Brynlee, without hearing her voice, without knowing where they stood.

He leaned against the cold wall outside her room, running a hand through his hair. His mind was a tangled mess of anger and confusion. He had been there for her, had fought for her, and now she was shutting him out. What was he supposed to do with that?

"Reed?" A voice interrupted his thoughts, and he looked up to see Dare standing a few feet away, his expression sympathetic. "You okay?"

Sawyer shook his head, a bitter laugh escaping his lips. "Not really."

Dare nodded, understanding without prying. He had been there, had seen the raw emotion in Sawyer's eyes as he carried Brynlee out of that house. "She'll come around, Sawyer. She just needs time."

"That's what they keep telling me," Sawyer muttered, his frustration boiling over. "But what if she doesn't? What if she never wants to see me again?"

Dare sighed, stepping closer. "She's been through a lot. More than most people can even imagine. She's scared, maybe even ashamed. It's not about you, Sawyer. It's about her trying to piece herself back together."

Sawyer knew Dare was right, but it didn't make it any easier. He had faced down killers, navigated some of the darkest corners of humanity, but this—being shut out—was something he wasn't prepared for.

"She'll see you when she's ready," Dare continued quietly. "And when she does, you'll be there for her, just like you always have been."

Sawyer nodded, the anger and hurt still simmering beneath the surface. He wanted to believe Dare, wanted to hold on to the hope that Brynlee would eventually let him in. But each day that passed made that hope a little harder to cling to.

"Yeah," he said finally, his voice low. "I just wish I knew when that would be."

Dare gave him a pat on the back before heading down the hall, leaving Sawyer alone with his thoughts. He stared at the door to Brynlee's room for a long moment, his heart aching with the weight of everything he couldn't say to her.

Finally, with a heavy sigh, he turned and walked away, the sound of his footsteps echoing down the sterile corridor. He would give her time, as much as she needed. But deep down, he feared that time might be the one thing that would push them further apart.

CHAPTER
FIFTY-TWO

Sheriff Dare Jensen stepped into Brynlee's hospital room, his boots scuffing lightly against the sterile linoleum floor. The room was quiet, save for the soft hum of machines and the muted beeping of the heart monitor. Brynlee lay in the bed, her face pale against the white sheets, her eyes closed as if trying to block out the world.

Dare hesitated for a moment, taking in the fragile sight of her. He had seen her grow up, watched her go from a carefree girl to the strong, independent woman she was today. But now, she looked so small, so vulnerable. It was a stark contrast to the Brynlee he knew, the one who always had a quick smile and a sharp retort.

She stirred as he approached, her eyes fluttering open. When she saw him, she managed a weak smile, though it didn't reach her eyes.

"Sheriff," she greeted softly, her voice hoarse from disuse.

"Hey, Bryn," Dare replied, pulling up a chair beside her bed. He settled in, trying to keep his tone light. "How you holding up?"

Brynlee shrugged, the movement small, almost imperceptible. "I'm still here."

Dare nodded, knowing better than to push. He glanced around the room, searching for a way to ease into the conversation.

"Sawyer wanted to come," Dare began slowly. "I know you don't want to see him right now. He understands. He just wants to make sure you're okay."

Brynlee's expression tightened, and she looked away, her fingers picking at the edge of the blanket. "I can't see him, Dare. Not like this."

Dare dropped into the chair next to the bed. "I get it, Bryn. You've been through hell, and you're still dealing with it. But you should know, he's not going anywhere. He'll be waiting for you when you're ready."

She didn't respond, just kept her gaze focused on the blanket, her fingers stilling.

Dare sighed, deciding it was time to share the news he'd come to deliver. "I wanted to let you know we figured out what caused the leak at your salon."

That got her attention. Her eyes flicked up to meet his, a flash of curiosity breaking through the numbness. "What was it?"

"Elisa," Dare said, his tone grim. "Zane's new girlfriend. She's the one who cut the brake lines on your car too, and drugged you at the bar."

Brynlee's eyes widened in shock, her breath catching in her throat. "What? Why?"

"Apparently, Zane still had feelings for you," Dare explained gently. "Each time he brought your things back, he was hoping to see you again, maybe even work things out. Elisa didn't take too kindly to that. She decided to take matters into her own hands."

Brynlee's face paled further, and she looked down, her

hands clenching into fists. "I didn't... I never wanted him back. I never gave him any reason to think..."

"I know," Dare said quickly. "This isn't your fault, Brynlee. None of it is. Zane made his choices, and Elisa made hers. They're the ones responsible, not you."

She nodded slowly, the information sinking in. "Thank you for telling me."

Dare smiled faintly, relieved that she was taking it as well as could be expected. "You're welcome. We're going to make sure she pays for what she did."

Brynlee swallowed hard, the weight of it all pressing down on her. After a long moment, she looked up at him again, her eyes searching his. "How's Sawyer?"

Dare's heart ached at the vulnerability in her voice. "He's holding up okay," he replied honestly. "But he's worried about you. Wants to see you for himself."

She shook her head quickly, the panic returning to her eyes. "I can't. Not yet."

Dare nodded, understanding. He stood up, giving her hand a reassuring pat. "It's okay. He'll wait. You take all the time you need."

Brynlee's lips trembled, and she gave him a small, grateful smile. "Thanks, Dare."

He smiled back, though it didn't reach his eyes. "You take care, Bryn. And remember, when you're ready—he'll be there."

With that, Dare turned and left the room, leaving Brynlee alone with her thoughts. She had a long road ahead of her, but he also knew that with time, she'd find her way back. And when she did, Sawyer would be there, just like he promised.

The drive home from the hospital felt like an eternity. Brynlee sat in the back seat of the Laynes' car, her head resting against the cool glass of the window, watching the world blur past. Her body was physically present, but her mind was elsewhere, lost in the dark labyrinth of her thoughts.

Mrs. Layne kept glancing back at her, concern etched into every line of her face. "Are you sure you're okay, sweetheart?" she asked gently, her voice tinged with worry.

Brynlee managed a small nod, not trusting herself to speak. She wasn't okay—far from it—but she couldn't bring herself to say the words. The pain, the fear, the overwhelming sense of violation—it all swirled inside her, too vast to put into words.

Her father drove in silence, his hands gripping the steering wheel a little too tightly. He was trying to be strong for her, but she could see the tension in his shoulders, the way his jaw was set in a hard line. They had both been so kind, so supportive, but all she wanted was to be alone.

When they finally pulled up to her duplex, Brynlee felt a strange sense of relief mingled with fear.

"Do you need anything before we go?" Mrs. Layne asked as they helped her out of the car and up to her door.

Brynlee shook her head, fumbling with her keys as she tried to keep the tears at bay. "No, I'm fine. I just... I need to rest."

They exchanged a look, both of them clearly reluctant to leave her alone, but they respected her wishes. "Okay, honey," Mrs. Layne said softly. "We'll be just a phone call away if you need anything. No matter what time it is... You're always more than welcome to call or come over."

"I won't," Brynlee whispered, though she knew she wouldn't. She couldn't. She needed to be alone, to retreat into herself where it was safe.

She forced a smile, a ghost of her former self, and watched

as they reluctantly left. The moment their car disappeared down the street, she quickly stepped inside and locked the door behind her, the sound of the deadbolt clicking into place oddly satisfying.

Brynlee leaned her back against the door, her heart pounding in her chest as she surveyed the small, cozy space that had once been her sanctuary. Now, it felt suffocating, the walls closing in around her. She took a deep breath and walked to the windows, yanking the curtains closed with trembling hands. She couldn't stand the thought of anyone seeing her, of the outside world intruding on her fragile sense of control.

The silence in the house was deafening. It pressed in on her from all sides, amplifying the memories she was trying so desperately to keep at bay. The basement, the ropes cutting into her skin, the terror that had consumed her—it was all too vivid, too fresh. She sank down onto the couch, her body curling in on itself as if she could make herself disappear.

She didn't even want to think about the salon. That was where it all started, where everything had gone so horribly wrong. If it weren't for that damn leak, she never would have met Burt Johnson. She never would have been kidnapped, never would have endured the horrors that followed. The very thought of stepping foot back in that place made her stomach churn.

Thankfully, Melanie had taken charge. Brynlee had received a text earlier letting her know that all her appointments had been canceled for the foreseeable future. Melanie was handling everything, ensuring that the business didn't fall apart in her absence. It was a small comfort, knowing that at least one part of her life was being taken care of, but it didn't erase the guilt she felt for abandoning her clients, her responsibilities.

But she couldn't face it. She wasn't ready to step back into the world, to pretend that everything was okay when it wasn't. Not yet.

Brynlee buried her face in her hands, her body trembling as the tears finally came. She cried for everything she had lost, for the sense of safety that had been ripped away from her, for the woman she used to be and wasn't sure she'd ever find again.

And as she cried, the darkness in her mind deepened, swallowing her whole.

CHAPTER
FIFTY-THREE

Sawyer paced in his living room, glancing out the window every few minutes like a restless caged animal. He hadn't seen Brynlee in almost a week—not since she'd been released from the hospital. The memory of her pale, bruised face as she hobbled into her duplex was seared into his mind, and it gnawed at him every day. He couldn't stand it anymore, the not knowing, the helplessness.

Her family came and went, but their visits were always brief. A car would pull up, a figure would disappear inside, and not long after, they'd be gone, leaving Brynlee alone again. It was as if she was pulling herself deeper and deeper into a shell, and no one could reach her.

Every morning, he'd check the backyard, hoping to see her outside, hoping for some sign of life. But all he found were her flowers, once vibrant and full of color, now withering and dying. He'd tried to care for them, watering them when he could, but he wasn't sure it made a difference. They seemed as lifeless as Brynlee had become.

His patience was wearing thin. She was shutting herself off from the world, and it was killing him to watch it happen. He knew she was hurting, but the longer she stayed hidden away, the more he feared she'd never come back. The thought of losing her—truly losing her—was unbearable.

By the time the sun had dipped low in the sky, casting long shadows across the yard, Sawyer had made up his mind. He couldn't just sit and wait any longer. Fuck it. If Brynlee wouldn't come to him, he'd go to her.

Less than a minute later he found himself at her back door. This time, he didn't bother knocking. He hesitated only briefly before reaching for his lock-picking kit, an old skill he'd picked up years ago. He knew it was a breach of trust, but he couldn't shake the feeling that she needed him more than she needed her privacy right now.

The lock gave way with a soft click, and he pushed the door open, then stepped inside. The house was eerily quiet, the air heavy with the scent of lavender and something else—something that made his stomach turn with worry. The curtains were drawn tight, blocking out any hint of daylight, leaving the room shrouded in shadows.

His heart pounded as he moved through the house, his footsteps muffled by the thick carpet. The living room was dark, the only light coming from the flicker of the television, casting a dim glow across the room. And there, on the couch, curled up in a ball, was Brynlee.

She was wrapped in a blanket, her body hidden beneath layers of pajamas, her face pale against the dark fabric. But it wasn't her appearance that stopped him in his tracks—it was her hair. It was bright pink, a shocking, vibrant color that stood out in the gloom.

Sawyer's breath caught in his throat. Brynlee had always had a flair for the dramatic, but this... this was different. This was a cry for help.

He forced himself to act calm, to keep his voice steady.

"What the hell happened to you, Bryn? You look like a Troll doll."

Her eyes snapped open, the fire in them unmistakable despite the shadows under her eyes. "Fuck you, Sawyer," she spat, her voice hoarse.

Sawyer bit back the urge to soften his tone, to tell her everything would be okay. Instead, he pushed her, knowing she needed to release whatever was boiling inside. "Is this your grand plan? Lock yourself away, let everything fall apart, and pretend like it doesn't matter?"

She glared at him, sitting up slowly, her movements sluggish and heavy. "You don't know anything about what I'm going through."

"Maybe not," he shot back, taking a step closer. "But I know this isn't you. You're not the type to hide, Bryn. You're stronger than this. Why the hell won't you fight?"

She swung at him then, and her hand connected with his cheek, the slap echoing through the small space. "I hate you!"

"Stop acting like a damn coward!" he goaded her.

A scream of rage welled up her throat as she launched herself forward and pummeled his chest. Her eyes filled with tears, and she tried to blink them away, but it was too late. The walls she'd built around herself began to crumble, and she finally broke.

Sawyer caught her as she collapsed into his arms, sobs wracking her body. She buried her face in his chest, her fingers clutching at his shirt as if he was the only thing keeping her from drowning.

He held her tight, his hand stroking her back in soothing circles as he whispered in her ear. "I'm here, honey. I'm always here."

Brynlee's sobs finally quieted, leaving only the sound of their breathing, the echo of her pain lingering between them.

The room was still, the air heavy with unspoken words and raw emotion. Sawyer held her close, feeling the rapid thud of her heart against his chest, matching the frantic beat of his own.

He wasn't sure who moved first—whether it was him leaning down or her reaching up—but the next thing he knew, Brynlee's lips were on his, her hands gripping the back of his neck as if she couldn't bear to let go. The kiss was desperate, fueled by everything they'd been holding back, a collision of anger, sadness, and something far more primal.

Sawyer let her take control, surrendering to the force of her need. This wasn't the time for questions or doubts. Brynlee needed this—needed him—and he was powerless to deny her. Her fingers tangled in his hair, pulling him down to her, and he followed willingly, their bodies pressed together in a fevered embrace.

They stumbled toward the bedroom, the path familiar yet charged with a new urgency. Clothes were shed in hurried motions, discarded carelessly onto the floor as they lost themselves in each other. There was no finesse, no slow build-up—just a fast and frantic coming together, a release of all the pent-up emotion that had been simmering beneath the surface.

Sawyer felt her nails dig into his back, the sting grounding him in the whirlwind of sensations. Her breaths came in quick gasps, mixing with his own as they moved together, the intensity of it all almost too much to bear. But he didn't stop, couldn't stop, until finally, they reached the edge together, collapsing into each other as the tension shattered and left them spent.

They lay tangled in the sheets, both exhausted and sated, the remnants of their passion still crackling in the air. Sawyer held her tight, his arms wrapped around her as if he could keep her safe from everything that threatened to tear her apart.

He didn't want to let go, didn't want to lose this moment, this connection that felt so fragile and yet so vital.

She was nestled against his chest, her head resting just below his chin, her breathing slowly returning to normal. He could feel the dampness of her hair against his skin, the vivid pink strands a stark contrast to the darkness that surrounded them.

"You really do look like a Troll," he murmured, his voice thick with affection.

Brynlee snorted, her hand reaching up to playfully tug at the hair on his chest. "You're such an ass."

"Ow!" Sawyer couldn't help but smile as he untangled her fingers and pressed a kiss to the top of her head. "I didn't say it was a bad thing. You know, I always thought the pink one was the cutest."

She huffed a laugh, the sound soft and real, and it was like a balm to his soul. Her body trembled slightly, and he could feel the tension in her muscles, like she was bracing herself for something. Sawyer tightened his hold a fraction, pulling her the tiniest bit closer.

"It's only temporary," she murmured. "I just... I couldn't just go on like nothing happened."

She sighed deeply, pulling away just enough to look up at him. Her eyes were red-rimmed, the remnants of tears clinging to her lashes. But there was a new determination in her gaze, a need to unburden herself, and Sawyer knew better than to interrupt.

Brynlee swallowed hard, her fingers nervously twisting the edge of the sheet. "Blonde hair, blue eyes. I fit his type perfectly." Her voice cracked, and she blinked back tears. "After everything, I just couldn't stand it. I had to change. I had to do something drastic to feel like I had some control."

Sawyer's heart ached as he listened to her. He hadn't realized the depth of her trauma, the way it had seeped into every aspect of her life, forcing her to take drastic measures just to feel safe again. He reached out, brushing a strand of her newly pink hair behind her ear, his touch gentle, reassuring.

"I thought if I changed my hair, maybe... maybe I wouldn't feel so vulnerable," she continued, her voice gaining strength as she spoke. "Maybe it would erase what happened."

Sawyer remained silent, letting her speak, knowing she needed to get it all out.

Her voice grew softer, haunted. "I remember being in that basement. It was so cold... I thought I was going to die down there."

Sawyer's chest tightened as her words cut through him. He could see the fear in her eyes, the way the memory of it all still had a hold on her. She was trying so hard to be strong, but the weight of what she had endured was too much for anyone to bear alone.

"I was so scared, Sawyer. He made me watch... Him and Fallon... It was awful. And I felt so relieved when he didn't... " Tears welled up in Brynlee's eyes, and her voice broke as she continued. "But then I felt guilty, too, because... He hurt her so badly. I can still hear it..."

Another shiver racked her body. "All I could think about was getting out, getting us away from there. I thought... I thought I'd never see you again."

That last admission shattered something inside Sawyer. He pulled her back into his arms, holding her as tightly as he could without hurting her. He could feel the shudders running through her, the way she clung to him as if he were the only thing keeping her from falling apart.

"I'm so sorry, Bryn," he whispered, his voice thick with emotion. "I should have been there. I should have—"

"No," she interrupted, shaking her head against his chest. "This isn't your fault. None of it is. You saved me. You got me out of there."

Sawyer felt helpless, the agony of her pain cutting through him like a knife. He wished he could go back in time, do something—anything—to spare her from what she'd endured. But all he could do now was hold her, keep her close, and let her know she wasn't alone.

"I'm here," he murmured, pressing his lips to the top of her head. "I'll always be here, Bryn. You don't have to go through this alone."

Brynlee's tears slid free, her body trembling in his arms. He stroked her hair, feeling the unfamiliar texture of the dye beneath his fingertips, a reminder of the lengths she'd gone to in an attempt to reclaim some sense of control.

"It doesn't matter what color your hair is," he whispered. "You're still you. You're still Brynlee, and you're stronger than you know."

She didn't respond, but she didn't need to. The way she relaxed against him, the way her breathing slowly evened out, told him that, for now, she felt safe.

And that was all he wanted—to give her that small piece of peace in a world that had tried so hard to take it away from her.

CHAPTER
FIFTY-FOUR

Brynlee sat on the edge of the couch, staring at the walls that had become her refuge over the past few weeks. She had barely ventured out since leaving the hospital, the thought of facing the world again filling her with a gnawing anxiety. But she knew she couldn't stay hidden forever. Life had to go on, even if it meant confronting the things she wanted to forget.

A knock on the door broke her thoughts, sending her pulse into a tailspin. She closed her eyes. No. It was over. She had nothing to worry about anymore.

Pushing down the fear, she swallowed hard and stood, then moved toward the door. Her hand froze on the knob, and she drew in a deep breath before opening it. Zane stood on the other side, his expression a mix of guilt and regret.

"Hey, Bryn," he said softly, his eyes searching hers. "Can I come in for a sec?"

"Zane," she replied, forcing a small smile. "Come in."

He stepped inside, his movements hesitant, as if unsure of his place. He had been a part of her life for so long, but now, with everything that had happened, the distance between them felt insurmountable.

"I wanted to talk to you," Zane began, his voice tight. "To apologize. For everything."

Brynlee nodded, her heart aching with the weight of their shared history. She could see the remorse in his eyes, the regret for what his relationship with Elisa had cost them both.

"I'm sorry, too," she said, meaning it. "But we need to move on, Zane. I need to move on."

Zane's shoulders sagged, and he nodded slowly. "I understand. I just... I wanted you to know that I'm sorry. I never meant for any of this to happen."

"I know," Brynlee said, her voice gentle but firm. "But it did. And I think it's best if we go our separate ways."

Zane looked at her for a long moment, his expression unreadable. Finally, he nodded, accepting the reality of her words. "I wish you the best, Brynlee. Truly."

"Thank you," she whispered, watching as he turned and left. The door closed behind him with a soft click, and Brynlee felt a strange mix of relief and sorrow. It was the end of something that had once meant so much to her, but it was also a necessary step forward.

The next morning, Brynlee stood outside her salon, her heart pounding as she stared at the familiar sign above the door. Blissful Beauty had been her sanctuary, her passion, and now it felt like a place she barely recognized. But Melanie had been keeping it alive in her absence, and Brynlee owed it to her friend to at least try to get back to some semblance of normalcy.

She pushed open the door, the familiar scent of shampoo and hairspray washing over her. Melanie looked up from behind the counter, a wide smile spreading across her face.

"Bryn!" Melanie rushed over, pulling her into a tight hug. "I'm so glad to see you."

"Thanks, Mel," Brynlee said, hugging her back. "I don't know what I would've done without you."

Melanie pulled back, her eyes sparkling with warmth. "You don't have to thank me. I'm just glad you're okay."

Brynlee smiled, though it didn't quite reach her eyes. "I'm trying. It's just... hard."

"I can imagine," Melanie said softly. "But you're strong, Bryn. You'll get through this."

Brynlee nodded, swallowing the lump in her throat. "I hope so."

The day passed slowly, each moment a battle against the anxiety clawing at her insides. She went through the motions, greeting clients, helping with appointments, but by the time the afternoon sun began to dip in the sky, she was exhausted. She thanked Melanie once more, promising to be back the next day, before finally heading home.

As she pulled into her driveway, she spotted Sawyer standing on her porch, his hands tucked into his pockets. He turned as she approached, a warm smile spreading across his face.

"Hey," he greeted her, his voice a balm to her frayed nerves.

"Hey," she replied, stepping up onto the porch.

Sawyer opened his arms, and Brynlee stepped into them, a calm descending over her. He wrapped her in a tight embrace, and for a moment, the world outside melted away. It was just them, standing together, the unspoken bond between them stronger than ever.

"Welcome home," Sawyer murmured against her hair.

"Thanks," she whispered, closing her eyes as she soaked in the comfort of his presence. "It still feels so weird... Coming home to an empty house."

After a moment, he pulled back slightly, his eyes searching hers. "Speaking of... My lease is up in a few months."

Brynlee's heart skipped a beat, her gaze jumping to his. "What?"

Sawyer hesitated, his expression unreadable. "I've been thinking about moving."

The words hit her like a punch to the gut, and she struggled to keep her voice steady. "Moving?"

"Yeah," Sawyer said, looking down at her. "I've been considering it for a while now. Thought maybe it was time for a change."

Brynlee's throat tightened, and she looked away, trying to process the sudden wave of emotions crashing over her. The house already felt empty without Scooter, and now the thought of losing Sawyer too was almost too much to bear.

Before she could voice her fear, Sawyer spoke again, his tone lighter. "Thinking about finding a house this time. Maybe we could get another cat."

Brynlee blinked, her gaze snapping back to his. "We?"

Sawyer shrugged, a small smile tugging at his lips. "Or I'll get a cat, and you can come visit."

She studied him, searching his eyes for the meaning behind his words. "Visit the cat... or you?"

He grinned, the playful light back in his eyes. "Both of us. Or... you could just come with me."

Her heart fluttered, and she found herself unable to look away from him. The offer hung in the air between them, filled with the promise of something new, something hopeful.

"I don't know," Brynlee said, her voice barely above a whisper.

"Just think about it." He trailed his finger down her cheek. "Take all the time you need."

The fear that had been gnawing at her receded slightly, replaced by a warmth that spread through her chest. For the first time in weeks, the future didn't seem so daunting. It felt like there might be a way forward after all.

She leaned into him. "What would I do without you?"

Sawyer's smile softened, and he brushed a strand of hair behind her ear. "You'll never have to find out."

EPILOGUE

Not too far away...

The man's eyelids fluttered, and he blinked his eyes open, confusion clouding his mind. The world around him was a blur, a haze of shadows and sharp lights that made his head spin. He tried to move, but his limbs felt heavy, unresponsive. His breath hitched as his vision slowly cleared, revealing his own reflection staring back at him from a polished metal surface above.

Panic set in as he realized he was lying on his back, completely nude, strapped to a cold metal table. His heart pounded in his chest, the sound echoing in his ears as he tried to comprehend what was happening. He could feel the chill of the metal seeping into his skin, the biting cold of the straps cutting into his wrists and ankles. He yanked at them, desperation fueling his movements, but they held firm, unyielding.

His breath came in ragged gasps, the rising terror making it difficult to think. He craned his neck, trying to get a better look at his surroundings, but the room was dimly lit, shadows dancing along the walls. The smell of antiseptic hung heavy in the air, sharp and sterile, adding to his growing sense of dread.

Suddenly, movement in his peripheral vision caught his attention. His head snapped to the side, eyes widening as a figure emerged from the shadows. A woman, her face obscured by a medical mask, moved closer to the table. In her hand, she held a scalpel, the blade gleaming ominously in the dim light.

"W-What... What are you doing?" he stammered, his rusty voice cracking with disuse, and drenched with fear.

The woman didn't respond. She merely tilted her head, her eyes narrowing slightly as she studied him, as if contemplating where to begin. The scalpel in her hand glinted as she shifted her grip, holding it with a practiced ease that sent a shiver down his spine.

"Please," he pleaded, his voice trembling. "Let me go. I haven't done anything—"

Her eyes flicked to his, and for a moment, he thought he saw a flicker of something but it vanished as quickly as it had appeared. She reached out with her free hand, tracing a line down his chest, her touch cold and clinical.

"Let's begin, shall we?" she murmured, her voice low and devoid of warmth.

His eyes widened in horror as she brought the scalpel to his skin. The cold steel pressed against his flesh, and he screamed, the sound raw and primal, reverberating off the walls of the small room. The blade sliced through his skin with sickening ease, parting flesh like paper. The pain was immediate, searing, a white-hot agony that blotted out all coherent thought.

He thrashed against his restraints, the metal biting into his skin as he struggled to escape. But there was no escape, no mercy. The woman worked with methodical precision, the scalpel gliding through his flesh as if she were performing a routine procedure.

His screams filled the room, each one louder and more desperate than the last, but she didn't falter. Her movements were calm, deliberate, as if she had done this a thousand times before. Blood pooled beneath him, warm and sticky against the cold metal, the metallic scent mingling with the antiseptic in the air.

His vision blurred with tears, the pain overwhelming his senses. He could feel himself slipping away, consciousness teetering on the edge as the agony became too much to bear. The last thing he saw before darkness claimed him was the woman's eyes, cold and unfeeling, as she continued her work with a surgeon's precision.

And then, mercifully, everything went black.

Thank you so much for reading the Secrets of Brookhaven Series! Keep an eye out in 2025 for the first book in the Ava Brooks Mystery Series!

ALSO BY MORGAN JAMES

THRILLERS AND MYSTERIES

SECRETS OF BROOKHAVEN

Out of Sight

Out of Breath

Out of Time

ROMANTIC SUSPENSE

QUENTIN SECURITY SERIES

Twisted Devil – Jason and Chloe

The Devil You Know – Blake and Victoria

Devil in the Details – Xander and Lydia

Devil in Disguise – Gavin and Kate

Heart of a Devil – Vince and Jana

Tempting the Devil – Clay and Abby

Devilish Intent – Con and Grace

Quentin Security Box Set One (Books 1-3)

Quentin Security Box Set Two (Books 4-6)

*Each book is a standalone within the series

RESCUE & REDEMPTION SERIES

Friendly Fire – Grayson and Claire

Cruel Vendetta – Drew and Emery

Silent Treatment – Finn and Harper

Reckless Pursuit – Aiden and Izzy

Dangerous Desires – Vaughn and Sienna

Cold Justice – Nick and Eden

Rescue & Redemption Box Set One (Books 1-3)

RETRIBUTION SERIES

Unrequited Love – Jack and Mia, Book One

Undeniable Love – Jack and Mia, Book Two

Unbreakable Love – Jack and Mia, Book Three

Pretty Little Lies – Eric and Jules, Book One

Beautiful Deception – Eric and Jules, Book Two

Hidden Truth – John and Josi

Sinful Illusions – Fox and Eva, Book One

Sinful Sacrament – Fox and Eva, Book Two

Retribution Series Box Set 1

Retribution Series Box Set 2

Retribution Series Box Set 3

The Complete Retribution Series

ABOUT THE AUTHOR

Morgan James is a USA Today bestselling author of thrillers and romantic suspense novels. She spent most of her childhood with her nose buried in a book, though she now loves to weave stories of her own. When she's not writing, Morgan can be typically be found experimenting in the kitchen (making a mess more often than not). She currently resides in Ohio and is living happily ever after with her husband and their two kids.

Keep up with Morgan and stay up to date on sales, giveaways, and new releases at AuthorMorganJames.com

Shop her books at MorganJamesBookShop.com

* 9 7 8 1 9 5 1 4 4 7 4 0 3 *